MURDER IN THE RUE ST. ANN

MURDER IN THE RUE ST. ANN

A Chanse MacLeod Mystery

GREG HERREN

alyson books
los angeles

© 2004 BY GREG HERREN. ALL RIGHTS RESERVED.

MANUFACTURED IN THE UNITED STATES OF AMERICA.

THIS TRADE PAPERBACK ORIGINAL IS PUBLISHED BY ALYSON PUBLICATIONS,
P.O. BOX 4371, LOS ANGELES, CALIFORNIA 90078-4371.
DISTRIBUTION IN THE UNITED KINGDOM BY TURNAROUND PUBLISHER SERVICES LTD.,
UNIT 3, OLYMPIA TRADING ESTATE, COBURG ROAD, WOOD GREEN,
LONDON N22 6TZ ENGLAND.

FIRST EDITION: OCTOBER 2004

04 05 06 07 08 a 10 9 8 7 6 5 4 3 2 1

ISBN 1-55583-817-0

LIBRARY OF CONGRESS CATALOGING-IN-PUBLICATION DATA
HERREN, GREG.
    MURDER IN THE RUE ST. ANN : A CHANSE MACLEOD MYSTERY / GREG HERREN.—1ST ED.
    ISBN 1-55583-817-0 (PBK.)
        1. PRIVATE INVESTIGATORS—LOUISIANA—NEW ORLEANS—FICTION. 2. NEW ORLEANS
(LA.)—FICTION. 3. GAY MEN—FICTION. I. TITLE: MURDER IN THE RUE SAINT ANN.
II. TITLE.
PS3608.E77M87 2004
813'.6—DC22   2004052919

CREDITS
• COVER PHOTOGRAPHY BY KEVIN MACKINTOSH/STONE COLLECTION (MAN) AND FROM BRAND X PICTURES (STAIRCASE).
• COVER DESIGN BY MATT SAMS.

THIS BOOK IS DEDICATED TO PATRICIA BRADY,
A GREAT LADY AND A TERRIFIC WRITER.

AND OF COURSE, TO PAUL.

"DELIBERATE CRUELTY IS NOT FORGIVABLE."

—Tennessee Williams, *A Streetcar Named Desire*

PROLOGUE

For the tenth time in less than two hours, he peered out through the blinds.

The digital clock on the VCR read 11:13. Of course today would be the day the mail came late. He took a sip from his Diet Coke and let the blinds close as he turned away from them.

The entire house was dark, despite the high sun outside. All the blinds were closed tight. He liked the gloom; there was something comforting in the darkness. Even before, he'd liked the dark. He almost tripped over a pizza box filled with hardened crusts. He swore, sending the box skidding across the rug with a reflexive kick. It hit a couple of empty cans somewhere out there. He didn't care.

He followed the blue light from the blank screen of the television around the end table and sat down on the couch, picking up the remote for the VCR off a pile of old issues of *TV Guide*. He hit the play button with his index finger. After a brief pause and a whirring sound, the tape began playing again.

A faint smile played across his lips and he settled into the sagging sofa cushions. This was his favorite tape. He'd practically memorized it in the six months since it had come in the mail. He never tired of watching it; some days he watched it as many as six or seven times.

His left hand drifted down to his pierced left nipple, and he started to pull on it just a little bit. His breathing became more shallow, and his surroundings faded into the far corners of his consciousness. He no longer smelled the litter box or the mound of garbage on the coffee table—fast-food bags and soggy paper cups and partially full coffee mugs where tiny gardens of mold had begun to grow.

The sound of someone groaning filled the room. He pressed the volume button, and a little green graph crossed the bottom of the screen. The groaning got louder. He tugged harder on the nipple ring. His eyes gleamed as the camera moved in for a close-up of a reddened face, once handsome, now hideously twisted in pain: Veins bulged in the forehead, the eyes were scrunched close, and the mouth an open grimace limned with spittle. His cock began to stir inside his white underwear, and his predatory smile grew wider.

The camera pulled back from the face to reveal a muscular pair of legs gripping the head. As the legs flexed, cords of muscle rippled beneath skin that was smooth, hairless, and tan. The camera continued to pull back until the full bodies of the two men filled the frame. The man being squeezed was young—maybe in his early twenties, possibly even as young as nineteen. He was wearing a tight pair of purple squarecuts. Even as he tried to shift his position and slapped at the legs wrapped around his head, his erection was clearly visible.

"Come on, you little bitch," panted the man with the advantage. *"Give up or I'll crack your skull."*

"No way," the younger man said. *He let out a howl as the other man applied more pressure.*

The boy was beautiful, certainly, with no body fat to obscure the muscle in his gleaming body. But it was the other wrestler the man with the remote liked best—his curly black hair and bright blue eyes, the small patch of wiry black hair in the center of his sculpted pecs, the wet hair under his armpits, and the hard muscles in his legs.

Cody Dallas, gay wrestling superstar.

He owned all twelve of the tapes Cody appeared in; he knew them frame by frame. The scene he was watching now, part of the match between Cody Dallas and Jay Robbins, was one of the hottest. Somehow, Jay managed to overcome the strength of Cody's powerful legs; in about another half-minute he would manage to escape for a brief moment. But he wouldn't be free for long. Cody would eventually get him down again, tie up his legs, and flip him into a Boston crab. Jay would hold out for a few moments, suffering beautifully, resisting mightily, before finally surrendering. Jay lost two straight falls, and after the second submission, Cody stripped him of the purple squarecut, straddled Jay's face and pulled it up into his crotch. No doubt, after the match Cody fucked Jay Robbins until he screamed with pleasure.

It was, he thought, too bad it happened off-camera. He would have gladly paid more to see that.

His cock was fully hard now. He slipped his hand under the elastic waistband and stroked himself. Jay was still moaning on the screen.

He imagined himself in the same position; Cody's legs of steel around his head, demanding submission from him, his ears ringing, the blood rushing to his head, refusing defiantly to submit to the pressure. *"Come on, you little bitch,"* he heard Cody whisper into his ear. *"You know you're going to, so why make it harder on yourself?"*

But he would hold out even longer than Jay, because he'd want Cody's legs around his head forever. He'd never want Cody to let go. That was his chief fantasy: to wrestle Cody, to take on the video superstar.

He knew he couldn't beat Cody in a wrestling match. Cody was too skilled, too strong, and too talented. But it sure as hell would be fun to try—to be that close to him, to feel his skin, to smell the funk of his sweaty armpits, the musk from his crotch.

The sound of a vehicle out front interrupted his reverie. He hurried back to the window and cracked the blinds a bit. The little mail Jeep had stopped at the foot of his drive. Today it was the girl with the lazy eye, in her uniform of blue shirt and darker blue shorts and a pith helmet. She wiped sweat out of her eyes as she searched through a white plastic tub and finally retrieved a couple of envelopes.

Pay dirt. One of them was a manila envelope, which could only be the new Cody Dallas tape.

His pulse racing with excitement, he grabbed a pair of sweatpants and stood at the front door. He waited for the Jeep to pull off so he could run down the driveway and claim it at last. Ever since he'd

3

ordered it, he'd cursed himself for not having paid more for overnight delivery. Every day he'd waited, he'd berated himself, watched Cody's older tapes and fantasized about the new one on its way.

Finally, after what seemed an eternity, the girl with the lazy eye got back into the Jeep, pulled out of the driveway, and disappeared around the curve in the road. Barefoot, he ran down the driveway, opened the mailbox, and pulled out his prize.

Yes, it was from Full Nelson Productions.

He tore it open right then and there, not caring if someone came driving along to see him, standing there in just sweatpants in the hot afternoon sun. Like all of Full Nelson's tapes, this one was in an unmarked tape box. He slid it out and read the label on the cassette.

MUSCLESTUD CHALLENGE 12:
JAY ROBBINS VS. KEVIN MARSHALL
SHAYNE GOODWIN VS. JAMIE WEST
GUNTHER SCHMIDT VS. MAX MANN
CODY DALLAS VS. MARK MILLER

As usual, they saved the best for last.

Humming to himself, he managed not to run back up the driveway and into the darkness of the house. Once inside, he peeled off the sweatpants and hit the eject button on the VCR. He took out the old tape and slid in the new one. He walked back to the couch and slid his underwear down and off. His hands trembled with excitement. He'd been looking forward to seeing this tape since he'd first seen it advertised on Full Nelson's Web site last week. Mark Miller was tough—a good-looking blond with a great attitude and a body to match. On the Web site, the bout was billed as a "Battle of the Unbeatens—the Match You've All Been Waiting For."

The Web page for the match featured some incredibly hot action shots from the match. After he'd ordered the video, he found himself going back to the Web page time after time, getting aroused, beating off until he came with a shout, his body trembling. He closed his eyes. His heart was racing. It was time.

He hit play on the remote, and the usual cheesy music began as the tape rolled. He hit fast-forward to get through the opening credits. The television screen flickered as the first match began. Jay Robbins got his ass kicked, as he always did. This time he wore an orange Speedo as he got tossed about and finally beaten by Kevin Marshall, an imposing black muscleman in an incredibly brief white bikini. Even in the fast-forward mode, he could tell Jay suffered magnificently, as he always did. When that match was over, Jay lay broken on the mat, Kevin Marshall flexed, his foot on Jay's prone form.

And now it was Shayne Goodwin's turn to destroy an opponent. Shayne had been his favorite until Cody Dallas's debut. Shayne was tall, lean, and muscular, and had a shaved head. He always wore a tiny blue squarecut to emphasize his amazingly round, hard ass. He didn't lose very often, but it looked like this time he was going down. Jamie West was the same height but outweighed him by about twenty pounds of hard, defined muscle. Jamie also seemed to have no problem with breaking rules during the match; he choked Shayne and grabbed his balls whenever he was in trouble. Sure enough, after Shayne won the first fall, he lost the next two.

It was a good fight—one he would have to watch and savor at regular speed sometime in the future.

The next match was clumsily staged. Both guys were new to the sport and the holds were obviously faked. They had flawless bodies. Maybe at some point, with more experience, they might be able to wrestle a real match, but now they were strictly making a video for the pleasure of the viewers.

He hated watching matches like that. He preferred to watch real matches, with real holds and real pain.

And finally, that mess was over, and Cody climbed into the ring to warm up and stretch. He clicked from fast-forward to play and let out a long sigh.

His erection was so hard it almost hurt.

He reached for his bottle of poppers and inhaled. As the rush spread through his body, his skin became sensitive and his nipples stood up hard and firm.

Cody wore a tight yellow bikini that rode up a bit on his hard ass. The yellow showed off his tan to perfection. He was perfection.

Then Mark Miller climbed through the ropes and removed his blue satin jacket. He wore a black squarecut. He had a head of thick blond hair, a pretty face, a great body, but he was nothing compared to Cody.

"So, you're the great Cody Dallas," he said with a big grin.

Cody struck a double biceps pose. "Yeah."

"You've never lost."

"Nope."

Mark's smile grew. "Until now."

"You're dreaming."

"Well, bring it on then, big guy."

They started to circle each other, one feinting toward the other, then backing off without locking up. Cody made a sudden lunge and managed to get one of Mark's legs, which he lifted and twisted. Mark fell backward and landed on the mat with a thud. Cody planted his own leg and twisted Mark's around his own. Mark let out a shout of pain and slammed his fist into the mat whenever Cody applied more pressure. This hold lasted for a minute or so, until Mark managed to get some leverage. He used his free leg to kick Cody square in the chest. Cody lost his balance and his grip, falling backward into the ropes. Mark sprang to his feet, and as Cody came forward out of the ropes, Mark drove his right hand into Cody's abs.

Cody doubled over and fell to the mat, groaning.

He reached for the bottle of poppers and inhaled again as *Mark began to work over a prone Cody. He dropped his elbows and then his knees into Cody's exposed and vulnerable abs. With each blow, Cody convulsed and moaned. His eyes were closed, his face grew dark red, and sweat poured down from his hairline. Finally, Mark grabbed a handful of hair, dragged Cody to his feet, and shoved him into a ring corner. Mark started to drive his right knee into Cody's abs, which were starting to bruise.*

"Come on, Cody, kick his ass," he muttered as he reached for the bottle of poppers again. Cody *never* lost! This Mark guy was good and sexy, and he had a serious attitude—he grinned like a little boy on Christmas morning each time he drove that knee in again—but Cody would come through. He *always* did.

Mark stepped away, and Cody slid down to the mat. Then Mark kicked Cody in the side. Cody slid out under the ropes and dropped to the floor.

Mark posed, flexed both arms over his head, and wiped sweat off his forehead. He looked into the camera, making his lightly furred pecs bounce while he growled.

In the background, he saw Cody use the lower rope to pull himself up to his feet.

He watched as the camera zoomed in on Cody's ass. It was truly magnificent—round and hard, and the yellow bikini had slipped into the crack, like a thong. The exposed cheeks were white against Cody's tan line.

His erection slapped up against his lower abdomen. He held the poppers to his nose again and inhaled deeply.

Cody climbed through the ropes. Mark stopped flexing and started toward Cody. Cody leaped into a perfect drop-kick and his bare feet slammed into Mark's chest. Cody rolled in the air to land on his back and quickly spring back to his feet. Mark fell backward, hit the ropes, and bounced forward back into the center of the ring. Cody connected with a powerful fist to Mark's abs, then Mark crumpled. Cody grabbed Mark by the head, launched into the air, and drove Mark's forehead into the canvas. Mark twitched once. Cody rolled him over with his foot, straddled his chest, and flexed as Mark shook his head, trying to reorient himself.

He picked up the remote and hit the pause button, and the picture froze into an awesome still. He started to stroke himself. He imagined Cody sitting on his chest, just like in the video. He imagined staring right up into Cody's crotch, where the yellow Lycra was soaked with sweat. As his eyes traveled up, he saw the beads of sweat glistening in Cody's curly black torso hair. A drop of salty water dangled from the elbow of Cody's flexed right arm.

He stroked faster.

When he was close—when only a few more strokes would bring him to climax—he stopped.

He pressed himself deeper into the spongy sofa; his breath came

in quick gasps. When his breath and his heartbeat returned to normal and the throbbing in his cock subsided to a dull ache in his balls,
he picked up the remote and hit the play button again.

On the television screen, Cody stood and sauntered to a neutral
corner and leaned back against the ropes while Mark slowly got up,
shook his head ,and stretched a bit. Then he walked to the center of
the ring and grinned at Cody.

"You're good," he said, *"but not that good."*

Cody just shrugged. "Apparently good enough."

*Mark beckoned him with his fingers. "Come on, muscle boy, let's see
if you can keep it up."*

*Cody just ignored the taunts, another reason he loved him so much.
It was hot when the other guys taunted each other at times to get their
blood and testosterone pumping. But Cody was impervious to trash talk.
He preferred to coolly and methodically go to work and taking his opponents apart.*

*Mark suddenly sucker-punched Cody. The entire second fall went that
way. Cody was barely able to mount any kind of offensive. When he did,
Mark pulled some dirty trick to lay him out again. After a few minutes of
this, Cody finally submitted to a brutal standing backbreaker.*

He didn't touch himself during the entire second fall. He didn't
enjoy watching Cody get worked over. It didn't happen very often,
but when it did, he usually fast-forwarded through it. This fall
would definitely be a fast-forward moment in the future.

*The third fall started with Cody losing his cool. He was furious—
it was plain in his face. He pounded the padding in the corner as he
watched Mark flex for the mirror. Taunting never moved him into anger,
but falling victim to dirty tricks certainly did. If Cody ran true to form,
he would blast Mark to pieces with superior wrestling skills and some
dirty tricks of his own to further humiliate the loser who dared get in the
ring with Cody Dallas.*

He inhaled some more of the poppers, and his dick began to
throb again. He started stroking slowly as Cody tortured Mark
through hold after hold.

Cody trapped Mark in the corner, kneed him in the gut, and then snap—marred him out to the center of the ring. Mark landed flat on his back with a groan. Both men were covered in sweat and Mark grew more wobbly with each move. He couldn't last much longer. Cody methodically wore him down, the way he did all of his opponents. He punished them until they couldn't fight on, until they lost the will to continue.

His smile got bigger, and he rubbed his cock faster.

Here it comes, he thought, as Cody moved in for the kill.

His breaths started coming faster.

A big grin on his face, Cody was almost within reach of his victim. The end was near for Mark Miller. Cody looked into the camera and paused for a moment to flex his arms; the muscles strained against the skin. He drew closer...

His body began to stiffen.

And as he reached down, Mark reached up and slammed Cody in the balls.

He tried to stop himself, but he felt the climax, could tell he wouldn't be able to stop it.

Cody collapsed in agony to the mat and tried to crawl to the ring apron. Mark came after him and landed a kick on Cody's lower back, driving him back down to the mat. Mark grabbed him by the legs and twisted them into a figure four, a big grin on his sweating face.

He screamed "NO!" as his body convulsed. White gobs shot up into the air, his body rocked stiffly, and cum spattered his chest and stomach.

And Cody was pounding the mat, submitting, his face red and twisted with pain. He'd lost the match...

"No," he whimpered as his spasms subsided, each one slighter and shorter than the one before until finally they stopped.

And Mark flexed for the camera and held his arms clasped over his head in victory. "I'm the man, I'm the man," he chanted for a few seconds. He cast a disdainful glance at Cody, motionless and moaning. After a few seconds, he walked over to Cody and grabbed him by the hair. "Who's the man, bitch?" he screamed into Cody's face, spit flying.

Cody recoiled from him. "You...you are."

"Sir!"

Cody screamed the words back at him, then Mark slammed Cody's head down into the mat again. Cody moaned, his back arched and his body convulsed.

"No." he whispered. He reached for the remote, hit STOP, and found himself staring at a rerun of *Designing Women*. "No," he said more loudly, standing up. "No!" He raised his voice still louder.

It *couldn't* be. Cody Dallas *never* lost.

Who the fuck did this Mark Miller think he was, to cheat that way and then taunt the greatest wrestler in the world? Anger surged through him. He kicked the coffee table aside and lunged for the VCR. Cans and paper crashed off the table as it slammed into the reclining chair.

He stabbed a finger at the eject button, and when the tape popped out he threw it against the opposite wall and screamed, "NO!" Spittle flew from his lips. He heard his heart pounding in his ears. It couldn't be. Cody never lost. So what if Mark Miller fought dirty? Other guys—better wrestlers with hotter bodies and more attitude—also fought dirty and Cody always beat them. This wasn't possible. It had to be a *fix*—it just couldn't be.

He sat at his desk in the kitchen where his eMac was purring. He was connected to the Internet twenty-four hours a day, thanks to the cable company. He typed www.codydallas.com and clicked FIND. The little wheel spun as the engine searched for the site. Finally, the black background loaded. But instead of the picture of Cody posed in a red bikini that usually greeted him, there was simply a white box with blue text:

Dear Fans:

I wanted to thank all of you for supporting my wrestling career over the past few years. Your kind e-mails have picked me up whenever I was having a bad day.

But the time has come to hang up my tights and retire from the ring. It wasn't an easy decision for me to make, but I recently became involved with someone, and we've been growing more and more serious. I want to focus all of my time and energy on this relationship, and one of the changes I have had to face is that I don't have time for a wrestling career anymore at this time.

Again, thank you.

Your brother in wrestling,
Cody Dallas

Retired? Boyfriend?

"No," he whispered. "No."

He shook his head to clear it. He bit down hard on his lip until tears filled his eyes. He wiped away the tears and stared at the computer screen.

"No, Cody, I won't let you leave me," he said, smiling to himself.

Now he understood. Cody had thrown that match, had *let* Mark beat him as a farewell to his fans. But Cody didn't understand. He loved Cody not because he was an undefeated wrestler but because he was a hot, sexy guy with a great attitude. Cody was more than just a fantasy. The other wrestlers—they were okay. They had great bodies and nice faces. Some of them had great attitudes and some of them seemed to enjoy wrestling. But there wasn't anyone else like Cody. He was the handsomest, the sexiest, the *best* wrestler. Even when he was losing, Cody was having a good time. He could always tell Cody was losing on purpose to make the match more interesting.

Cody had thrown that match. Mark Miller was unbeaten, but there were matches he should have lost. But not Cody. Cody had gone out on a losing note, which was just wrong. What thanks was that to his loyal fans? He should have gone out on top.

His eyes narrowed as he stared at the screen. No, he couldn't just let this stand.

It doesn't end here, he thought, his eyes gleaming in the darkness. *No way, this isn't the end of things, Cody can't just leave his fans in the lurch like this...*

CHAPTER ONE

I took a streetcar named St. Charles down to Canal, crossed the street, and walked down to Royal.

It was eleven o'clock in the morning on one of those splendidly sunny September days that makes you glad to be alive. Taking the streetcar had been a good idea. The long heat of summer had broken, and the air was crisp and in the mid seventies. The sky was that blue unique to New Orleans, with wispy white clouds scattered across its expanse. There was just a hint of cool moisture in the air. There were a lot of people milling around the sidewalks on Canal, a good sign for the tourist season. Canal used to be the main shopping drag of the city, with huge department stores like Maison Blanche and D. H. Holmes. Those were long gone. They had either gone out of business or fled to the suburbs and now it was mostly hotels, fast food, and Foot Lockers.

There were hopes that putting the Canal streetcar line back in place would stimulate a recovery for the street. So far, all the construction work had simply made the Quarter difficult to get to from uptown. Add to that the chore of trying to find a place to park that would get me a ticket in two hours, and I was kind of glad I was having car trouble. The streetcar down and a cab home was very simple.

Not that riding the streetcar didn't bring its own set of aggravations. If the cars ran on any fixed schedule, I'd never been able to figure it out. You could wait for one for half an hour, and then three in a row would show up, all packed to the gills. The streetcar ostensibly operated as public transportation, but was also a de rigueur tourist attraction. There was no way of telling when you'd be able to catch one with a place to sit. But when you did, it was nice to find a window seat on a sunny day and enjoy the city clacking by.

I knew my car was on its last legs. I'd had it for over ten years, and the transmission was starting to go. My boyfriend, Paul, was all for my getting a new one. He didn't like my red Cavalier. I think it embarrassed him in some way. He always offered to drive his car if we were going anywhere. I tried to explain my attachment to the car to him once, but he didn't get it. It was the first thing I'd ever really owned on my own, the first truly expensive thing I'd ever bought and paid for. I'm not one of those people who get into cars. For me, they've always just been a way to get from point A to point B. I'm also a creature of habit. My next car was most likely going to be a Cavalier. They're good cars that last. I sometimes had the impression Paul wanted me to get something more expensive and stylish, but that was too bad.

I looked at my watch as I started to walk up Royal Street. I was running a little late for my appointment, which is usually not like me. Then again, I'd been acting like someone else for a few months. Maybe being in a relationship had changed me. I hadn't been in one since college, and that was a long time ago. It had ended badly, with hurt feelings all around, and I didn't ever want to go through anything like that again. My memories probably weren't completely accurate—there had to have been *some* good times. But those memories were gone. It probably hadn't been as bad as I remembered it. I'd managed to quit smoking (well, I still snuck one every now and then), cut back on the pot, and had even started taking my workouts a lot more seriously.

These changes were all due to Paul Maxwell, my boyfriend. He didn't like my smoking, and he *really* disapproved of the pot smoking. He was right, of course. You can't argue with the Surgeon General. Cigarettes were damaging my health. And the pot, well, I'd heard it was illegal.

Paul and I had also become workout partners, which I hadn't thought I'd like. But it was fun, actually. I'd always thought my workouts were tough, but they were a piece of cake compared to

Paul's. He also encouraged me to eat better. Since we ate most of our meals together, he usually cooked one of his healthy dishes. I didn't mind, and because my muscles were getting bigger, I was getting more defined than ever, and my abs were starting to really show. I liked the way I looked in the mirror now. My clothes fit in an entirely different but better way. I've always been a pretty big guy—I played scholarship football at LSU, for Christ's sake—and other guys seemed to like that. But now my body was becoming hard, solid muscle, and even more people seemed to take notice. I found women smiling at me on the street or in the grocery store. I got faster service in the bars. It was pretty cool.

But every once in a while I really craved a bacon cheeseburger.

Maybe after this appointment I can go have one at the Clover Grill, I thought as I dodged a couple of tourists looking at a map and jabbering in German at each other. The thought made my mouth water. I hadn't cheated on my diet in a while, I reasoned, so I was entitled to a treat. Paul's theory of diet included rewarding yourself with something fattening and bad for you every once in a while, but he never seemed to indulge, so when I cheated, I did it when he wasn't around.

Call it diet adultery.

My appointment was at Domino's, an unopened club in the 700 block of Bourbon. It had opened briefly during Southern Decadence, but closed to complete renovations and improvements immediately afterward. It was a good location close to the corner at St. Ann, which put it in easy walking distance of the gay bars. It was a dance club trying to go for both the gay and straight markets. A lot of straight people, mostly women, frequented Oz and the Parade for their great dance music, but the straight boys stayed away. Domino's planned to court straight people who liked to dance along with some of the gay boys, too.

I was meeting Dominique DuPré, the owner/manager. She hadn't said why she needed a private eye when she'd called, but I was going to find out soon enough. I'd done an Internet search on her after she made the appointment. She was in her early thirties, had been divorced fairly recently, and had enjoyed some moderate success as a dance music diva. She'd never made the big leagues like Donna Summer or Madonna, but she had a big gay following. Her biggest dance hit was a song called "I Don't Want You Anymore"; it had gone to number five on the Billboard dance charts. She'd been interviewed in a gay national glossy, but the article read like the typical straight celebrity in the gay press interview. She loved her gay fans, she loved performing in gay bars, and did a lot of AIDS benefits—the typical kind of crap.

I was wearing a pair of black jeans and a yellow short-sleeved cotton pullover that fit a lot tighter than it used to. I caught a glimpse of myself in the reflection of a gallery window and grinned. My shirts were all getting tight in the chest and shoulders. I stopped to look at myself for a while, until I saw that one of the street mimes was watching me. Embarrassed, I dumped my change into his hat and hurried up Royal.

The guy dressed as a hand grenade was standing in front of Tropical Isle on the corner of St. Louis and Bourbon, and he was trying to urge the passing tourists to come in. I always wondered about that guy. *What do you do for fun at night when you spend your days dressed as a hand grenade?* I paused there on the corner for a minute. The Lucky Dog vendor on another corner was making a chili dog for a man in a business suit. A beer truck rumbled by, followed by a couple of cabs and a very slow-moving convertible blaring rap music and filled with white teenagers. When it went past, I saw it had Mississippi plates. College kids. They were probably from USM over in Hattiesburg, out playing hooky for the day in the Quarter. *It must be great going to college in close proximity to New Orleans,* I thought with a grin.

I'd escaped down here from Baton Rouge plenty of times.

A woman started to sing into a microphone somewhere down the block. She was singing an old Aretha Franklin hymn, "Sweet Bitter Love," which has always been one of my favorites. The singer was no Aretha, but her voice ached with pain as she sang every word in a deep register that was almost a growl. I started to walk in the direction the suffering voice was coming from, which was the way I needed to go. As I got closer to Domino's, the voice grew louder.

I walked in the front door. Just inside the foyer there was a door to my left and a hallway directly in front of me. There were five stairs that led to a window marked CASHIER. That would be the entrance then. The door to my left was open, revealing a room decorated almost entirely in dusty, slightly faded red velvet. I could hear people moving things around. Ignoring the proper entrance, I went in.

The room was big. Everything was covered with red velvet—upholstery, walls, even the carpet. The red velvet wallpaper ran up the wall about six feet from the floor,; it was faded, torn, and stained. Yellow-painted Sheetrock, water-stained and cracked in places, went the rest of the way to the ceiling. A dirty black iron chandelier hung from the ceiling in the center of the room, and cobwebs waved in the air between the sconces. To the right of the room was a long bar. Behind it, against the mirrors, glasses and bottles were stacked. There was a guy with really broad shoulders in a white T-shirt and a long black ponytail shining glasses and adding them to the pyramid in front of him. On the other side of the room two guys holding walkie-talkies smoked cigarettes. Both wore tool belts that hung below their waists.

Beyond that room was what had to be the dance floor. It was pitch dark back there. At the far side of the dance floor was a stage. A woman stood on the stage and sang into a microphone—hers was the voice I'd heard from the street. She was tall, dark and rail thin. She wore a tight knee-length black skirt and a sleeveless black silk blouse, with enough buttons open to expose some cleavage. A spotlight shone directly into her face, giving it an unearthly glow. Her eyes weren't open, and her hands were at her sides as she began to raise her register to make the bridge, each note came louder and higher than the one before. I wondered if she'd make it all the way when feedback squawked, hurting my ears.

"Goddamn it!" she screamed into the microphone. "Can't you assholes get this right?" She glared up at the wall above the entryway before jumping off the stage. She tossed the microphone back onto the stage, and a loud thump echoed through the space. She headed directly to the room I was standing in, and her low black heels clicked on the floor. Her face was furious—eyes wide, lips compressed into a tight line. She walked to the bar and drummed her long red fingernails on the shiny wood surface. "Give me a Wild Turkey, Sly."

The ponytailed guy poured her half a glass of bourbon, and noticed me as he put it down in front of her. "Something I can help you with, bud?" He had an anchor tattooed on his right forearm, a mermaid on the left. Thick eyebrows over a broken nose gave him a thuggish look, but his voice was friendly.

"Maybe." I stuck my hand out. "My name is Chanse MacLeod, and I have an appointment with Dominique DuPré."

"Sly." He shook my hand, then gestured to the woman. "You're looking at her."

The woman took a long swallow and closed her eyes to savor it before she turned to look at me. She was easily six feet tall, and her slenderness made her seem taller. Her arched eyebrows were actually penciled on. Her eyes were big, round, and a deep chocolate brown. Her cheekbones were high and hinted at a Native American in her bloodline somewhere. Her hair was pulled back into a tight bun. She had a white rose behind her left ear. "I'm Dominique DuPré."

"A pleasure to meet you." I walked over and shook her hand.

"You want a drink?" she asked.

"Coke's fine." Sly filled up a glass with ice and squirted Coke out of a hose until the glass was full. He popped a maraschino cherry and a straw into my drink, then slid it across to me.

Dominique gave me a half-smile, saluted me with her glass, and downed the rest of the Wild Turkey. She closed her eyes for a moment, then opened them, letting out a satisfied sigh. She smiled at me. "Self-medication, Mr. MacLeod. Otherwise, I'd be completely insane."

I didn't say anything.

"Come on." She stood up. "Let's go up to my apartment."

I followed her as she walked back across the dance floor. Almost every step of the way she shouted an order to whomever she passed. They would nod or give her a thumbs-up and go back to what they were doing. We walked around the stage, and she opened a door into a hallway behind it. We stepped into a cement stairwell lit by fluorescent lights, which made the gray walls and stairs even more depressing. As she started climbing the stairs, she said, "I suppose I should have this meeting in my office, but I am fucking starving, and I have to eat something. Care to join me? I made fresh chicken salad last night."

I hesitated. That bacon cheeseburger at the Clover Grill still sounded awfully good, but even with mayonnaise, chicken salad would have a lower fat-gram content and ultimately be a better decision. I laughed at myself. Since when did I start caring about fat grams?

Since Paul started pointing it out to you—that's when.

"Yeah, that sounds great. Thanks." Why not? People tend to open up more over food. And the bacon cheeseburger would take an additional ten minutes on the StairMaster at least to burn off. Yeah, better to have the chicken salad. I hated the goddamned StairMaster.

She smiled at me. Her smile was amazing. It was huge. Her mouth was large, and when her lips moved into a smile to reveal large, even white teeth, it seemed to almost take over her face. She smiled with her teeth apart, making the allusion of a shark's mouth even stronger. There was no menace in her smile, though, just joy. She seemed to be the kind of woman who liked to smile and liked to laugh loudly, long and hard.

We climbed up past two landings. It was a long way up and the stairs were steep. My calves were starting to burn a little bit, and my breath was coming a little more shallowly. She showed no signs of slowing the higher we climbed. She bounced from step to step—and in heels, no less. Her butt swung out with each movement, first to once side, then the other. She waited for me at the top. "It's quite a climb," she said charitably when I finally dragged myself up the last step.

I just nodded, humbled, as I caught my breath. I thought I was in better shape than that. She unlocked a large warehouse-style door and swung it out and open. She flicked a switch, and light filled a cavernous space. The floor was hardwood, polished to a shining mirror's surface. The overhead lighting came from four wrought-iron chandeliers, each with little flame-shaped bulbs that hung in a straight line from one end of the loft to the other. The blades of ceiling fans began to rotate, creating an artificial breeze. Various pieces of unmatched furniture were strewn around the room; there had been no visible attempt at feng shui. A love seat was under a small window facing the river. A black leather couch with several worn spots in it was in the middle of the room and a couple of boxes in front of it apparently served as a coffee table. An ashtray, a couple of dirty plates, empty soda cans, and newspaper pages were scattered on top of them. Boxes and cartons were stacked in groupings that betrayed no sort of order. Some open boxes lay open on their sides, spilling out clothing, towels, or sheets. In one corner there was a wrought-iron bed half hidden by a Chinese screen with a fire dragon design in red, black, and orange emblazoned on it. In another spot was a white screen with several lighting instruments in front of it. A lone bar stool stood crookedly in front of the screen, as though it were waiting for someone to pose on it. Dominique's shoes clicked on the hardwood as she walked over to a little kitchenette area.

There was a stack of framed prints leaning against one wall. The print in front was a black and white photograph of a nude man with rippling muscles sitting sideways on the crooked stool as he brushed through his hair with his right hand. His head was tilted back, which made his abdominal muscles rigid as a washboard. His legs were strong and muscular, and just a wisp of pubic hair peeked above his hip. His front foot balanced on one of the rungs, and the other hung to the floor. But the most arresting thing about the photograph had to be the model's eyes. Wide-open and staring at the camera over his near shoulder with an air of nonchalant innocence, they were luminous and almond-shaped and framed by long lashes that curled slightly. The eyes seemed to stare into my soul.

"Those aren't his real eyelashes." Dominique handed me a plate with a sandwich cut in half and surrounded by a handful of potato chips. A lengthwise slice of pickle nestled on the far edge of the plate. She laughed. "Everyone falls in love with his eyelashes, but they're false. I applied and curled them myself. Something to drink? I have beer, whiskey, iced tea, or Diet Coke."

"Iced tea." She poured me a glass, then grabbed her own plate and led me to a small wrought iron table with a glass top. We sat down. "Did you take the picture?"

"Yeah. Photography is a kind of hobby of mine, a different way to express myself and be creative other than music." She took a bite from her sandwich and peered at me. "You've got an interesting face. I'd like to photograph you sometime." She reached across the table and grasped my face by the chin, turning it one way, then the other.

I was flattered. "I might take you up on that sometime." *Wait'll I tell Paul,* I thought. Paul was a good-looking man. Whenever we went out, people hit on him, tried to buy him drinks, grabbed his ass, or touched his biceps. Nobody ever seemed to notice me when Paul was around. And Paul could be a little mean sometimes. Well, not mean, but unintentionally thoughtless. Even when he told me I looked good, there was always a criticism involved. "Those pants look great on you," he'd say, "and just think how great they'll look when we tighten your butt up some more."

So this was kind of a minor triumph. I wasn't *that* ugly.

She let go of my face and smiled. "Let me know." She winked at me. "Anyway, you're probably wondering why I called you." I nodded. "Have you heard of me?"

"I know you had a couple of hit dance records." I didn't really want to go too far into my research on her. I assumed this was an ego-driven question anyway.

My assumption was on target. She smiled again and fairly squirmed with delight. "Thank you. Anyway, I probably could have been bigger, but the *business* of show business, I just hated. I didn't

want to be really famous, you know. I just liked making good music."
She shrugged. "But my single-minded devotion to my career turned
me into someone I didn't like. I did whatever the record company
and my agent told me to do—the interviews, the public appear-
ances, all of that stuff. It ended up costing me my marriage." She
finished the second half of her sandwich, lit a Virginia Slim, and
blew smoke into the blades of one of the ceiling fans. "After I filed
for divorce, I had to stop and take stock of my life. I loved music, but
music had taken over my life, and for what? So I could sleep in
motels every weekend and wake to find myself on a plane or in a car
heading for the next show? So I could maybe sell a few more CDs?
Anyway I made a decision to get out of the business. I've always
wanted to own a nightclub, so I decided on this place."

"Why New Orleans? Are you from here?"

She laughed. "Hardly. I grew up in Buffalo, if you can imagine
that. My father was a French-Canadian merchant seaman named
Pierre Levecque, and my mother was from the Dominican Republic.
I wasn't born Dominique DuPré—I became her. My real name is, of
all things, Clarette Levecque. I always liked New Orleans when I
came here to perform, I liked the people and the energy of the
French Quarter. So I got myself some partners and sunk my life
savings into Domino's." Another plume of smoke jetted upward.
"And now someone is trying to ruin me."

"How's that?" I leaned forward.

"Somebody doesn't want me to open this club," she said with a
shrug. "The battle I have had over the liquor license—you don't
even want to know how awful that was. We've been reported I don't
know how many times to the city for code violations, which has further delayed the opening. And we weren't in violation of any codes!
But all the work had to stop until the city inspectors came in and
checked things out, and they never come quickly. We've lost weeks.
I was hoping to be open for Southern Decadence…" She let her voice
trail off. Then she looked me square in the eye. "My public relations
company thinks the gay bars are trying to keep me from opening."

"Why would they do that?"

"The competition, I guess." She shrugged again. "As far as I can tell, there's plenty of room for bars in the Quarter, don't you think?"

"One would think."

"Mark Williams, my PR guy, is convinced that the owners of the other bars here are trying to sabotage my club." She sighed. "Two nights ago someone cut the power cable. That took another whole day to get repaired. Then someone called the phone company and got our phones turned off." She stood up. "I'm losing money every day this club stays closed, Chanse. I mean, I didn't mind it so much when they were causing trouble for me with the liquor board or the city inspectors—that was easy enough to rectify even though we lost time. But this other stuff has got to stop." She sat back down and slammed her fist onto the table. "I won't have it!"

"So, what do you want me to do for you?"

"I want you to find out who's behind this all." She smiled. "I can deal with it, but I have to know what I'm dealing with.

I explained my rates to her and got the contract I'd prepared out of my briefcase. She got up and grabbed a checkbook from a desk drawer. She wrote the check with savage strokes, tore it out, and tossed it to me. She took the contract from me, read through it, and then signed her name in the same bold strokes before she handed it back to me.

"I'll need a copy, if you don't mind," she said evenly.

I folded the check and slipped it into my wallet. "Of course. Mind if I fax it to you?"

"That's fine." She wrote down the number and handed it to me.

I stuck my hand out to her. "Pleasure to meet you."

She hesitated for a moment, then shook it. "Please find out who is trying to ruin me, Chanse."

"I'll do my best, Dominique." I put the contract back into my briefcase and stood to go.

"Talk to Mark," she said as she led me to the door. "He'll tell you everything you need to know."

CHAPTER TWO

The Pub and Oz stood on opposite corners of Bourbon Street where it crossed St. Ann. The façades of the large clubs seemed to glower at each other in the sunshine as their rainbow flags waved in the breeze. I stood there for a minute and stared first at one, then the other. Oz was getting a beer delivery. The afternoon bartender, a gorgeous Cajun-looking man with black hair and muscular forearms stood in the doorway and talked to the delivery man, who was smoking a cigarette. There were several people drinking and talking in the Pub, and I heard a Christina Aguilera remix.

How could there not be room for another dance club at this end of Bourbon Street? Both bars, despite their closeness, did good business. It always seemed to me they benefited from their proximity to each other; most people paid the cover at both places and wandered between the two all night long. On holiday weekends, the street between them was bumper-to-bumper with men. Surely it wouldn't hurt to have another club just a short walk away? People wouldn't choose one over the other—they hadn't so far. Besides, a lot of people I knew stayed away from the crowds during the holidays. Another bar might just lure more of the locals to come down and party.

The office of Attitude PR was in a Creole cottage on St. Ann, around the corner from Domino's and about halfway up the block in the direction of Dauphine Street. Unlike the other buildings on the block, it wasn't on the sidewalk. Instead, it was set back behind a small yard and blocked off from the sidewalk by a shoulder-height brick wall with broken glass imbedded in cement along the top. Just inside the wall, a huge flowering magnolia was visible through the wrought-iron gate, which opened under a roll of a razor wire. I was just reaching for the buzzer on the gate when the front door opened.

What on earth is Paul doing here? I wondered as he shut the door behind him and came down the steps at a brisk clip. He stopped for a brief moment when he noticed me outside the gate. But then a big grin spread across his face. "Hey, honey," he said, opening the gate and kissing me on the cheek.

"Hey." I brushed his arm with my hand. He was wearing a nice pair of pleated khaki shorts with a black ribbed tank top. Curly black hairs sprouted at the base of his throat. An errant black curl hung down on his forehead. He had a strong nose, and bluish-black shadow on his cheeks and chin from not having shaved that morning. *He has the most beautiful blue eyes,* I thought. "What are you doing down here?"

"Oh," he said. He glanced back over his shoulder at the door. "The guy who puts out *Attitude* wanted me to pose for the cover of their magazine. Isn't that cool?" He gave me his big, winning grin again.

"Really?" Whatever I had been expecting to hear, it wasn't that. I stood there, thinking, trying to remember what the covers of *Attitude* looked like. I'd never really paid much attention to the magazine before. I noticed in passing. Sometimes I'd thumb through one in a bar when I was waiting for Paul to meet me, but I never kept it. I either left it where I found it or threw it in the trash on my way out.

I did recall the covers were full-color and glossy, and sometimes I thought the cover models were hot. I tried to remember what they wore, if anything. I was blanking on that.

He looked at me, his grin growing. "Are you surprised?"

"Well…" Not really, now that I was thinking about it. So much for being asked to pose by Dominique. If she ever met him, she'd forget all about me posing for her. Of course, someone would want to put him on the cover of a magazine. Paul was a hot guy, a lot more attractive than me. His body was more defined, more proportionate, thicker. He could put on anything, look sexy, and get people to look at him. He was built as well as any stripper or porn star I'd ever seen. Better than some, in fact. He looked just as good in his underwear as the guys on the boxes it came in. And then his face and hair, his eyes—he was a great-looking guy. It made sense for someone to want him to model. He *belonged* on magazine covers and underwear boxes.

"You don't want me to do this?" he asked. His smile faded just a little bit, but his dimples were still there.

"I'd rather you didn't, to be honest," I replied. I felt my face getting hot. An image flashed into my mind—stacks and stacks of *Attitude* magazines. In my mind's eye I saw guys leering at Paul's picture, talking about how hot he was, how they'd like to fuck him or suck his dick or…

"Why not?" he asked. His eyebrows arched over imploring eyes.

"Well," I said, "I don't like the idea of people beating off to your picture." That sounded stupid and childish, even to me. I regretted it as soon as I said it.

Paul folded his arms, and his thick black eyebrows knit together over his strong nose. "I would be wearing shorts at the very least, Chanse."

I could tell by his tone he was getting annoyed, and I felt my own annoyance building. "Paul, what I'm saying here is I don't like the idea of other guys looking at you that way."

"So, you'd rather I gained weight?" He pulled at the straps of his tank top. "Should I stop taking care of myself and wearing clothes like this?"

"Don't be stupid." I took a deep breath. "It's hard enough as it is."

He tilted his head. "What's hard?"

"Paul…" I tried to find the right words, to try to salvage this conversation. "You know you're hot, Paul. Well, all I'm saying is—"

"So, what you're saying is you still want me to look good, but you don't want anyone else looking at me." His smile was gone completely. He started to bounce on his toes, and veins popped out in his biceps.

"Well, it bothers me." There, I'd said it.

"Why?" He looked at me like I was crazy. "Why would that bother you?"

The lightbulb went on. "You like having people look at you."

He tilted his head to one side. "Don't you?"

"Well, yeah, but…" I floundered. It *was* nice. I'd have been lying if I said otherwise. It felt good to have someone look at you in that appraising way, to try to imagine what's you'd look like naked, to *want* to see you naked. But that wasn't why I worked out. It wasn't why I was following Paul's diet, his workout. "Why isn't it enough that I look at you? Why do you need validation from other people?"

"Chanse, that's not what this is about." He shook his head. "I'm proud of the way I look…and look at how you've been hitting the gym lately!"

"I'm getting myself into better shape for you, Paul, not for people to look at me."

He shook his head. "Chanse, you shouldn't be doing all of this for me." He tapped me in the center of my chest. "You should be doing it for you."

I didn't know what to say to that. "Are you going to do it? Pose, I mean?"

"Are you asking me not to?" Paul replied.

It sounded like a test question, one where I could pass or fail. Fuck it. "Yeah, I guess I am."

"Then I guess I need to think about this." He glanced at his watch. "I've got to get running."

"Where?" I couldn't believe what I'd said, or the whiny way it had come out.

He frowned at me. "I told you I have some things to do, Chanse." He shook his head. "You want to meet for dinner at seven? Juan's Flying Burrito?"

Juan's wasn't on our diet. "Yeah. Sure."

He winked at me. "Well, you knew I've posed before. And I've posed nude, Chanse, but this isn't going to be. So just relax, okay?" He started to walk away, then stopped. "Let me ask you this, Chanse.

Does other people looking at me bother you because you don't want them to look at me, or does it bother you because you would rather they looked at you?"

I just stared at him. After a moment he shrugged and walked away.

I watched him until he rounded the corner at Dauphine. I didn't know what to think. Maybe he was right—maybe I *was* jealous when people looked at him. But if the situation was reversed, I didn't believe he could honestly tell me he wouldn't feel the exact same way. I loved him and thought he was the most gorgeous man I'd ever seen, but couldn't he understand how *tiring* it was always to be made to feel inadequate? To see guys checking out your boyfriend and knowing they're thinking, *Why is he with that guy?* And it would only get worse if he posed for that magazine cover. And what was this "I've posed nude" shit? Why was I just now finding out?

What *else* hadn't he told me?

The gate hadn't shut, so I walked through it and up the stairs. I knocked on the door. I heard footsteps, then a slender young man opened the door. He had large green eyes, short black hair parted in the middle and gelled stiff, and a rather large nose the rest of his face dropped back from. He was slender, maybe 140 pounds, and wore baggy jeans and an orange T-shirt with an iron-on patch of Lynda Carter as Wonder Woman on it. In a very soft voice he said, "May I help you?" Behind him I heard a male voice say something I couldn't make out, followed by a high-pitched girlish peal of laughter.

"I'm looking for Mark Williams. My name is Chanse MacLeod"— I reached into my back pocket for my badge—"and I'm working for Dominique DuPré."

He nodded, without giving the badge the courtesy of a glance. "She called to let us know you'd be coming." He held the door open, and I walked into a large room. A chandelier hung from a sixteen-foot ceiling. The desks were slapdash things made out of particle board. Several of them were scattered about the room, with computers on top of them. Equally cheap-looking chairs, garbage cans, and lamps accompanied them. A man and a woman were seated in chairs on the opposite sides of two desks that had been pushed together. Loose papers and file folders covered their shared work space.

The man was in his early forties, with bangs brushed forward over a receding hairline. He had brown plastic-frame glasses that dangled halfway down a wide, almost squashed-looking nose. The lenses were large and thick. The glasses had been glued together several times at the bridge. The man was laughing, his eyes were narrow slits, his mouth gaped open and his head shook. He was wearing a gray T-shirt with ATTITUDE written across the chest.

The woman facing him had blond hair in dreadlocks. She wore a baggy, faded blue men's shirt over cut-off men's brown polyester pants. Her feet were in sandals. She turned her head and faced me. Her face was round, her cheeks full with deep dimples, and her eyes were round and black behind severe black plastic-frame glasses. She was also smiling. "Hey, come on in!" she said.

My eyes wandered to the walls. They were covered with framed posters, which were actually blown-up *Attitude* magazine covers. I recognized a hot muscle boy who'd been on *The Real World,* a muscular young Hispanic soap star, and an adorable young guy I'd seen dancing on the bar at the Pub a few times. He had almost tempted me to break my long-standing rule about not tipping dancers. There were several others I didn't recognize, but they were all young and beautiful and shirtless.

"Our past covers," said the guy who'd let me in. "My name is Zane Rathburn. I'm the artistic director. That's Ghentry Rutledge, who's the editor of the magazine"—he pointed to the man in glasses, who nodded"—and Julian Eastwick, our sales director."

"Eastwick as in *Witches of,*" she said in a girlish voice. She couldn't be much older than twenty-three. Her nose, lower lip, and tongue were all pierced, and I spotted a tattoo of Wile E. Coyote on her unshaved calf.

I nodded to her. "Nice to meet you."

"I'll tell Mark you're here," Zane said. He then walked across the room, knocked on a door, and walked into another room.

I sat down. "So what's it like working here?" I asked Ghentry and Julian just to make conversation. It was better than just sitting there staring at each other.

Julian tossed her dreads with a grin. Silver braces shone on her teeth. "I like working in a queer environment. I like having a job where my boss doesn't expect me to take out my jewelry, wear my hair in a certain style, or keep my tattoos covered." Her blue eyes were serious. "I have a college degree, man, in English. And the only job I can get is being a salesperson. Wasn't what I was expecting when I was paying my tuition." She shrugged. "I could have gotten this job without a degree, but it's fun working here."

"Yeah." Ghentry leaned back in his chair with his hands behind his head. Nicely shaped muscles moved in his arms. "I've had a lot of shitty jobs I hated that paid better than this, but we have a good time. I don't mind coming to work, if you know what I mean."

"Cool," I said. I've always thought enjoying your work was a lot more important than money. I'm not cracked out to be an employee, which is why I'm self-employed.

The door opened again. Zane came back with another man. I stood back up.

"Mr. MacLeod?" A blue-eyed man stepped forward with his hand extended for a shake. He had thick dark-blond hair clipped about an inch above the top of his head. His eyebrows were brown and had been shaved apart over the bridge of his straight nose. There were some tell-tale lines starting to show around his eyes and mouth, but they were hardly noticeable. His cheeks were dimpled, his lips full and thick, and his teeth straight and white. He was a little over six feet tall, and probably about 190. He wore a tight black T-shirt with ATTITUDE printed on it. His tight, faded jeans had a rip at the left knee.

I shook his hand. His grip was fraternity-trained strong. "Call me Chanse," I said.

"And you call me Mark." He clapped me on the back. "Come on into my office so we can talk."

31

He shut the door behind me. His office was completely different from the outer one. It was decorated in mahogany, brass, and glass. The walls were painted a dark green. There were no posters on the walls. The large desk was immaculate with everything neatly stacked and carefully ordered. He sat down in his chair, leaned forward, and cupped his chin in his hands. "What they're doing to Dominique is terrible, isn't it?" he said, shaking his head slightly.

I sat down, pulled a notebook from my briefcase, and flipped it open. "Just who is doing what to Dominique?"

"I know she told you about the trouble with the liquor licenses." He shook his head. "You'd think the other clubs would welcome another one into the fold. More clubs means more people. I managed to get the club open for Southern Decadence, and you couldn't tell a difference—*all* the bars were full."

"So you all managed to get it open for Decadence? How?" Paul and I had gone out during Decadence but had never gone beyond the St. Ann line on Bourbon. It hadn't even crossed my mind. That dividing line between gay and straight Bourbon Street, invisible as it may be, was fixed in my head.

He nodded. "We got them a special-event license. She couldn't stay open for twenty-four hours, but she could open at nine as an event and stay open till six in the morning. She did a bang-up business too."

"And the other bars see this as threatening?"

He held up his hands. "I don't understand it, Chanse. It doesn't make much sense. I have friends who bartend at Oz, and they say it was the busiest Decadence there ever. My friends at the Pub say the same thing. Business was up everywhere. But both bars are trying to keep her from opening."

I scribbled that down. "And you've told Dominique this?"

"She doesn't believe me." Mark shrugged. "They're nice to her when she sees them, and act friendly, so she can't believe they'd do her dirty like that." His eyes hardened. "She doesn't realize how things work here in the Quarter. How much do you know about the bars?"

"Not much." I'd been to all of them, but didn't know much about them. Some of the bartenders and bar backs I recognized, but for the most part I didn't know their names. I didn't know who owned or managed either the Pub or Oz. I knew the same company owned Rawhide, Lafitte's, Good Friends, and the Clover Grill, but I didn't know the company's name. The bars were just a place to go, drink, and meet guys. Since I'd met Paul, I'd gone mainly to drink and dance, back when we went out. Paul and I had taken to staying home more and more.

Who owned or ran the bars hadn't been of much interest to me.

"It's a savage, cutthroat business," Mark said, shaking his head. "I'm telling you, Chanse, look no further than the bars."

"Do you have any proof? Have any threats been made?"

"They're way too smart for that."

This wasn't much help, so I stood up. "All right. Thanks, Mark. If I have more questions—"

"Please give me a shout. I want to help in any way I can."

I walked over to the door.

He stood up. "Sometimes…" He hesitated.

I stopped. "Yes?"

"I wonder if it's because she's black."

I froze with my hand on the doorknob. I'd wondered if this was going to come up. Since I'd first laid eyes on a publicity still of Dominique on a Web site, I'd hoped it wouldn't.

Race is a complicated issue. Most white people like to think it isn't anymore. The Civil Rights movement had been a success, and all the problems of black people were finished, over, done with. They could vote, they could go to college, and they could get any job they wanted.

But the vast majority of black folks in New Orleans were still unemployed or working at minimum-wage jobs. Black women still worked as maids and paid companions in the Garden District and Uptown; some of them worked for the families their mothers had worked for before them. The majority of the bellmen and porters at the hotels of the Quarter were black men. Burger flipper, grocery bagger, drugstore counter help, waiter and waitress, convenience store clerk—these were jobs to which the Civil Rights movement had opened the doors.

If most white people liked to think that the problems were over, they did so only by ignoring the evidence of the poverty and desperation all around them.

Which most of them did.

But the blacks knew better. They were living it. Maybe they'd come a long way, but they still knew. They saw the way some white people looked at them. They noticed how when three or four of them walked together on the sidewalk white people would cross to the other side. They knew store security followed them every time they walked into Saks Fifth Avenue at the foot of Canal Street. It wasn't out of the question for Dominique's troubles to stem from the color of her skin.

I looked back at Mark. He wore a smug half-smile, as if he were playing me. When he saw me look back, his face acquired a serious expression.

I felt myself getting mad and gripped the doorknob. *This guy's an asshole,* I thought, when I finally turned the knob and walked out. The three people in the outer office were focused on their computer screens and didn't look up as I passed through and walked out the front door.

I crossed over to the Pub and ordered a Coke from a blond bartender who was chatting with a couple of guys at the other end of the bar. A video for a Pink remix flickered on the video screens above the bar. There were only a few other guys in the place, grouped around a table here and there. A guy played a video poker machine, and was not doing well apparently. He pushed another twenty into the money slot.

I noticed the stack of free papers and magazines piled on a ledge on the other side of the room. I set down my Coke and walked over there. Sure enough, there was a stack of *Attitude* magazines next to some issues of *Ambush* and *Guide*. I picked one up and walked back to the table.

Attitude was digest-size and full-color. The name was spelled out in lowercase letters in rainbow colors across the top. A shirtless young hunk smiled at me from the cover. He was generically beautiful in the way so many young guys are, with muscles rippling under deeply tanned skin. His loose jeans hung low on his hips with just a few strands of curly pubic hair teasing their way out. I opened the magazine and started paging through it. I'd picked it up before but hadn't paid much attention to it. There wasn't much to pay attention to, actually. There wasn't ever anything to read in it. You could tell not much thought went into the articles. They just served as filler to make an excuse for ads and full-page color photographs of beautiful, nearly-naked young men. What was the point? You might as well go buy a porn magazine—at least then you got to see bare ass and hard-ons.

About halfway through I realized I'd already seen an ad for Domino's when I found myself looking at another one. I carefully started paging backward. Yeah, there it was: an ad for Domino's, with a photograph of a mass of sweaty, shirtless dancing muscle boys taken from a balcony above and a graphic of a two-one domino in the upper right-hand corner. At the bottom it simply said DANCING AT DOMINO'S—HOT MUSIC AND HOT GUYS. I turned back to the other one. A beautiful shirtless young man with dark hair and brown eyes, leaned against a balcony pole with the Domino's sign hanging over his head. Again, the ad said HOT MUSIC AND HOT GUYS at the bottom.

Why on earth would you buy two ads in the same magazine? I wondered as I kept paging through. Almost at the back of the issue, right before the classifieds with the hustler ads (with photos and ages that never changed regardless of what magazine ran them), there was another ad for Domino's. It featured another generic-looking pretty boy wearing a tiny squarecut swimsuit and dancing on a bar, with the same tag line.

Three full-page ads in a thirty-two page magazine: I'd never seen anything like that before. And that look on Mark Williams's face when he didn't think I'd seen him. Was he just playing the race card, or was there some truth to it?

And just how the hell did he know Paul, and where had he run into him? Did he just walk up and ask a stranger to pose for a magazine cover? It didn't seem like Paul not to tell me something like that happened. I mean, I was pretty thrilled when Dominique asked me to pose for her. I would have told him. Maybe he knew Mark from before he met me.

I knew Paul was from Albuquerque, from an Irish Catholic family. His mother was actually from Ireland. I liked to hear her accent when she called for Paul at my place. She was always friendly and nice to me. I'd never spoken to his dad, but Paul always spoke fondly of him. He also had three older brothers and an older sister. They were all married and had kids. It seemed like every other week or so Paul was flying off to a birthday celebration for one of his nieces or nephews. His flight benefits as a gate agent for Transco Airlines at Louis Armstrong International Airport made that possible. He'd been a flight attendant when we'd first met but had gotten assigned a ground job when we started getting more serious about each other. I knew he'd come out of a five-year relationship with a doctor in Dallas when we met. I knew he liked to go to the gym and work out. I knew he'd been a jock in high school, and his red and black high-school letter jacket was still hanging in his bedroom closet. I knew his family was perfectly fine with his homosexuality.

I didn't know he'd posed nude, though. I didn't know who else he might know in New Orleans. He'd never introduced me to any of his coworkers or friends.

Come to think of it, that was kind of odd.

I crumpled up the magazine and threw it in the trash.

CHAPTER THREE

The Vieux Carré Commission is the second-oldest preservation society in the country. The state constitution of 1921 was amended in 1936 to create the commission, and specifically charged it with the preservation of the quaint traditional architecture of the Quarter. It's hard to imagine, but back then the Quarter had degenerated into little more than a slum. There had even been talk of bulldozing it as an eyesore. It's hard to imagine today anyone taking such a suggestion seriously—the French Quarter *is* New Orleans.

The commission took to its job with a vengeance. The way the French Quarter looks today is thanks primarily to them. People who run afoul of them, of course, refer to them as the "Quarter Gestapo" and abuse them to anyone who will listen. Most people don't. Any changes or renovations to the exterior of any building requires their approval. They can fine property owners and even place liens. The Quarter is responsible for generating a bundle of tourist dollars— and Louisiana needs every penny it can get. Without the estimated billions in revenues generated by the Quarter, the entire state would be a Third World country.

Working at the VCC had to be a thankless job. No matter what you did, you were bound to piss someone off.

The VCC offices are located in the Eighth District Police Department, on the corner of Royal and Conti. The Eighth District has probably one of the most beautiful police buildings in the country. Painted peach, with massive white columns built into the façade, it looks like an old pre–Civil War plantation manor house. A little café next door serves coffee, beignets, and sandwiches to din-

GREG HERREN

ers on a patio set off by the wrought-iron fence surrounding the building. On nice days those tables are full of tourists wiping powdered sugar off their faces. How many other police stations in the country have an al fresco café on their grounds? Only in New Orleans, I'm sure.

Police motor scooters were lined up like soldiers inside the black wrought-iron fence to the left of the big gate. I noticed, with a little amusement, that some of the license plates had expired, and I grinned at the thought of a scooter cop being ticketed by a fellow officer for expired registration. That would be one way to meet your monthly quota of tickets.

I hadn't been stationed at the Eighth District when I was a cop—I'd worked the Garden District. That might sound like a cushy assignment, but that jurisdiction also included the area around the St. Thomas Housing Project. It was strange to cruise around the elegant streets shaded by massive swamp oaks only to respond to a crack shooting a half-mile away. Just a few blocks from the storied mansions were some of the most miserable living conditions in the country. But that was New Orleans for you—every neighborhood, no matter how posh and expensive, abutted an area that was seedy and scary. One block could have houses recently renovated, with beautifully landscaped gardens and smelling of money, while one block away were ramshackle houses a good wind could blow over, with garbage piled up in front of them and old women in faded house dresses sitting in rusty chairs on the sagging porches trying to catch a cool breeze as they fanned themselves with newspaper.

When I was a cop, I lived in the Quarter in a carriage house behind a huge old mansion on Dumaine Street between Chartres and Royal. I loved my apartment, and its close proximity to the bars. Every restaurant in the Quarter seemed to deliver, so I never had to use my ancient gas stove. I'd always wished I were stationed at the Eighth District, in that graceful building with chandeliers and polished hardwood floors. I never regretted leaving the force, but I did feel a bit of a pang as I climbed the hanging stair to the second floor.

38

It would be so cool to report for work here every day, I thought.

There was a lot of activity when I walked in—cops coming in and out, talking into their radios. Much as we liked to pretend otherwise, the tourists in the Quarter were easy prey for pickpockets and muggers. They'd drink too much, wander down a dark street, and find themselves at the end of a gun. There was an occasional shooting, and the residents weren't safe from break-ins, either. That was why the fences around houses down there had broken glass imbedded across the top or razor wire to keep out unwelcome guests. Every once in a while, a horrific crime would unite the usually contentious Quarter residents into an angry mob marching on City Hall. A few years back, the employees of a restaurant on the edges of the Quarter were massacred before it opened for the day. The killers managed to get a couple thousand dollars out of the safe. Afterward, residents hung signs from their balconies warning the tourists: THE QUARTER IS A HIGH-CRIME ZONE: BEWARE. Things had gotten better since then; the crime rate had fallen, and people felt a little safer walking the streets at night.

But you still had to be careful.

I climbed the steps and walked into the VCC office. I knew someone who worked at the VCC, and I figured if anyone knew what was going on with Domino's, she would. I asked the receptionist—a pretty young redhead in her early twenties who gave me a big smile when I walked in—if Ruth was in. The redhead asked me to take a seat, picked up her phone, and called back to Ruth's office. I paged through a copy of *New Orleans* magazine while I waited. The phone rang, and the young woman said, "Mr. MacLeod, go ahead. It's the last door on the left."

Ruth Buchmaier Solomon was the younger sister of Greg Buchmaier, the scion of the Buchmaier jewelry empire. The Buchmaiers were a New Orleans institution since before the Civil War. Their original store was still on Canal Street, even though they now had several scattered throughout the city and the suburbs. Greg's life partner, Alan Gardner, owned Bodytech, my gym in Uptown. I liked Greg and Alan a lot, even though Alan had a tendency to gossip. Greg was more quiet and reserved, always thinking. Even when he was looking at you and his mouth was moving, making conversation, his mind seemed a million miles away. I'd met his sister, Ruth, at several parties at Greg and Alan's big mansion in Uptown.

Ruth was a graduate of Tulane Law and had passed the bar, but she had never practiced law except on behalf of the VCC. She'd worked there as an intern while in law school, and they'd offered her a job when she graduated and passed the bar. "It's better to work for a cause you believe in," she'd told me once while she was waiting for the bartender at one of her brother's parties to refill her vodka martini, "than to just practice law for the hell of it."

She didn't really have to work at all. She came from money and then had married more. She loved the Quarter and fought for its historic heritage with the tenacity of a tigress. She was very petite and pretty, with short, thick brown hair and a lovely olive skin that didn't require a lot of makeup. She had a birthmark just above the left side of her mouth and lustrous, round brown eyes framed with long lashes. She was what we in New Orleans called a "party friend"—someone you never saw unless it was at a party or a function with a cocktail in her hand. I'd always liked seeing her. When I attended a party and saw her there, I always made a beeline for her side. She had a raunchy sense of humor that never failed to take me by surprise because she looked every inch the Uptown aristocrat. She was the perfect person to stand beside in a room full of people you don't know. She knew everyone and everything about them—and was more than happy to share her wealth of knowledge. What she didn't know, she'd make up. Once I accused her of fabricating something. She grinned at me, threw her arms out in a dramatic gesture, and said, "But, darling, this is New Orleans! Anything can happen here!" You never could be sure if the gossip she shared was true or not, but that was part of the fun.

"Chanse!" She squealed as she came around the desk to present her cheek for me to kiss and then her body to hug. She was maybe five foot three, so I had to bend down for her to wrap her arms around me. She wore a white silk blouse over a gray skirt that matched the jacket flung over the back of her chair. "I couldn't believe it when Christy buzzed me to say you were here asking for me." She sat back down and crossed her legs. "I'm so sick of all this crap—what a pleasant break from all of this." She gestured to the pile of paperwork on her desk with a dismal frown. "I swear, sometimes I just want to get in a cab, head to the airport and buy a ticket for *anywhere*."

"It's nice to see you." I took a seat. "How are you doing?"

It took her about five minutes to fill me in. Her husband, a psychiatrist, was thinking of going on sabbatical and writing a book. "A novel, can you imagine? Suddenly, he thinks he's a creative genius." Her youngest daughter was turning into such a terrible flirt—she was going to be trouble as a teenager. "Every morning I have to send her back to her room with turpentine to take the paint off." Her older daughter had taken to wearing white makeup and black clothes—she was probably going to be a lesbian. "Not that there's anything wrong with that—at least then I don't have to worry about her getting pregnant in the backseat of some horny boy's car." Their pool was almost finished, though her contractor was a nightmare to work with. "You'll have to come to the party I'm going to throw when it's finished. The guest list is going to be limited to people who look good in swimsuits—you can be sure of *that*." She was thinking about having another baby, but if her husband was going to take a sabbatical, she really couldn't yet. Still, she was afraid if she waited much longer it would be too late.

"How polite you are, listening to me run on and on." She took a deep breath and smiled. "But enough about me. How are you? How's that new boyfriend thing working out?"

"Good," I said. I'd known Ruth for years, but it wasn't like she was a confidant. Besides, the last thing in the world I wanted was to become part of her cocktail-party repertoire for someone else's entertainment.

Her eyes narrowed for a second, and her smile faltered just a little. When it reappeared, it didn't quite look real. "So, what brings you to see me?" The friendly gossipy tone was gone from her voice.

Shit. I needed her in gossip mode. "Why is Dominique DuPré having trouble with her nightclub?" I grinned at her. "I figured if anyone would know, you would. Have you heard anything?"

She raised a perfectly plucked eyebrow to let me know it wouldn't be that easy. "I know she's having some trouble with her liquor license."

"Is that pretty standard for a new club?" I asked, sitting back and crossing my legs. "I figured a liquor license wouldn't be a big deal."

She glanced at her shut office door, then back at me. "No, it's not. It's not a piece of cake—liquor license applications get turned down all the time, but she had some strange things in..." She paused, shaking her head. She leaned back in her chair and folded her arms. She bit her lower lip and made her decision. "Apparently, Ms. DuPré's background check turned up some things that concerned the liquor board."

"Such as?"

"They voiced some concerns about her ex-husband." She leaned forward over her desk and lowered her voice. "You didn't hear this from me, okay?" I nodded. "Some of his, um, *clients* raised some eyebrows."

"And why would that be?"

"He's been known to defend people the"—she swallowed and looked over at the door again—"the, um, *Feds* consider *connected.*"

Whoa. "He's a mob lawyer?" If this had anything to do with organized crime, I was out of it. This was way out of my league. I enjoyed my life, thank you very much, and planned to keep going for a while.

She shrugged. "It's possible, and so the Liquor Board was understandably cautious. But the Feds couldn't give any concrete evidence to the Liquor Board because they just suspected the guys were connected, and Dominique's husband managed to get them off." She sighed. "There were also some questions about her backers—I know one was a holding company out of the Caymans that couldn't be traced anywhere for a while." She scratched her chin. "But the money trail was finally cleared up, above reproach, and so the lady got her license."

"There have been some allegations that possibly other club owners on Bourbon Street are trying to cause trouble for her," I said as I leaned forward. "Do you think that's a possibility?"

"Oh, please," she said. "Like they don't have better things to do?" She laughed, shook her head, and looked me right in the face. "I've heard those stories, too, Chanse, and they don't hold water. I mean, I don't like some of those guys personally, and I don't like some of the things they do, but this is too much, even for them. And like I said, like they have the time to create this level of harassment."

"Someone is causing trouble for her," I replied. "Someone cut her power line the other night."

She didn't answer and looked out the window for a moment before she turned back to me. "Off the record—Well, this whole conversation was off the record, am I clear?—I personally think Ms. DuPré is trusting the wrong people, if you know what I mean."

"Come on, Ruth, don't play with me. What are you talking about?"

She got out of her chair and walked over to a filing cabinet. She removed a file from the top drawer and sat down. "Someone is trying to cause trouble for her. But I don't think it's who she thinks it is." She opened the file and passed a piece of paper over to me. "What do you think of that?"

It was a fax. It read:

Dear Ms. Solomon,

It's come to our attention that a new club is opening on the 700 block of Bourbon Street—one that is going to cater to a young clientele, is going to have live entertainment, and is going to draw crowds of people down to that end of the street.

While this block is zoned commercially, the location of this club has always been occupied by restaurants before...and as this block is very close to a highly residential section of the Quarter, we are very concerned about noise, more trash, and more crowds of drunken people spilling into the quiet of our neighborhood.

During the Labor Day Weekend, there was a considerable amount of noise emanating from this club. Is the Vieux Carré Commission satisfied that this club has adequate soundproofing? The Quarter doesn't need another loud club at this end of Bourbon Street!

A Concerned Neighbor

I looked up at Ruth. "Do you often get anonymous complaints faxed to you?" I read it again. "I mean, with all the nuts in the Quarter..."

She laughed and rolled her eyes. "You'd be amazed at what we get here, and unfortunately, it's the position of the VCC that every complaint we receive has to be checked out by a city inspector." She made a disgusted noise and scratched her head. "If I didn't have to deal with all of that crap, everyone would be amazed at how much I could get done."

"And how many of these have you received?" I asked. "About Domino's?" I placed the fax back on her desk.

"At least one a day since early July," she replied, "when the renovations started." She put the folder down. "We received complaints about noise, about signage, about you name it. And every one of these has to be checked out." She tapped her index fingernail on the file folder before leaning back in her chair. "Chanse, I went down and met with Ms. DuPré personally about the number of these complaints. To say that she was hostile to me would be an understatement. I can certainly understand her hostility; she thinks she is being harassed, and this is costing her money. Why she didn't get that being a bitch to me wasn't going to help her cause is beyond me." She leaned forward. "But what I really didn't understand was why her public relations agent needed to sit in on our meeting, or why he did most of the talking for her." She smiled. "Have you met him yet?"

"Mark Williams."

"Ah, yes. Mark Williams. What a jackass." She rubbed her temples.

"I didn't care for him either, frankly."

"Domino's has been quite a headache for me—I would prefer we not get any more complaints. So I did some checking of my own." She gave me a predatory smile. "He annoyed the hell out of me."

I may not have known Ruth well, but I knew better than to be on her bad side. "And?"

"Williams represents himself as the head of Attitude PR. However, he is not an owner or a partner in the business, it is registered solely in the name of a Zane Rathburn, whom I haven't met. The company was originally just the magazine, but then it changed hands a few months ago—it used to belong to a Philip Davis of Meridian. I contacted Mr. Davis, who informed me he had merely put up the money for the business, and it had been a steady money loser for him, so he was preparing to shut the company down when Zane Rathburn approached him about buying him out. Then it became Attitude PR, and Mark Williams began hawking himself to merchants in the Quarter as a PR rep."

"So, he has no qualifications to do public relations?" I asked. I remembered how subservient Zane had been to Mark. He'd acted more like an employee than the owner of the business.

"And all of these faxes"—she shoved the file across the desk at me—"came from the same fax number."

I hoped my shock didn't show on my face. "What? Do you know whose fax it is?" I made a mental note of not only the outgoing fax number and Ruth's too.

She nodded. "Vieux Carré Mail Service." Ruth opened her purse and pulled out a pack of cigarettes. "Hell, come down and have a smoke with me. There's some things I'd rather not talk about in the office."

I followed her back down the staircase. Several of the men who passed us going up gave her a second look. Her tight black skirt hugged her hips, and her black heels gave her body the sway that always gets men to look back. She pushed her way out the front doors and leaned up against the gate by the sidewalk.

"Listen, Chanse, you didn't get any of this information from me, okay?" She lit the cigarette and smiled at a couple of uniforms walking past us. Her smile faded, and she turned back to me, gesturing with her cigarette. "I casually asked Dominique once how she came to find Mark Williams and Attitude PR. He showed up at her place the day we got our first complaint and offered to help her out with it. He said he knew how to 'deal with the VCC.'" She flicked ash. "Chanse, you know as well as I do how hard it is for an outsider to adapt to New Orleans. Put yourself in her place. You've got millions riding on this club, investors to answer to, and you're in a strange city trying to navigate through the murky waters of permits and zoning and so forth. Every day your club is closed you're losing a lot of money. A local shows up and offers to help take care of things for you—and he proves himself by coming up with a solution so you can get open for Southern Decadence—why wouldn't you hire him?"

"Seems like an awful lot of trouble to go through to get a client, though," I said. I watched her inhale. I'd quit smoking a few months earlier, but still hadn't gotten past the need. I still snuck one every once in a while. Everyone told me it gets easier, but it hadn't yet. I swallowed and resisted the urge to bum one from her.

"Well, from what I've heard, Attitude PR is in serious financial trouble—a lot of debt and not enough money coming in. Williams spends an awful lot of money." She shook her head. "For example, this concert they put on at Domino's last week? Well, they paid for the hotel rooms and airfare for the band, did all this advertising, and Attitude's total payout? Dominique lets them keep the cover charge, she gets the bar. They charged ten dollars and had maybe a hundred people. That's a thousand dollars gross-and I can tell you that didn't cover the airfare." She laughed. "Not exactly good business, you think?"

"No. It doesn't make any sense at all," I replied, thinking, *Why make a deal where you are constantly losing money?*

"I have to tell you, I don't like that guy." She crushed the cigarette out with her foot. "The first time I met him, I didn't like him. I can't explain it. He just rubs me the wrong way. I like her—she's great, if a little misguided, but I think she's smart enough to figure it all out for herself." She smoothed her skirt as another cop went past us. "And if not, oh, well. Businesses come and go in the Quarter all the time."

"Thanks, Ruth," I said. I leaned down and hugged her.

"Good seeing you." She kissed my cheek. "You and your boyfriend must come over for dinner soon. I'm dying to meet him."

"Call me," I said as she walked back, knowing she wouldn't.

Vieux Carré Mail Service was just a few blocks up Royal Street from the Eighth District building, so I figured I might as well scope it out while I was in the Quarter. I walked down Royal. The sun was getting low in the sky, and long cold shadows crept across the street. The temperature had dropped into the high sixties, and I was cold. I stopped and got a cup of coffee to warm me up and headed toward the little shop.

Vieux Carré Mail Service was one of those spots where someone can rent a box and have mail delivered there. The shop also accepted packages from the overnight carriers, sold stamps and postcards, did box packaging and shipping, and so on. I've never understood how a place like that can make money, but there were several different ones scattered all over town. One service that was offered, I noticed when I walked in, was to fax things for only fifty cents a page.

I waited until the woman at the counter was through with an impatient balding man who kept looking at his watch until the woman was finished with him. "Yes?" she asked me with a tired smile. She was in her late fifties, and her hair hung to her shoulders. It was dyed an unnatural shade of black. A pack of Camels was tucked into her smock pocket.

I pulled out my little notebook. "Is this your fax number?" I read the number off to her.

"Uh-huh. Why?"

I gave her a warm smile and showed her my badge. "I'm trying to track down some faxes that were sent from this office."

"Oh…" She walked to the back and returned with a black three-ring binder. She set it down on the counter in front of me. "We track our faxes—the number they are being sent to and who sent them."

I looked at the binder. "May I?" I asked.

"Knock yourself out," she said as she walked around from behind the counter. "I'm gonna step out and have a quick smoke."

The door shut behind her. I opened the notebook and scanned the first page of a simple ledger recording the time, the fax number, and the name of the sender. I flipped to the back and started to work my way forward, looking for familiar names. And on July 27, there was the entry: Mark Williams and Ruth's number. I turned the page. Two more the next day and so on. I walked over to the copy machine and started copying the pages. The clerk was still out on the sidewalk. I didn't think it was necessary to copy every page, but a few would suffice to prove my point.

When she opened the door and came back in, the notebook was back on the counter and I was picking through the postcard rack. "Find what you needed?" she asked as she went around behind the counter again.

"Yeah. How much are copies?"

"Five cents each."

I pulled out a quarter and placed it on the counter. "I made five."

"Cool." She rang it up and put the quarter in the drawer. "You want the receipt?"

I shook my head no, walked out, and looked down the street for a cab. It didn't take long—maybe five minutes—and I was on my way home. My cab driver wasn't one of the talkative ones, fortunately. I just stared out the window and tried to figure out what Williams's game was. He was losing money on the shows at Domino's. How much was she paying him? It seemed like all of this was an incredibly complicated way to go about drumming up business—and an expensive one. I paid the cabbie when we arrived at my place, went into my apartment and turned on my computer.

The Internet had changed the private eye business significantly. I used to have to manually do research—filling out forms and paying fees to get information. Now, all I had to do was go to some Web sites designed specifically for private eyes to get that information within seconds. The easiest way to start was with the Social Security number, but I didn't have Williams's. So I logged into a business license Web site and plugged in "Attitude PR." Just as Ruth had said, it was listed with the state as a sole proprietorship under Zane Rathburn. I then checked their payroll tax logs. Interesting. They only had two employees listed: Zane Rathburn and Mark Williams. Bingo! There was the Social Security number for both. I copied down Williams's and went to another site, one that listed criminal records. Just on a hunch, I typed in Williams's Social Security number. A few moments passed while the computer searched through the site's records, and then it came up.

I whistled. Ten years ago Williams had been convicted of credit card fraud in Savannah. He'd served five years before being paroled, and his parole had been completed three years later. He was twenty-four when he was convicted, which made him thirty-four now. I printed out the report and signed off the Internet.

I got a Dr. Pepper out of the refrigerator. I made copies of the report and then some copies of the faxes Ruth had received, matching them up to the report.

Not bad, I thought as I sat back down at the computer. I called Dominique's office. After a few rings her voice mail picked up. "Dominique, I've found out who's behind the harassment. I haven't figured out why yet. Give me a call when you get this message and let me know how you want me to proceed. I'll go ahead and fax my report to you." I hung up and did just that.

As the pages passed through the fax machine, I patted myself on the back. Hired this afternoon, case solved by late afternoon.

Damn, I'm good at my job.

CHAPTER FOUR

It was almost six when I finished faxing my report to Dominique. I put my copies of everything into a binder labeled DuPré, Dominique and tossed it into my out tray. I stood up and stretched. My back cracked from being hunched over the keyboard. If I was meeting Paul at seven, I was going to have to hurry.

It took me roughly about half an hour to shower, shave, and get dressed. The whole time I kept thinking about this situation with Paul. By the time I walked out my front door, I had worked myself into a knot of tension. Juan's Flying Burrito was on Magazine, about four blocks from my apartment. There was no point in risking taking the car, and besides, it was a nice autumn night. I started walking up Camp Street. Coliseum Square was filled with people and their dogs.

I felt a little tightness in my stomach. In the six months Paul and I had been seeing each other, we'd never had a disagreement until this thing today. We got along so well it was almost eerie. Yeah, maybe it was because I just went along with whatever he wanted, but it wasn't like anything had ever been unpleasant. I didn't mind changing my eating habits or working out harder at the gym. Quitting smoking wasn't a bad thing, and I already felt a difference in my lungs. I felt healthier and looked better than I had since I was a teenager.

So why did it bother me so much to have Paul pose for a magazine cover? It's not like it was *Genre* or another magazine distributed nationally. For Christ's sake, it was just a little local glossy bar rag, really. It was kind of stupid to react so intensely. Paul was a great-looking guy. Yeah, it kind of bothered me that so many guys stared at him, wanted him, flirted with him, tried to make eye contact and all the other annoying things guys will do to try to get into someone's pants. And to be completely honest, most of the time I liked the fact Paul was such a turn-on for other guys. It felt great to have someone that everyone else wanted. *You might like him, you might want him, but he's going home with me.* But every once in a while it made me wonder, *Why is he with me?* And he did hurt my feelings every once in a while with his casual, off the cuff remarks about the way I looked.

But being on a magazine cover was different. Guys didn't see Paul in bars and then run home and jack off remembering what he looked like. In the pages of a magazine, he was there to be objectified. The whole point of the photos would be to arouse the viewer, to get him hard, and beat off to the pictures. That bothered me. Maybe I was being irrational, but regardless, if it bothered me, Paul would just have to just accept my discomfort and not pose. It just seemed, well, *intrusive* to me.

Juan's wasn't crowded yet. It was a small place—long and narrow. Heavy metal music I didn't recognize blared through their sound system. Juan's was a hip place, popular with college students and that age group. I could do without the loud music, but I liked their food. I grabbed a booth in the front and sat facing the front door. I instantly wished I had a cigarette. I was about ten minutes early, and Paul was always at least ten minutes late. I picked up a *Gambit Weekly* and started paging through it. I was in the midst of another article about the juvenile detention facility at Tallulah when I looked up with a start.

When and where had he posed nude, and why?

That question had gone right past me in all the fuss about the *Attitude* cover.

And just why exactly was I only finding out about that now?

I should *know* things like that about my boyfriend.

We'd met about six months ago at Oz. I'd seen him earlier that day at my gym. At Oz, he was dancing on stage, shirtless, the black hairs on his hard torso were slick with sweat. I went out on the dance floor and we wound up dancing together. He was flying high on Ecstasy, and we ended up going back to my place. He told me he was a flight attendant for Transco Airlines, which is based out of its hub in Dallas. He'd just taken an apartment in Uptown and was commuting. He paid partial rent on a three-bedroom house in one of the Dallas suburbs that he shared with five other flight attendants, but he wanted a place of his own to be by himself when he had time off. He'd been seeing a doctor in Dallas, but that was coming to an end.

We clicked. The sex was phenomenal, and we started seeing each other whenever he was in town. We took a trip to South Beach. We'd decided to stop seeing other people in July, about a month after we'd met, when he transferred to the ground crew at Armstrong International. He'd gotten the job with Transco when he was twenty, seven years ago—when he'd dropped out of Arizona State. Apart from that, we never really talked a lot about his past, and it was weird I'd never met any of his friends.

Maybe he's ashamed of me.

I sat up straight with a jolt. No, that couldn't be it.

Be fair, I said to myself as three young guys in their twenties walked in. They were wearing baseball caps backward and sleeveless T-shirts. Baggy shorts hung to their knees. *You never talk about your past, so why should he talk about his?* Only my best friend, Paige, knew about the Ryan disaster in college, and we never talk about it. Paige didn't even know any details of my pre-LSU life other than that I was from a little town in East Texas.

Then again, I'd never posed butt naked for a camera before. He *should* have told me about *that.*

I'd never told Paul much about my past, mainly because he seemed rather uninterested in it. One time, when we were lying covered in sweat, our bodies entwined on top of the covers, still slightly out of breath from the sex, I sat up to take a drink of water. Paul reached out and touched a scar at the bottom of my left lower back. "What's this from?" He traced it with his fingers.

I'd winced, pulling away from his touch as though it hurt. "I'd rather not talk about it." He just shrugged and never brought it up again. He never asked me anything about my past. It just never came up—not that there was a hell of a lot for me to tell.

The loud music changed. It was an old Def Leppard song: "Armageddon It." I smiled. I'd been how old when that song was a hit? I'd been fifteen, in high school, already starting on the football team. My success at football had changed everything in my away-from-home life. I'd always been big for my class, so kids never picked on me, but most of the kids stayed away from me. I don't know if they sensed somehow that I lived in a trailer park, or if they picked it up from my Sears catalog clothes that never fit right. The clothes always looked okay at the start of the school year, but after a few washings they started looking ragged. My mother wasn't big on laundry, and as she hated to iron, she never did it. She didn't like to clean either. My fifth grade teacher once sniffed and said to me, "I can smell the packing plant on you." My dad worked at the meat processing factory and came home every night to drink himself senseless. He usually ignored us kids, unless we got in his way or he was in one of his moods.

That changed when I went out for football. I didn't have much interest in it, frankly, but practice was from 3:30 to six after school, which meant I wouldn't get home until almost seven. I would have practiced longer. I knew enough about football from having watched it on television every weekend I could remember. I'd always done well in gym class, but I took to football like I was born to play. I was fast, I could hit hard, I could catch, and I was hard to tackle. I started as a wide receiver when I was a freshman, and in our first game caught two touchdown passes. Even my dad, who made it pretty clear I was nothing but an expense to him, was excited. After the game, when I was heading with the team for the locker room, he came down and clapped me on the back, a big grin on his face. "Way to go, son!" he said, and I could smell the liquor on his breath. I just smiled and went in to shower.

Monday morning was like going to school in a parallel universe.

Everyone was nicer to me, even the teachers. People saved seats for me in class. At lunch, I was invited to sit with the starters and the cheerleaders. I sat down next to T.J. Ziebell, a sophomore who started as a running back but was also backup quarterback. T.J.'s dad owned the local newspaper and a couple of the oil fields around town. They lived on a huge ranch on the side of town farthest from the trailer park I called home. It might have been the other side of town, but it might as well have been a different planet.

T.J. was one of the best-looking boys at Cottonwood Wells High. He was always going steady with some pretty girl, but seemed to trade them in every month or so. He had curly reddish-brown hair, golden skin with freckles across his nose and cheeks, gray eyes, and a grin so wide you couldn't help but grin back at him. He also had a beautiful body. I'd been sneaking peaks at him in the locker room since football practice started with two-a-days back in August. His torso was tanned but hairless, the skin smooth as silk. A trail of curly hair led down from his navel to the waistband of his underwear. He had hair on his legs below each knee, but above his legs were just as smooth as his stomach. He wore tight bright-white underwear with a gold stripe on the waistband just above a navy blue stripe. He had the roundest, hardest, most perfectly curved ass I had ever seen. I could stare at it for hours. At that point I knew I was attracted to boys, but still wasn't sure what boys could do together other than beat off or get blow jobs. But I knew I was turned on by T.J.'s ass and wanted to touch it, squeeze it, hold it.

At night, in my narrow bed, listening to the blaring television in the living room and my father's alcohol-induced snores, my hand would slip into my own underwear as I fantasized about T.J. I wished one day we'd become best friends, love and care about each other, walk around naked in front of each other, go skinny-dipping, wrestle, and then one day...

Sitting next to T.J. at the lunch table was almost too much for me.

And we did become friends. I still don't know if I was a pet project or something for him, but he took me under his wing. I went to dinner at his house. He drove me around in his car, a Mustang convertible. We hung out together, and for once, T.J. didn't have a steady girlfriend.

Every once in a while we'd double-date. T.J. always arranged these, telling me about it later. I wasn't about to complain. I didn't have to ask anyone out, and it was a perfect shield for me. T.J. never asked if I liked my date, and we didn't pay much attention to them anyway. As I observed other couples on dates, I began to feel T.J. was using the girls to cover up us being together all the time.

Hope springs eternal in a young heart.

"Are you ready to order, sir?"

I looked up at my waitress. She was maybe twenty-one, about five foot nine with a long, sturdy body. She was wearing hip-hugging brown polyester pants under a clingy, cropped black top that revealed the compass tattooed around her pierced navel. She wore no makeup and little round glasses set in black plastic frames. "No, someone is meeting me. I'm early." When I looked at my watch, I was startled to see it was already a quarter after seven.

Paul was *always* late. That was something else I knew about him. It drove me crazy. I fucking *hate* being late.

"Something to drink, then?"

I started to order a Coke, then stopped myself. *Sugar.* "Iced tea with lemon."

She nodded and walked away.

I fought my irritation. It was just Paul. You'd think someone who had worked for an airline for seven years would always be on time. Paul even joked about it. "I single-handedly keep Transco from being the most on-time airline," he would laugh. "If they want to improve their ranking, they should fire me." It never seemed to matter what time he started getting ready, he always managed to be late. He could start getting ready three hours before we had to be somewhere, and we'd still wind up arriving half an hour late.

Even when I was a kid, I was always on time. Having to be someplace meant getting out of the trailer and away from my parents, so

I always left early. When I started getting invitations to parties in high school, I was without fail the first guest to arrive, sampling the food and making awkward conversation with whoever was throwing the party as he or she put last minute touches on things. T.J. always teased me about it. "You always do as you're told, Chanse? Someone tells you 'Be there at seven' and you obey?" He'd flash me that grin.

Any command you want to give me, T.J., flashed through my mind every time he'd say it.

I was on time the night I went over to T.J.'s to study history during my junior year. He picked me up in the convertible outside the entrance to the trailer park, where I always had him meet me. He'd met my parents at football games and was always extremely polite while I burned with embarrassment. His parents never reeked of liquor. His mom always smelled of some nice perfume and was always made up perfectly and dressed nicely. Even when she was just wearing jeans and a sweatshirt, she seemed to radiate class. His father wasn't as friendly as his mom, but he was always nice. He would ask me about the team and school—things like that—even though I could tell he wasn't interested.

On the way over to T.J.'s house, the stereo was blaring Def Leppard, and he was singing along over the roar of the wind. In the passenger seat I obliged by playing air guitar to go with his vocal, chiming in on the chorus. We both had big stupid grins on our faces. I always liked spending the night at his house. We'd both sleep in his king-size bed. I got to get long looks at him in his underwear. While he slept I would lie there, unable to sleep, listening to the even rhythm of his breathing and wishing I had the nerve to do something—anything—but was always too afraid.

He wore a white mesh Texas Longhorns tank top and tapped his hand on the car door in time with the drum. RayBans hid his eyes. His curls danced as he bopped his head as he sang.

The house was dark as we pulled up the long driveway. "Where are your folks?" I asked as we got out of the car. He had an older sister, Karen, who was at school in Austin.

"Dad had a thing in Dallas, and Mom went with him." He flashed that grin at me again. "We got the whole place to ourselves." He laughed. "Party time, ol' buddy."

The Ziebell place didn't intimidate me anymore by then. The house was huge, something out of a movie—two stories with a wide veranda and big, round stone columns. A fountain bubbled in the front yard, and the veranda was lined with Mrs. Ziebell's huge rose bushes. The living room was as big as our entire trailer.

We tossed our backpacks on a chair by the front door and headed back to the kitchen, where T.J. snagged a six-pack of Coors Lite out of the refrigerator and led me out back to the pool. He kicked off his shoes and socks, cracked a beer, and tossed me one. I pulled off my own shoes and sat down, my feet dangling into the warm pool water. He flicked a switch and the pool flooded with lights. He went back inside and turned on the stereo: "Appetite for Destruction" by Guns N' Roses. He came back and sat down next to me, his feet plopping into the pool. He grinned at me as he pulled a joint out of his pants pocket. He lit it and handed it to me. We sat there, our feet dangling in the water, smoking the joint and drinking beer as the sun faded in the west.

T.J. had introduced me to pot. I'd never smoked it before I started hanging out with him. I liked it a lot. Being stoned made everything easier. I could even deal with my parents when I was stoned. We'd smoke a joint in the morning before school, which made the whole school thing easier to deal with. If it wasn't football season, we worked out with weights every day after school and would get stoned after. During season, we only smoked on weekends.

I opened my third beer as T.J. stood up and took off his shirt. "Let's go swimming. I feel sticky."

"I didn't bring anything to swim in."

He grinned at me. "I ain't wearing nothing."

I stood up and took a swig out of my beer. It took my addled brain a few seconds to comprehend what was happening. *T.J. is suggesting we skinny-dip,* I thought as my shirt came up over my head. The moment I'd prayed for was finally here. This would be it, the first step—getting naked together alone. I'd never been naked in front of just one other person in my life at that point. At least not since I'd started bathing myself. This was it.

I glanced over at T.J. as I slid my jeans down. He was standing there, hands on hips, with just that bright tight white underwear on. Once I folded my jeans and set them down, he slid the underwear down and off.

I was just starting to take mine down when I realized I had an erection.

I stopped, stricken. I looked up at T.J. and he was grinning at me. "Damn, Chanse, you got a hard-on?" He laughed. "No big deal, I get 'em all the time. You wanna go into the house and take care of it in the bathroom?"

I slid my underwear down. It was now or never. My voice shook. "Do...do you wanna come with me?"

His grin faded. His eyebrows went up then back down as his face relaxed. He half-closed his eyes and looked out over the pool. "No, I don't think I do."

Mortified, I turned to retrieve my jeans and slipped, falling over the edge into the pool. I clipped my lower left back on the side on the way. It bled pretty bad. T.J. helped me clean it up and bandage it.

It never came up again, and T.J. didn't treat me any different. We both acted like I'd never said anything.

But he never invited me over when his parents weren't home again.

"What time are you expecting your friend?"

My waitress was still smiling, but she didn't seem sincere this time. I looked at my watch: 7:39. Damn him, he was almost forty minutes late!

He just refused to understand how rude it was to keep someone waiting, but even this was bad for Paul. He tried to be punctual when it was me he was meeting—he rarely was later than fifteen minutes, maybe twenty. I longed for a cigarette. Back when I smoked, I'd chain-smoke while I waited for someone—even lighting a new cigarette off the butt of the one I'd just finished.

He must really be pissed at me.

I shrugged. "I guess he isn't coming," I told the waitress. I stood up and slipped a five on the table. "Sorry to tie up the table for so long." I'd go home and order a pizza, I figured, and wait for him to call. I'd be damned if I'd call him when he'd just stood me up.

She patted me on the arm, a sympathetic smile on her face. I got the sense she'd been stood up before. "Something must have come up," she said, giving me a halfhearted smile.

"Yeah, sure, thanks." Nothing like having a total stranger feel sorry for you.

I walked out the front door onto Magazine Street and stepped into the little grocery store on the corner at St. Andrew. I bought a pack of cigarettes and a lighter and lit up one up as I headed up Sophie Wright Place. If Paul showed up and I was gone, good enough for him. How fucking insensitive.

So, I'd never told him about T.J. and how I got the scar. Big deal. That was an embarrassing story. I was ashamed of it. Yet his attitude toward posing bare-ass didn't suggest he was ashamed—it seemed more like he was proud of it. So, if there wasn't a reason to be ashamed of it, why not tell me?

My cell phone rang as I crossed against the light on Felicity. I flipped it open. The caller ID read NOPD. I turned it on. "MacLeod."

"Chanse, it's Blaine." Blaine Tujague was an old friend of mine on the police force. We'd gone through police training together, and he'd just gotten promoted to detective. His voice was lowered. "Do you know any good lawyers?"

"Well, yeah." I'd done some work for a gay lawyer named Loren McKeithen. "Why? What's going on?"

"Good, you better call one." I could hear the hubbub of the police station behind him. "They've brought Paul in for questioning."

"What?" The Camp Street bus roared by and spewed toxic black fumes. "I could have sworn you said Paul was brought in for questioning." I couldn't have heard that right. That didn't make any sense.

"He has been, Chanse! That's why I'm telling you to call a lawyer." His voice remained hushed but became more urgent. "He's going to need one."

"Why have they brought him in?"

"Suspicion of murder."

I almost dropped my phone. "Blaine, this isn't funny." Blaine had a weird sense of humor and loved to play jokes on people—and sometimes he went a little too far.

"No joke, Chanse."

"Just who is he supposed to have killed?" I felt the knot in my stomach tightening, as I waited for Blaine to start laughing and say "Gotcha!"

"Some guy who lived over on St. Ann," he replied instead. "Name of Mark Williams. You know him?" He sighed. "Anyway, get a lawyer down to the Eighth District station. Pronto."

CHAPTER FIVE

I don't remember walking the rest of the way back to my apartment. My mind was in another place completely. I just felt nauseated, worried, sick. I think I almost stepped out in front of a Kenwood water delivery truck, but I wouldn't swear to it. Somehow I managed to get my keys in the door and go in. I vaguely remember calling Loren McKeithen and interrupting his dinner. Loren switched immediately into lawyer mode and promised to get down to the station immediately. "I'll call you later," he said and hung up. I toyed with the idea of going down there, but there was no way in hell they were going to let me in to see Paul. Blaine might be able to swing it, but he'd just got promoted and I didn't want to get him in trouble. The only person who could get in to see him was his lawyer—to get more than that Loren would have to threaten to go to a judge. I hung up the phone and just sat in the dark for a little while.

Paul couldn't kill anyone. That was just ridiculous.

How well do you really know Paul? An insidious voice asked from the back of my brain. *You didn't know he was a nude model, did you? You don't know anything about him—he could be a fucking serial killer for all you know. There could be all kinds of things in his past you know nothing about it, you fucking idiot.*

I turned on the computer and the desk lamp. "I can't do this," I said to myself out loud. I couldn't invade his privacy like this.

Don't you want to know? That insidious voice was back. *Don't you have a right to know? He'll never know you checked him out. He probably thinks you did already. And why didn't you do this before? What kind of detective are you?*

The kind who wants to trust his boyfriend...

Hating myself a little bit, I logged onto the Internet.

I went to a search engine and typed in Paul's name and social security number.

I paused before I clicked 'send.'

The nature of my job is to be suspicious. People lie pretty easily, and the ones who claim never to lie are the worst. Every word out of their mouths is a lie. I never take anyone I meet during an investigation at their word. That's just asking for trouble. Stories *always* have to be checked out and independently verified before I take it as gospel. And New Orleans is a city where people frequently take liberties with the truth. Some folks could be quite entertaining, even though their lies were so outlandish and over-the-top there was no way they could be true. New Orleans seems to attract people who come here to escape from their pasts and begin afresh. Their histories become what they wish they'd been. After a while, they've told the lies so long they begin to believe them.

I'd taken Paul at his word. I hadn't checked him out. *Why was he different?* I wondered.

Because you're supposed to trust and believe in your boyfriend, that's why.

I took a deep breath and clicked the mouse.

The engine I was using showed previous addresses. It wasn't always accurate; it only showed mailing addresses. I sat, stared at the screen as the site looked up Paul's information. The program dinged when the search was finished and the page was loaded. Sure enough, it showed Paul's current address as his apartment up on Valence Street, with two former addresses in Dallas and the one prior in Tempe, the student apartment where he lived during his brief stint at ASU, and before that Albuquerque.

I printed out the page of his former addresses, then went to a basic Web search engine and typed in his name. I cursed myself for being stupid. What did I expect to find about him on Google, anyway? After a few seconds, the results came up.

The first page of results obviously were in reference to several other Paul Maxwells. I knew Paul couldn't be a professor of psychology at Washington State, nor was he a dancer on Broadway. I scrolled to the bottom of the page. The last one read simply: "Paul Maxwell, one of Top Rope's biggest stars as Cody Dallas, recently…"

Cody Dallas? I grinned. That had to be a porn star name.

For the hell of it, thinking it might be funny to tell him about it later, I clicked on the link. It took me to a Web site called Ilovefullnelson.com. The front page loaded, and then the window flashed off as a subpage loaded. A headline appeared, in caps and all red: "CODY DALLAS RETIRES! EXCLUSIVE!!"

The notice looked like something you'd see in a grocery store tabloid. I started to close the window—obviously, this couldn't be my Paul Maxwell—but I decided to wait and see what this guy looked like. He couldn't be as good-looking as my Paul.

Some text appeared, and next to it a picture began to load. I started to read the text. Cody Dallas was apparently a video star of some repute for a company named Full Nelson Productions. But now he was giving up the business, and the Web site revealed, for the first time, his real name: Paul Maxwell.

Paul's going to get a kick out of this, I thought, deciding to print the whole thing once it finished loading. We'd laugh about this when…

When he gets out of jail?

Of course he was going to get out of jail. It was all a misunderstanding—it had to be. Paul couldn't kill anyone. He might not have told me a few things about his past, but I'd know if he was a killer. He couldn't even kill the damned cockroaches that got in from outside and ran across the floor.

The picture finished loading and my mouth went dry.

It was Paul, wearing a low-cut red bikini that left little to the imagination. His hands were behind his head, his arms flexed, his abs standing out in bas-relief. You could clearly see the outline of his genitals through the bikini, and his dick was hard.

He was smiling.

I knew that smile quite well. My heart sank and my stomach twisted.

I looked at the text again.

*Cody Dallas, long one of the biggest stars under contract to Full
Nelson Productions, recently announced his retirement from
the scene.*
   *"It's kind of hard to top the video I just shot with Mark Miller,"
he says with a shy smile. "I'd like to go while I'm still on top."*
   Pun fully intended, of course.

I clicked to the next page. I stared at the screen.

Action pictures loaded. Paul in a black bikini. Paul wrestling
Mark Miller, who wore white. One picture showed Mark Miller
pulling Paul to his feet by his hair. The bikini had crept into the
crack of his ass, revealing both round hard cheeks. I kept shaking my
head, trying to make sure I was looking at the right thing, trying to
get my brain to accept what I was looking at. It just wouldn't com-
pute, on any level. Then, taking a closer look at Paul's opponent, my
blood ran cold.

Mark Miller was Mark Williams.

I pushed my chair away from the desk, staggered into the bathroom, and threw up.

It was Paul—my Paul, all right—and he and Mark Williams
obviously knew each other much better than he'd led me to believe.

How many other lies had he told me?

This was more than just not telling me about his past—he lied
about knowing Mark Williams. *What had he said? Oh, yeah: "The guy
who owns the magazine wants me to pose for the cover." Not "I knew him
from before—I fucking made a goddamned fucking porn tape with him."*

I washed my face and brushed my teeth, staring at myself in the
mirror.

That was something else I knew about Paul—he liked wrestling.
If there was a wrestling show on television, he wanted to watch it.
It wasn't anything I'd ever really gotten into. When I was in college, some of the guys in my fraternity were into it, ordering pay-
per-views, but I'd never bothered with it much. Yeah, the bodies of
some of the guys were great, and it was nice seeing huge, muscular

men running around in tights—kind of hot in a way—but it was always so obviously fake I couldn't deal with it.

But Paul loved it. Every once in a while when we were in bed, he'd ask me to restrain him physically, but I'd never given it much thought. I liked holding him down while he struggled against me— it always seemed to make him really horny and the sex even hotter. Watching wrestling shows with him was interesting. I never paid much attention; I just daydreamed while he watched and kept a running commentary. He often critiqued the wrestlers and com- plained about the obvious cartoonish elements. I didn't mind watch- ing it with him. It never stirred my interest, but every so often there was a hot guy I'd watch, which was kind of fun, but their hitting each other with chairs and ladders and so on was just dumb.

I walked into the kitchen and got a beer. I pulled the cigarettes out of my pocket and lit another one. At this point, what did my smoking matter? *Yeah, just try to lecture me now,* I thought as I walked back into the living room and sat down at the computer.

At the bottom of the page was a link that said ORDER THIS TAPE NOW!

I clicked on it without a second thought.

A window popped open: WOULD YOU LIKE TO ORDER MORE CODY DALLAS TAPES? I clicked on YES, and a list popped up. I clicked on three more, adding them to the shopping cart.

What the hell? Why not? Didn't I have the right to see what my boyfriend got up to on videotapes? Just another interested customer, like God knows how many others there were. I ordered the tape. I typed in my American Express number as quickly as my shaking fingers could move. I clicked on OVERNIGHT RUSH DELIVERY, author- izing an additional twenty-dollar charge on the card. After I clicked SEND, the confirmation e-mail arrived.

I bookmarked all the pages and logged off the Internet.

Then I turned on the overhead light and ceiling fan in the living room.

Not only is he a nude model, he also has just "retired" from a lucra- tive video-wrestling career. And what else? A murderer?

My phone rang. I got to it on the third ring. "MacLeod."

"Hey, Chanse, it's Loren." He let out a breath of air. "They've booked him, and they're keeping him overnight as a guest of the parish. He'll been arraigned in the morning. I'm pretty sure I can get him out on bail, though."

"How bad is it?"

"I won't lie to you, Chanse. It looks pretty bad. You got any cranberry juice?" Loren was a vodka-and-cranberry drinker.

"No."

"You do have vodka in the house?"

"Yeah."

"All right, I'll stop on my way over and get some cranberry. You need anything?"

"No…" Then something occurred to me. "Yeah, get me a pack of Marlboro Light 100s. In a box."

"See ya in a few."

I walked into my bedroom and reached up onto the closet shelf. I felt around for a while before I found the old Cuban cigar box with my pot stash in it. I hadn't smoked pot in almost three months. Paul thought I'd thrown it all away, but I hadn't. I'd kept it. Keeping some in the house where I could get to it whenever I wanted to was how I was getting through life. It was a challenge every day to see if I could handle everything without having to get stoned at night in order to deal. Once Loren was gone, I'd roll myself a big fattie.

I'd probably smoke the entire pack of cigarettes as well.

Paul wouldn't like it, but he could just get over himself. Like he was anyone to criticize my bad habits. I didn't pose naked. I didn't make wrestling porn tapes. I wasn't all over the fucking Internet in a tiny little bikini with my dick hard. I wasn't so big a star that my retirement required a press release and an interview on a Web site.

Who the fuck *was* my boyfriend? Was he a murderer?

As I sat there on the bed, my head and heart were pounding.

The doorbell rang. I grabbed the bottle of vodka from under the sink on my way to answer the door.

"You expect me to drink that cheap-ass vodka?" Loren said,

giving the bottle in my hand a withering look. "For shit's sake, MacLeod, get out the good stuff."

"This is the good stuff."

He handed me the bag with the cranberry juice in it and sighed. "I don't think that bodes well for my fee." He walked past me and sat on the couch. Loren was short, maybe five foot five, but stocky. He wore silver wire-frame glasses and had toffee-colored skin and gray hair cut short. He was dressed in a light pistachio-colored suit with a white shirt underneath the jacket. He lit a cigarette and looked for an ashtray.

I'd first met Loren at a gay-and-lesbian business social held at Cobalt on St. Charles Avenue. The invitation to attend had been unexpected, and I wasn't that interested in going, but when the night rolled around, I'd had nothing else to do. Paul was visiting his parents in Albuquerque and I was bored, so I decided to get dressed and go. I'd met Loren at the bar, where both of us were getting glasses of wine, and later ran into him again outside smoking. We started chatting, then exchanged business cards. After we'd met, he threw some business my way every once in a while.

Loren was one of those gay men who made you feel guilty. He was politically active—he often wrote briefs and legislation about queer rights to go before the state legislature. He never tired of trying to get me more involved in things like that—hell, I rarely voted—but he always kept after me. It was people like Loren who made life better for the rest of us.

I handed him an ashtray and went into the kitchen to make us both a drink. I made them about half liquor and half mixer.

"Now that's a drink," Loren said, making a face as he swallowed. "But this rotgut vodka is going to give me a headache in the morning."

I lit up another cigarette. It tasted incredible, a little piece of heaven just for me. *Fuck you, Paul,* I thought as I inhaled another lungful of relaxing smoke. "So what's the story?"

Loren took another swig of his drink. "It looks bad. He talked before I could get there to shut him up." He shook his head. "Why don't people know better?"

"Fuck." That was bad news. Never, ever talk to the cops without a lawyer.

"Well, this is what the police know." Loren sat back in the sofa, holding his cigarette. "At 6:15 one of the neighbors heard a shot and called 911. The cops who arrived on the scene a few minutes later found Paul standing over Mark Williams's body and holding a gun." He looked at me over his glasses. "I'm vastly oversimplifying to get the point across, all right?" I nodded. "They take him down to the station. They test him for powder residue. He comes up positive. But even before the test came back he told a story to explain it away. He claims he walked in, saw the gun, and picked it up. It went off, and then he saw Williams's body lying there. Then he called 911 on his cell phone."

Oh, God. I took a big swig of my drink, which burned. Loren was right, the vodka was shit. "How fucking stupid is he?" I growled. I clenched my fists. The cops would never believe a story like that— hell, I didn't believe it. *Nobody* could be that stupid.

"That's the key, Chanse." He toasted me with his glass. "Is he stupid enough to do something like that?"

"I don't know." And I didn't. I didn't know anything about him at all.

"Come on, Chanse." Loren stubbed out his cigarette and lit another. "You're his partner, for Christ's sake. If you don't know, who does?"

"Turns out I don't know a lot of things." I took another drink. This one went down smoother. "What do they say the motive is?"

"They don't need a motive yet. There's more than enough physical evidence to arraign him."

"Why was he there?"

"He told the police…and me…that Williams wanted him to pose for his magazine. He'd decided against it, went over to tell Williams so, and found the door open and Williams dead." Loren raised his eyebrows. "He saw the gun lying there, picked it up, and it went off. Williams was shot once, right through the heart, and the gun had only been fired twice, and the cops did find the bullet in the floor, like he said, so that part holds up." He sighed. "But I don't like it. It doesn't look good for him, not good at all. The cops are convinced they've got their killer, and you know what that means."

Yes, I did. Once the cops are convinced of a suspect's guilt, they are only interested in one thing—convicting him. Overworked and under a lot of pressure, they don't try very hard to find other suspects or evidence that points to someone else. I took a deep breath. "Did he say anything else about Williams? Other than the magazine stuff?"

Loren shook his head. "No." He cocked his head toward me. "Why? Is there more?"

I finished my drink. "He isn't telling you everything."

Loren placed his drink on top of a *TV Guide* on my coffee table. "What are you saying? Do you know the motive, Chanse? Fuck, fuck, fuck."

I walked over to the computer, logged on the Internet, and clicked on the page selling Cody Dallas's latest tape. The shots of Paul and Mark Williams filled the screen.

Loren, standing behind me, whistled. "Well, I don't see why that matters. So he made some porn?"

I touched the screen on Mark's face. "That's Mark Williams, Loren."

"Well, fuck. That complicates things."

"A little."

I turned and watched as he started pacing, chewing on his cigarette butt. "So they had a prior relationship. That doesn't mean anything." He was obviously just thinking out loud, so I remained silent. The vodka was starting to give me a buzz, and my stomach was empty. I was definitely ordering the greasiest, most fattening pizza Café Roma had to offer. Fuck the diet. Fuck the smoking. Fuck the gym tomorrow.

He stopped pacing and emptied his glass. "Another?" He held it out to me. He followed me into the kitchen and watched me mix his drink. He clapped me on the shoulder. "Consider yourself retained. Find out everything you can about this Mark Williams guy, and I'll talk to Paul tomorrow morning about it before the arraignment." He took the drink from me and walked back into the living room.

"About fees, Loren…" I asked from the doorway. I leaned against the frame, hesitating.

He gave me a look. "I can cut my normal fees because he's gay—that's not a problem. But I can't do this pro bono." He sat down. "I also know approximately how much he makes working at the airport. We can work out a payment schedule. That's no big deal."

I made a decision. "Well, I'll do it for free." Paul *couldn't* be a killer. He just couldn't. I rushed on, "I mean, he doesn't have the money, would probably have to borrow some from me, and it seems kind of stupid to have to borrow money to pay me."

"Honey," Loren said, "the only way I can get you involved in client-attorney privilege is to have you working for me on the case, and even then a judge could easily decide it doesn't apply, if the D.A. really wants to press it." He sighed. "Print out a contract; I'll retain your services for a dollar. I doubt a judge would want to know how much I'm actually paying you."

"That presents another problem," I said. *Think of it as work. Paul isn't your boyfriend; he's the client.* It was going to be hard to be objective.

"Which is?"

"I already have a client, one who has had business dealings with Mark Williams." It was getting easier: *Just another client, just another client.* "There may be a conflict of interest."

"Your client might have a motive?" A sly smile spread across Loren's features. His eyes gleamed. I could almost see the wheels turning in his head.

"I can't say, one way or another." I held up my hands. "But there might wind up being a conflict of interest."

"You don't have privilege in court, you know," Loren said as he lit another cigarette. I joined him.

"I know that. If called to testify, I will. But right now, I don't know whether my client has a motive or not."

"So there may *not* be a conflict of interest." Loren's eyes glinted.

"But one may came up." I pulled up my standard contract on the computer, typed in a little addendum about the possibility of my needing to dissolve the contract instantly and without explanation.

"You realize any information I dig up that you might use in court might be considered 'tainted' by the district attorney since I also have this other client. And if it turns out, by whatever chance, my client is guilty, it will be even more tainted by my personal relationship with Paul." Christ, what a fucking mess.

"I don't have to prove he's innocent, Chanse." Loren signed the contract after I finished printing it, opened his wallet and handed me a dollar with a lopsided grin. "There...consider yourself retained. And don't worry too much, okay? All I need is a shadow of a doubt, remember? The state has to prove he's guilty. My job is a lot easier than theirs. And if I can't get one single person on that jury to think Paul just might be innocent, then I'm not much of a lawyer, am I? And if you can't find me some evidence to help create that doubt, you're not much of a detective." When I didn't say anything, he sighed. "Look, Chanse, we're both very good at what we do. Take comfort in that." He picked up his briefcase and headed to the door. "Reasonable doubt, Chanse." He looked at me carefully. "What do you think, Chanse? Do you think he's guilty?"

"I don't know what I think, Loren." I opened the door for him. "Thanks, man, I really appreciate it."

"No problem, Chanse. I'll be in touch."

I watched him get into his Mercedes, waving as he drove off. I shivered. Yeah, he's probably right, I thought as I walked back into the apartment and got out the joint. I put one of Paul's Destiny's Child CDs in the stereo, sat down on the couch, and lit the J. He was a good lawyer, and I'm good at my job. But I knew the only way I could ever be satisfied was to prove him one hundred percent not guilty.

Christ.

Hell of a day, I thought, as I let the smoke out slowly. I took another hit and started to mellow out as the vodka and the pot began to work in tandem. I leaned back in the couch and closed my eyes. He had to be innocent. He had to be.

CHAPTER SIX

I didn't sleep well, which wasn't much of a surprise.

I thought getting stoned and having a few more drinks would take the edge off my anxiety and sufficiently anesthetize me, but I was wrong. All it did was put me into an obnoxious kind of unrestful half-sleep. My body was asleep, but my mind was racing. When the alarm went off at seven, I groaned and hit the snooze button, I was exhausted and wanted nothing more than to lie there all day. With my eyes closed, I argued with myself about getting up. I could stay in bed until Loren called me with the bail amount. I wouldn't have to shower to go see a bail bondsman or to go down to Central Lockup…they'd seen much worse down there than an unshaved and grimy gay man. In one of life's hateful little ironies, my mind was finally tired and begging for sleep. I let myself lie there for another half hour before I dragged my ass out of bed and put on coffee to brew while I showered.

I was just getting out of the shower when someone rang my doorbell. As this was computing in my foggy brain, whoever it was gave up on the bell and started pounding on the doorframe hard enough to rattle my windows.

The hot shower hadn't worked. I still had a bit of a pot hangover. I shook my head to clear the fog, but that didn't work. I stumbled as I put my robe on, still dripping wet. Not cool. *Maybe the coffee will help,* I thought as I opened the front door.

"And just when were you planning on telling me Paul was arrested?" Paige demanded, puffing on a cigarette. She was tapping her foot, one hand on her hip, her huge black purse slung over one shoulder. She pushed past me into my apartment.

Paige Tourneur was my best friend. We'd met in college at my fraternity, Beta Kappa, where she was my little sister. She now worked as a reporter for *The Times-Picayune,* a job she truly hates. She really wants to write romance novels and has been working on one for about three years.

Her reddish hair was disheveled, and her eyes were bleary from lack of sleep. She wore a tight, short black skirt under a cream-colored silk blouse. She wore heels that put her a little over five feet. The most striking thing about Paige was her eyes. The left was blue and the right was green. She always joked that if she ever got fired, she could always tell fortunes in Jackson Square.

"What are you doing up so early?" I asked. Paige hated mornings almost as much as she hated her job.

She held up a box of Dunkin' Donuts. "I brought breakfast, so you'd better fucking have coffee ready." She looked me up and down. "Oh, for God's sake, go dry off and put some clothes on." She plopped down on the couch, opened the box, and revealed a dozen donuts, all glazed. It's the only kind she'd eat. She grabbed one and looked at me. "Get me some coffee first, honey."

I walked into the kitchen and poured us both a cup. I brought it in to her and grabbed a donut. Donuts weren't on my diet either, but what the hell. I'd already blown the diet completely to hell already anyway. I walked back into my bedroom and pulled on underwear and sweatpants. I joined her in the living room and lit a cigarette.

Both of her expertly plucked eyebrows went up. "Smoking again? And donuts? What's going on?"

I blew the smoke into the ceiling fan. "Yeah, well." I shrugged. "I had a hell of a day yesterday."

"So I gathered." She picked up her third donut. "So what the hell is going on? At about five this morning I got a call from the city editor telling me Paul's been arrested and charged with murder. What the fuck, Chanse?" The city editor was a friend of hers. Paul and I had met him at a party in the summer. Nice guy—intel-

ligent and a little on the sloppy side because he was always thinking and not paying attention to little details like tucking in his shirt
and making sure he got every errant hair when he was shaving.

"I don't know, Paige." I grabbed another donut and took a bite.
Glazed donuts are heavenly. Why is it that everything really bad for
you tastes so good?

She sighed. "Come on, Chanse, this is Paige here. Remember
me? And this is not for publication, okay? Just tell me. Paul's my
friend, too, remember?"

"Look, I'd never even heard of Mark Williams until yesterday,"
I said. It hadn't been twenty-four hours yet. Jesus H. Christ.
"Yesterday morning Paul and I got up, went to the gym, and had
breakfast at the Bluebird. Then he said he had some errands to run,
and I had an appointment with a client in the Quarter." I sighed.
"The day really went to shit from there."

"Yeah, well." She tossed her head. "I think Paul's day ended up a
lot worse than yours. Go on."

"Back off," I said evenly. "That's not what I meant." I lit another
cigarette. It was like I'd never quit in the first place. I'd completely
forgotten about the delightful little buzz. "So, I was hired yesterday
by Dominique DuPré, you know her?"

"She's that singer opening a club on Bourbon Street." She sat
back, crossed her legs and pulled her skirt down. "So, what for?"

"Well, she hired me to find out who's causing trouble for her." I
went on to explain, without a lot of details, what was going on at
Domino's. "And who's coming out the front door of Attitude? Paul."

"So, you didn't know Paul knew Mark Williams till then?"

"I'd never fucking *heard* of him." The righteous indignation from
yesterday began to burn back through the fog. "So, Paul tells me this
Williams guy wants him to pose for the magazine cover, and we had
a bit of an argument."

She stared at me. "About what?"

It was my turn to stare at her. "I didn't want him to pose for
the cover."

She waved her hands. "Wait a minute, wait a minute." She leaned forward. "You're telling me you two argued about him posing for the cover?" When I nodded, she rolled her eyes, using her whole head and started laughing. "Oh, for Christ's sake, Chanse, that's priceless."

I don't like being laughed at. "I don't think it's crazy not to want my boyfriend half naked on a magazine cover," I said in a cold voice.

"I'm sorry." She reached over and patted my hand. "I shouldn't have laughed but, honey, it doesn't matter. I mean, really." She clicked her tongue. "Did you stop to wonder why Paul would want to do it?"

"He likes the attention," I said. I realized my lower lip was jutting out.

"Oh, honey." She shook her head. "Did it ever occur to you that maybe he needs the money?"

"He doesn't need the money!" I said. If Paul needed money, I'd know. She was really in outer space this time.

"You..." She paused, took a few deep breaths, then went on. "Chanse, do you remember what it was to be poor?"

"I'm not rich." I wasn't by a long shot. What the hell was she talking about?

"When was the last time you had to worry about making your rent? How you were gonna buy groceries? Where your next pack of cigarettes was coming from?" She lit one and exhaled through her nose.

"Paul's not broke, Paige. I'd know."

"Do you know how much he makes?" She scratched her head.

"No, I don't." We'd never talked about money.

"Some detective you are." She shook her head. "Look, honey, I'm sorry if this seems harsh, but you need to know some things. Paul only makes about ten dollars an hour. That works out to about $400 a week before taxes. So, every two weeks he brings home maybe about $600 or so. He took a huge pay cut to transfer to ground crew. He has to pay his rent, his utilities, his car payment, his insurance and buy food out of that. He's broke, Chanse."

"I..." I stopped myself and thought back. Come to think of it, I'd never seen Paul with cash. If we went out to dinner, he always paid with a credit card. When we went to bars, I always paid for our drinks and cover charges. That kind of thing never really bothered me; I just assumed that because Paul was so good-looking he was used to having someone buy his drinks, so I just always did. But come to think of it, every time we went to the clubs, Paul always hung back and let me go first when paying cover. Once we were inside, he would say, "Can you get me a drink, honey?"

It never occurred to me he might need money. Or that he'd taken a pay cut so he could be in my bed every night.

"Basically, he's been living on his credit cards." Paige got up and refilled her coffee cup without offering to do the same for me. She sat back down. "So, I'm sure if they offered him money, he jumped at it."

"How come you know so much about Paul's financial situation?" *And I don't?*

"Because, honey, I talk to him. About what's going on in his life." She ran a hand through her hair. "Paul's my friend."

I didn't like where this was going. "And just what is he to me?"

"Chanse, I know you love him...I'm not saying you don't." She shrugged. "What do you guys talk about?"

"I don't know. Just stuff."

"But apparently, never anything important."

"Why didn't he ever say anything to me about this?" I didn't understand. I was his *boyfriend,* for God's sake.

"Maybe he was embarrassed—I don't know." Paige stubbed out the cigarette, dug into her purse and produced her compact. She stared into the mirror for a bit, then freshened her lipstick. "For whatever reason, he didn't feel comfortable sharing it with you. Maybe he was afraid you'd be judgmental or something."

My mind was reeling. "I mean, if he was having trouble with the rent or something, he could have just..." I stopped for a moment, then went on. "He could have moved in here."

She started laughing. "Oh, that's rich, Chanse. It really is."

She was really starting to get on my nerves. "I'm serious!" I protested.

Paige reached over and patted me on the hand. "I know you are, honey, and I think it's great. But do you really think you're ready to live with him? I mean, come on, you didn't know about his money problems, you didn't know he'd modeled…"

"I didn't know he'd made wrestling porn videos." I folded my arms and gave her a satisfied smile. I'm sure he hadn't told her about *that*.

"Paul made wrestling videos?" she said after a few beats. She frowned, "Are these videos like a form of fetish porn?" I could see her mind working. "But what's wrong with that?"

Now it was my turn to stare at her. I'd heard her go off on numerous rampages against the porn industry and how it degrades women. "Are you serious?"

"Yes, I'm serious." Paige tilted her head to one side. "It does make sense in a kind of way—if he was really desperate, of course he would turn to his looks to make some money. Just be glad he didn't become an escort or something."

"How do I know he didn't?" I snapped.

She inhaled with a hiss. "I guess you should ask him. But these videos—I mean, were they just wrestling, like the WWF stuff, or were they actually wrestling sex?"

I shrugged. "I don't know—I haven't seen one." I didn't tell her I'd ordered some. "But the Web site described Paul, or Cody Dallas, as one of the 'superstars of the industry.'"

She whistled. "No surprise there." She laughed. "Paul's a hot guy, Chanse. If he made videos, people would buy them."

"What I don't understand is why I am just finding all this out *now*." I stubbed out my cigarette. "Would he have ever told me about this secret life of his? It's like I don't even know him, Paige."

"Relax, Chanse." Paige closed the box of donuts and pushed it away from her. "The most important thing right now is Paul beating this murder rap—we can sort all this other shit out later."

"Easier said than done," I noted.

"I know it's hard, but try not to be a complete jackass here, okay?" She leaned forward. "I know you're in shock—who wouldn't be?

Do you really think Paul killed this Mark Williams guy? I mean, put aside your own feelings. I get it—you've found out some things about Paul you didn't know. But just because he kept some things from you—and be fair, have you told him about your past completely?—now you think he might be a killer? Christ, Chanse, are you that big of an asshole?"

"Hey!" That was a bit unfair, I thought.

"Remove yourself from this situation. Pretend that you didn't know Paul from Adam, that this was a case Loren dropped into your lap. What would your initial impression be?"

I thought for a minute. "His story stinks, Paige. It's kind of hard to believe."

"Truth is stranger than fiction."

"If I didn't know Paul at all, after hearing his story, I'd think he's an idiot."

"Chanse..." she took a deep breath. "Hello? People *are* stupid. You were a cop. How many times have you seen people do stupid things? Mess up crime scenes? Isn't it entirely possible it could have happened the way Paul says it did?"

"I guess."

"Don't convict him because your feelings are hurt." She stood up. "I've got to get to work. I'll see what I can find out. What are you going to do today?"

"Well, his arraignment is this morning. Loren's pretty sure he can get him out on bail." I sighed.

"His arraignment is this morning?" Her eyes narrowed. "My God in heaven, Chanse. Why the hell aren't you down there?"

"There's nothing I can do until they set his bail."

"Chanse MacLeod!" She stood up. Her hands were trembling. "You are blowing this big time, bud. Paul's just spent the night in jail—not a pleasant experience under any circumstance—and he's going in front of a judge today. It might have been nice for him to see you in the courtroom."

"Court doesn't even open until 9:30." I looked at the clock on the VCR. It was just past eight.

"Okay." She reached over and took my hands. "Look, Chanse, you know as well as I do Paul couldn't have killed this guy. Get your butt down there. Be there for him."

"I am going to post his bail," I replied.

"Well, of course you are." She dropped my hands and together we walked over to the door. "I guess I'd better get to work. You give him my love, okay? And tell him to call me day or night, if he needs anything." She paused at the door, and reached up to kiss my cheek. "And remember: innocent until proven guilty, okay?"

I nodded. She smiled and walked down my front steps.

I walked back into the kitchen and got another cup of coffee before I got dressed. The whole time, everything Paige said kept running through my mind. Paul was broke. Paul needed money. And I'd been completely oblivious to what was going on with my boyfriend. I imagined Paul being led into the courtroom, looking around for my face but not finding it and wondering if I'd written him off. We'd had an argument, after all, and now he was accused of murder. Considering the kind of boyfriend I'd been so far, it wasn't a reach for him to imagine I'd abandoned him. *Man, oh. man, oh, man, this so sucked.*

Yeah, I was a complete failure as a boyfriend. Paul probably hated me.

I was checking my e-mail after I got dressed when my phone rang. It was Loren. "Chanse, bail's been set. Can you come up with the cash for the bond?"

"How much is it?" I closed my eyes, thinking about the money in my savings account. There was almost seventy grand in there.

"The judge set it at $200,000, so you need to come up with $20,000."

I closed my eyes. Twenty grand was a lot of money, and you don't get it back. You pay it to a bail bondsman, they put up a bond for the full amount, and you kiss your cash goodbye. Of course, the bondsman is taking a big risk. They have to come up with the full amount if the accused jumps bail, and they are dealing with accused criminals.

It was a little past ten when I walked out to my car. I climbed in and started it. "Come on, baby, run right today." I wasn't completely sure what was wrong with it, but I knew the problem was transmission related, and it usually started when I was out on the highway. Whenever I slowed down to exit and would get down to about twenty miles per hour, the gears wouldn't downshift property and the car would start lurching. Sometimes I could slip into neutral, and the engine wouldn't stall. Sometimes that didn't work, and I'd have to restart the car, gun the engine for a while, then shift into drive and hope it wouldn't stall again. Today wasn't a day I needed to deal with that. Fortunately, I wasn't going to have to drive very far or very fast.

The courthouse was on Broad Street, so the easiest way for me to get there was to head up Poydras. There was a Whitney Bank on St. Charles only a couple of blocks from my house. I parked, waited in line for a teller, and withdrew the money from my savings account. *Hang on, Paul, I'm coming,* I thought as I pulled back into traffic and headed down St. Charles to Poydras.

Broad Street is an area most tourists only see if they're really unlucky. It's not New Orleans at its finest. The area around the courthouse is a curious mixture of convenience stores, gas stations, fast-food restaurants, pawn shops, and bail bondsmen. There are very few trees or bushes, just unrelenting concrete. The gutters are full of trash—Quarter Pounder wrappers, empty beer cans, cigarette butts. I pulled into a small parking lot just past Loyola Street. There was a huge yellow sign outlined in yellow lightbulbs with those black letters that come on clear plastic squares: LEGUME AND MER-CEREAUX—BAIL BONDS. The building looked like a Quonset hut on stilts with an unfinished wood staircase leading to the door. All the windows had bars on them. The only car in the parking lot was a battered blue Toyota Celica that had seen better days; nevertheless, it had a Club attached to its steering wheel.

A bell rang when I opened the door. A black woman in her early forties, wearing a pair of jeans and a yellow cardigan, looked up at me from a file she was glancing through. She was seated at one of five desks, all of which overflowed with file folders and papers. There was a water cooler in a corner, almost empty, and the sleeve for paper cups was empty. "What can I do for you?" she asked. A nameplate on her desk read MAXI LEGUME.

I sat down in an uncomfortable plastic chair in front of her desk. "I, um, need to bail someone out."

She closed the folder. "How much is bail?"

"Two hundred thousand."

She whistled. "I can write that bond. What's the charge, murder?"

I nodded. She opened a drawer and passed me a form with a clipboard and a pen. I started filling it out. It was like a credit card application, with requests for six character references as well. "What's the name of the accused?" She started typing on her computer.

"Paul Maxwell," I said.

"Arraigned this morning?"

"Yes." I went back to my form while she typed away at her keyboard.

She stopped and looked at me as I tried to remember addresses and phone numbers for my references. "You know I can't take a check for the ten percent, right? Cash or credit card."

I put down the clipboard and balanced it on the edge of her desk while I pulled my wallet out of my pocket. I counted out the money and handed it over to her. She didn't recount it; she simply took it and walked into the next room.

I was finished with the form when she came back to hand me a receipt. "Okay, I've called over there. They should be bringing him down in a bit. Do you know where to go meet him—you are going to go meet him, right?" She took the form from me and began typing again.

"Yes."

"Get back on Broad and go back to the courthouse. There's a little frontage road right off Broad. You can't miss it—there are police cars parked everywhere—and then you're going to have to go right. You can't do anything else, but after you make that right turn, keep going straight. You can also go to the left, but that'll take you back to Poydras. The street you want is Perdido." She laughed. "Kind of appropriate, actually. Perdido means 'lost' in Spanish. Anyway, there's a parking lot right there. Park there and it's the building right behind the parking lot. Just go in the front door and you'll be in a waiting area. There's a place where there's a window, and you go tell the person there whom you're coming for, and at some point they'll bring him down."

"At some point?" I didn't like the sound of that.

"The best advice I can give you, Mr. MacLeod, is not to piss off the person at the window." She leaned back in her chair. "They are in no hurry to let people out, and if you do or say anything to rile them, they'll make you wait all day."

"Can they do that?" This was outrageous.

"They can do whatever the fuck they want to." She gave me a sad look. "I hope you brought a book or something to do."

"Well, no."

She shrugged. "Best of luck to you, then."

Her directions were perfect. I found the parking lot on Perdido all right, but then I got a little confused. There was a building right behind the parking lot, but there was no entrance to it right there. I walked up Perdido Street and finally found it. Two uniforms were sharing a cigarette outside, and I asked if this was where you went to bail someone out. Both nodded. I walked inside, and there was the waiting room. It had hardwood benches and plastic chairs from the 1950s—everything was orange, yellow, or red. There were several people sitting at various places throughout the room. *The Sharon Osbourne Show* played on an old television set sitting on a ledge just below the ceiling. The lighting was all yellow fluorescent and gave everything a sickly look. The floor was green tile with white streaks. I walked over to the window.

The woman sitting on the other side wore a police uniform. She had to weigh 300 pounds. She was paging through a tired-looking copy of *People* magazine. An open can of Coke sat next to a partially eaten bag of barbecue potato chips. Her gray-streaked brown hair looked greasy and was pulled back from her moon face. I stood there for a moment, watching her read about Brad and Jennifer, and finally cleared my throat.

She didn't respond.

"Um, excuse me?" I asked.

With a very deliberate, slow motion she closed the magazine and turned her head to look up at me. The expression on her face was sullen hostility. She said nothing and just stared at me for a few seconds, then she reached over and pulled a chip out of the bag, put it into her mouth and chewed it at the same slow, deliberate pace.

"Um, I just posted bail for someone," I said.

She kept looking at me in silence.

Remembering Maxi Legume's advice, I suppressed my rising anger. *Don't piss her off, Chanse. She's already got a serious attitude problem. She's just looking for someone to take it out on—don't let it be Paul.*

"Can you help me?" I injected a note of pleading in my voice.

"Name?" She reached for a clipboard.

"His name is Paul Maxwell."

She made a great show of looking at the list. "Name's not on here."

"Well, I just posted bail, so—"

"Have a seat and wait." She put away the clipboard and went back to the chips.

I swallowed my anger and forced myself to walk away. But I didn't have a seat. I went back outside and lit a cigarette. At this point, I seriously doubted Paul would give a rat's ass about my smoking.

I checked back again in an hour, but Paul's name still wasn't on the list. I sat down and watched television. I was hungry, but I was afraid to leave in case they released him while I was gone. The morning ticked away—*The Young and the Restless, All My Children, One Life to Live.* Every half hour I went back outside and smoked. Every hour I went back and checked to see if Paul's name was on the magic list.

General Hospital was starting when I went back to check again. At this point, I was ready to blow up at the fat bitch, so I was a little taken aback to see a pretty young black woman sitting there instead.

"Oh, Paul Maxwell?" She checked the list and smiled at me. "He's on his way down. Shouldn't be more than two minutes."

I almost collapsed in relief. *Finally.*

CHAPTER SEVEN

Paul walked through the door as it buzzed. He was rubbing his upper arms with his hands, as though he was trying to get warmer. He was in the same clothes he'd been wearing when I'd run into him in the Quarter, only now he looked more rumpled. His blue eyes were completely bloodshot. Stubble sprouted on his cheeks, chin, and upper lip. His curls were flattened on one side and stood out at weird angles from his head on the other side. His face looked bloodless and shiny in the sickly light from the fluorescent tubes overhead. "Oh, thank God," he said. His voice was low, and his eyes constantly blinked. He bit his lower lip. "Can you please get me out of here?"

He walked like he'd been kicked in the balls as we passed through the electric doors into the sunshine. His shoulders were hunched and his head was down.

"That was horrible," he said. He glanced over at me, then cast his eyes back down toward the sidewalk as we walked to the parking lot. "They *shackled* me, Chanse." He shuddered and stopped walking. He started shaking and put his head down and his hands on his knees as he tried to catch his breath. He made gagging noises. Not knowing what to do, I reached out and patted him between the shoulder blades.

A police car cruised by slowly. The driver watched us from behind mirrored sunglasses. Paul turned his head away. I nodded in acknowledgement, and the cop turned his gaze back to the road.

"Come on, honey," I said. "Let's go home. Are you hungry?"

He nodded. "A little bit. I didn't have dinner…" He broke off. "And this morning I couldn't eat the breakfast they gave us…oh, God." He shuddered again.

"Come on, let's get out of here."

We headed over to where I'd parked my little red Cavalier. Just when we reached the car, he stopped, threw his arms around me, and gripped me with all his strength. At first I just stood there as my ribs were crushed, and then I put my arms around him. His body shook. *He's crying,* I realized with a start. I squeezed him tight and stroked his hair. *Poor guy, I do love him,* I thought. I said, "It's okay, baby. Everything'll be fine, you'll see. Everything's gonna work out…"

He pushed away from me, wiped his eyes, and forced a shaky smile. "It'll have to be, won't it? I can't go back to jail. I'd rather die." He shuddered again. "I'd rather die, Chanse."

"You aren't going to jail," I said, almost to convince myself as well. I unlocked the car. "Come on, get in. Let's get you out of here and get you something to eat."

"I just want to go home," he said. He stared out the window as I turned onto Broad Street. "I'll just make myself a sandwich."

"You doing okay?" I patted his leg. It seemed hopelessly inadequate. I suck in these kinds of situations. I'm just not a nurturing person. I never know what to say.

He nodded. "It just doesn't seem real." He put his hand on top of mine and squeezed it. "Thanks for posting my bail."

"Yeah, well, just don't *jump* bail." I looked over at him. Even disheveled, he was handsome. I smiled at him. *No, he couldn't have killed anyone.* How could I even think that?

"I'm not going anywhere." He sighed. "I'll pay you back the money, Chanse. I swear."

I didn't say anything.

I pulled into a spot across the street from Paul's apartment. He lived on the second floor of a Queen Anne–style house on Valence Street between Prytania and Magazine. It was three stories, with an octagonal tower in its left front corner. The coolest thing about Paul's apartment was his bedroom, which was in the tower and surrounded by windows. The owners of the house were in the process of repainting it. The outside was stripped down to the bare wood with ladders and a maze of scaffolding decorating the sides. We went to the side door and climbed the wooden steps to his apartment.

Paul's had three big rooms, which were always immaculate. I never could figure out how he did it. New Orleans is a dusty city. I could dust my apartment in the morning and everything would be coated again by the afternoon-so I rarely tried. Paul's hardwood floors always gleamed like he'd just waxed them. Everything was in its place—nothing was where it shouldn't be. You'd never find a sock or a dirty pair of underwear underneath his couch.

He walked into the kitchen and put some seven grain bread in the toaster. I headed into the living room and sat on the couch. The living room windows were made of stained glass, the morning sun gleamed through the painted panes and bathed his white leather couch in reds, blues and yellows.

I never felt really comfortable in Paul's apartment. It was too tidy, clean, and neat. Unlike my own apartment, all his furniture matched. His end table gleamed. He always used coasters. It looked more like a show apartment than a place where someone actually lived, which was probably why we spent all of our time at my place.

I sighed and looked up at the print over the fireplace mantel. It was a beautiful nude in black and white. The model's head was turned away slightly from the camera and was in shadows. The model reclined on a divan with his legs stretched out in front of him. The muscles in his abs rippled, and his strong, hairless, marble-like legs stretched out leisurely.

With a start, I realized it was Paul. Why had I never noticed that before?

"You sure you don't want anything?" Paul called from the kitchen.

"Positive." I got up and walked closer to the picture. Sure enough, it was him. His hair had been cut short—buzzed Marine-style—and that brought out his cheekbones more prominently. His eyes were closed, his body was shaved smooth, and his muscles weren't as big. I turned and looked at another framed print that hung on the wall beside the fireplace. It was a rear shot, in black and white. The model's arms were up over his head, revealing the smooth definition in his shoulders and back.

And there was Paul's mole right above the right cheek. So much for my powers of observation—some detective I was.

Paul sat in the reclining chair with a tuna sandwich on a plate. He placed his glass of ice water on a coaster of green marble and cork.

"When did you pose for these?" I asked, gesturing at the two prints.

"When I was twenty-two." He took a bite of his sandwich. "I met a photographer at the gym in Dallas. That's how I got started modeling."

I didn't say anything else until he finished eating. He seemed to come back into himself with each bite. He'd also combed his hair. "How come you never told me you'd modeled?" *Nude,* I added silently.

He put the empty plate on the table and frowned at me. He pointed at the pictures. "Come on! I thought you knew! I mean, it's pretty obvious those pictures are of me, isn't it?"

He had a point. It wasn't his fault I was so fucking clueless. I'd seen them thousands of times, even commented on them. I'd envied him for owning them. Now, looking at them again, it was so obvious. I felt like an idiot.

"I mean, my body is shaved and my hair is different, and I'm bigger"—he gave a weak smile—"and of course I'm older, but you never recognized me?"

"No." *Enough of this,* I told myself. *Let it go. He's just a client—not your boyfriend—establishing his innocence is the most important thing—for now at any rate.* "You want to tell me what happened yesterday?"

He shuddered again, and his face paled. "I went to see Mark. I was going to tell him I wasn't going to do the cover shoot because it bothered you." He flashed a smile at me, as if to say *I'm such a good boyfriend.*

Whatever. "What time did you get there?" I asked.

"Oh, I don't know," he said. "I wasn't paying attention to the time." He frowned.

"After you saw him earlier, after you left me, where did you go?"

"What does that have to do with anything?" he asked, eyebrows going up.

"I need to know exactly where you went, what you did all day."

"Oh." He thought for a minute. "After I saw you, I went back uptown to the grocery store. I guess it was around noon. I was there for a while, then went home and checked my e-mail, and then I had some other errands to run." He rubbed his forehead. "I picked up my dry cleaning, went to Garden District Bookstore to get something to read, and went to the coffee shop on Magazine, to read and think."

"Which coffee shop?"

"The one by the A&P."

The Rue de la Course. I nodded. "And then?"

"That's when I decided to come back and tell Mark I wasn't going to pose for the cover."

"Where did you park?"

"On Burgundy between St. Ann and Dumaine."

"Did you see or talk to anyone between parking the car and when you got to his office?"

"I don't see how that matters."

I sighed. "Well, if you ran into someone and talked to them, and you seemed perfectly normal, it could be argued you weren't on your way to commit a murder."

"Oh," he said and scratched his head. "No, I don't remember talking to anyone."

"Go on."

"He lived in the carriage house behind the main house, you know? Where the office is? That dreadlocked girl, whatever her name is, told me to just go around there because that's where he was. I walked around, the door was open, so I knocked and went in." He shivered. "I tripped on something and almost fell. It was a gun. I bent down and picked it up, and it went off, and that's, that's wh—wh—when I saw him." His breath became more labored. He closed his eyes and took several deep breaths. "I didn't know what to do." He winced, remembering. "The gun was so loud, but it didn't sound real, you know? More like a firecracker or something, just louder—not like on TV. Then the next thing I knew the police were there, asking me questions, putting me in the police car..." he closed his eyes again.

"Why didn't you just call him?" I crossed my arms.

His eyes opened. "What?"

I crossed my arms. "You could have just called him, couldn't you? Why was it so important that you had to go see him in person?"

"I...I don't know." He was lying. It was easy to see. He wouldn't look me in the eyes, and his body language had shifted.

"Were you sleeping with him?" I asked, keeping my voice steady.

"*What?*" He stared at me. "Is that what you think?"

"I don't know what to think, to be frank." I sat down and took a deep breath. *Client—not boyfriend—client.* "Why don't you tell me?"

"I wasn't sleeping with Mark." He swallowed and leaned forward. "You have to believe that, Chanse. We were involved, yes, but that was over three years ago, and it didn't last very long."

"Why didn't you tell me that yesterday? Why did you pretend you barely knew him?"

He looked away from me. "Because you're so jealous."

"Jealous?" I stared at him. I couldn't believe what I was hearing.

"Yes, Chanse, *jealous.*"

"I'm not jealous!"

"Oh, yeah, right." He smirked at me. "Remember the last time we went to Oz?"

"What about it?" Now I was getting defensive. I thought back. It had been about a month or so—we'd taken to staying home or going to movies instead of dancing. I remembered having a good time and coming home about three in the morning and having intense sex.

"Don't you remember your hissy fit?" His voice sounded sad more than anything else.

"You mean that guy who was flirting with you?" That I did remember.

"I mean the guy that was *talking* to me."

We'd taken a break from dancing, and I'd gone to get us both a drink. Paul was standing in the front corner by the dance floor. When I looked over from the bar, I noticed a guy in the middle of the dance floor moving in Paul's direction. I watched as he walked up to Paul, put his hands on Paul's chest and started talking to him. The guy was good-looking—in his early twenties with that slim, smooth, boyish kind of body some guys are lucky enough to keep as adults. He was about my height, give or take. His beltless jeans hung low off his hips, and he wasn't wearing underwear. I paid for our drinks and walked back over. I glared at him until he got the hint and left. "Come on, that guy wanted to sleep with you," I said. "How could you think he wasn't flirting with you?"

"You think *everyone* wants to sleep with me," Paul replied.

I started to say "they do" but stopped myself. I closed my mouth.

"Don't think I don't appreciate it—it's really flattering," he continued. "But it's also kind of hard to deal with. I mean, when we go out I'm always afraid someone is going to talk to me and you're going to get pissed off. Do you have any idea how hard that is on me?"

Hard on you? I thought. *Has it ever occurred to you how hard it is to have everyone in the world want to fuck your boyfriend?*

I just stared at him. I struggled to get hold of myself. *Client, not boyfriend.* I took a deep breath. "Okay, okay, maybe I'm a little jealous. That's not the issue here." *The real issue is a little thing called a first-degree murder charge.* "You need to tell me the truth—everything, Paul. I can't help you if you lie to me."

"The truth." He looked at me and swallowed. "Chanse, I wasn't exactly a saint before we met, you know."

"I didn't think you were." *I just had no idea of the extent of your sins.*

"I met Mark online four years ago in a chat room." Paul rubbed his eyes. "He was living in Norfolk at the time. We traded pictures and started talking a lot when we were both online. Then we started talking on the phone, and I decided to fly up and visit him."

"Weren't you living with Jeff then?" Jeff was my predecessor—the doctor in Dallas.

"Jeff and I had an open relationship." He squirmed a bit in his chair. "I would have told you, but you never seemed to want to know anything about Jeff and me."

"Oh." He had tried to bring up Jeff from time to time, but I never encouraged it. "And I know how you feel about open relationships..." He shrugged.

It's no secret that I've never understood open relationships. My friend Blaine and his longtime lover had one. It never made much sense to me. Sex was such an intimate part of a relationship. I couldn't grasp how you could allow someone you loved to have sex with someone else—whenever they wanted, with whomever they wanted, and as often as they wanted. That wasn't what love was supposed to be like. "Go on," I said.

"Mark and I hit it off really well, so I went back up there a few times over the next year or so." He shrugged. "Then it just kind of petered out for us. We stayed friends, talking online or by e-mail, and I visited him once in a while, but the physical part was over a couple of years ago." He took a deep breath. "Mark is why I moved here, you know?"

"What?"

"I came here to visit him after he moved here last year and fell in love with New Orleans. That's why I decided to move here when Jeff and I were breaking up."

Christ on the cross!

"And then I met you." He shrugged. "And here we are."

I took a deep breath. *He's a client, I told myself again, not your boyfriend.* "And that's all there was to it?" *What about the wrestling career, buddy?*

"That's all."

"You need to tell me the whole truth, Paul," I said carefully, trying to keep my temper. *Client, not boyfriend. Client.* "If there's anything else—trust me, the police are going to go through your life with a fine-tooth comb. They don't have a motive yet, but they're going to be looking for one. Their case is pretty strong on the physical evidence, but…" I let my voice trail off.

"That's all." He shifted in his seat and wouldn't meet my eyes. He picked up part of his sandwich, looked at it, and put it back down again. He licked drops of mustard off a couple of fingers.

I couldn't look at him anymore. I turned my head and looked through the stained glass. *Please tell me*, I thought. *Please, please tell me.*

His silence was deafening.

"You're sure?" I had to say something, and I felt my anger rising. I gripped the armrests and squeezed them. *Stay calm, stay calm. Client, client, client.*

"Chanse, please." He wouldn't look at me.

Damn it. "Do you think the police won't find out about Cody Dallas?"

His face drained of color. "Oh…my…God. How do you…how did you…oh, my God." He buried his face in his hands.

"It's a little hard for me to believe your story when you keep leaving out important details." My voice was harsh. "If I found out about your little side career in videos, the police certainly will. Mark made videos, too, didn't he? In fact, your most recent match was against him, wasn't it?"

"Oh, God." He looked at me. "How…how did you find out?"

"I did an Internet search on you." *Deep breaths, easy now. Client… remember that, Chanse, don't lose control.* "Apparently, you did an online interview about your retirement from wrestling and revealed your real name."

His eyes widened. He shook his head. "No, I didn't."

"I read it, Paul." I ground my teeth, trying to keep my breathing measured.

"I swear to you, Chanse, I didn't do any interviews—like anyone would care that I was quitting." He gave a short laugh. "Besides, the last thing in the world I want is for people to know I'm Cody Dallas." He stood up. "Come on." He walked into the little room he'd set up as his office. His little white laptop sat in the center of it, hooked up to a disk drive and a printer. He turned it on and logged onto the Internet. He typed in "www.codydallas.net." I stood behind him as the site loaded. When it came up, there was the same picture of Paul, smiling in the low-cut red Speedo I'd seen on the other site. He pushed his chair back. "See?"

I closed my eyes. Christ, he even had his own wrestling Web site. I counted to ten, struggling not to lose my temper. I opened my eyes and read the text. It was basically an announcement that he was shutting down the site and retiring.

"When I started seeing you, I decided to retire," he explained. "That match with Mark was my last one. I didn't tell you about it...well, I didn't think you'd understand."

"Well, you were right about that. I don't understand." I folded my arms and walked over to the window. "I don't understand why you never told me about this wrestling thing. I don't understand why you never told me about modeling nude. I don't understand a lot of things, Paul."

"You're being unfair." He folded his arms, veins bulging in his forearms. "There's a lot I don't know about your past...stuff you've never shared with me."

"I never posed nude or made porn videos."

He made a face. "It wasn't porn."

"No, they were just videos for guys who are into wrestling to watch and enjoy, right?" *Like, I've just fallen off the turnip truck or something.* "Come on, Paul...they're beat-off tapes." *Why can't he just admit it?*

"You can be such an asshole," he said bitterly.

I bit my lip and closed my eyes. *Get back on track, Chanse.* "Okay. I'm sorry. But cut me some slack here, Paul...this is a lot to deal with." I sat down on the window ledge. "But you've got to understand something, my friend. You've got to be honest with me and Loren...completely one hundred percent honest. These charges against you are serious. You could get the death penalty.'

"But I didn't kill Mark."

"I didn't say you did. The police think so, though, and the evidence looks pretty bad. Now, why did you go over to see him in person instead of calling?"

"Well, I did want to tell him that I wasn't going to pose for the cover." Paul leaned back in his chair. "But I'd gotten this weird e-mail yesterday afternoon, and I wanted to talk to him about it."

"A weird e-mail?"

"From a fan of the videos."

"What was weird about it?"

"Well, for one thing, it came to my private e-mail account, not Cody's." He sighed. "On my Web site"—he gestured to the computer screen—"there was a link where fans could e-mail me direct, you know? I had a standard e-mail response I'd send them. It was weird someone contacted me direct...but you say some Web site posted my real name, right? That would explain it, I guess."

I walked over to the computer and typed in "www.ilovefullnelson.com." Once the page loaded, I clicked on the link to the Cody Dallas interview.

Paul stared at the computer screen. "Chanse, I never gave this interview. I've never even heard of this Web site before." He typed in "www.fullnelson.com" and explained, "This is the site for the company."

The page loaded. A large picture of a hot guy with a shaved head and goatee wearing a black leather thong came up. There were smaller pictures of muscular guys in underwear or Speedos wrestling down another side, with links to the videos the pictures were taken from. "Okay, we'll come back to that," I said. "What about this e-mail?"

He clicked on his mail icon, and his inbox came up. He clicked on one on the envelopes. The letter opened.

Dear Paul, or Cody, or whatever you call yourself now,
I've been a huge fan of yours ever since your first video was released. You are Full Nelson's sexiest wrestler and so handsome too. I've always wanted to meet you.

I can't believe you lost that match to Mark Miller and are retiring. I know you threw that match because you were retiring. What a shitty thing to do to your fans, those of us who have supported you and bought your tapes loyally all these years. The least you could have done was gone out on a high note instead of throwing a match to that arrogant, cocky son of a bitch. Mark Miller isn't fit to carry your Speedo, let alone beat you. That is such bullshit, bullshit, bullshit. But don't worry about that—he'll pay for it.

You, on the other hand, should be ashamed of yourself. One day you'll understand what you have done to your fans, and you'll be sorry.

There was no signature at the bottom. I whistled. "Huh."

"I wanted to talk to Mark about it." He sighed. "I mean, I've gotten weird e-mails before, but they were mostly from guys who wanted to wrestle me, date me, whatever. This was, I don't know, just weird. It kind of scared me."

"Most people who write threatening letters or e-mails generally don't ever do anything about it," I said. This was true—just venting their spleen usually did the trick for them.

"I knew I had some time before I was meeting you at dinner, so I decided to go down to the Quarter." He groaned. "Fuck, I left my car on Burgundy Street. It's probably been towed, huh?"

I sighed. "I'll take you over to the impound lot." It was under I-10 on Claiborne, right behind St. Louis Cemetery Number One.

He stood up, looking at me. "So, you don't think this guy who sent the e-mail could be dangerous?"

I shook my head. "It's possible, but I can't say for sure."

His voice dropped. "Do you think I killed him?"

I didn't answer, searching my head for the right answer.

"You do." His entire body began to shake, beads of sweat gathered on his forehead. His skin looked whitish. "You think I killed him!"

Something in me just snapped—I don't know, maybe it was all the tension that had built up. I started yelling at him. "How *can* I believe you? Tell me what the fuck I am supposed to think! I just found out my boyfriend has posed bare-assed! I just found out my boyfriend had a porn career I knew nothing about! What else don't I know about, huh? You have this whole other life I don't know about! Maybe you *are* a killer! How the fuck am I supposed to know? Tell me! Tell me what to believe!" Spittle flew in his face.

His eyes filled with tears. "You're hurting me," he whispered.

I stared at him and the anger drained out of me. I realized I was clutching his biceps. I'd been shaking him.

I dropped my hands to my sides.

"I think maybe you'd better go," he said.

His skin was turning greenish-purple, where my fingers had dug in.

I stumbled past him, out the front door, and down the steps, not stopping to breathe and trying not to think. I pulled my car keys out of my pocket, opened the door, started the car, and pulled away from the curb.

CHAPTER EIGHT

I stopped at a light on Magazine. My hands gripped the steering wheel so tightly my knuckles were white. My palms were soaking wet. My heart was pounding so hard and fast I could barely hear anything else.

The coffee in my stomach was turning to acid. I started to shake. *Calm down, Chanse.*

I took some deep breaths. I'd grabbed Paul. I'd hurt him. I'd left marks.

Inhale, hold it. Exhale. Get a hold of yourself.

My heart rate began to slow down. *Get control, Chanse.*

The wave of adrenaline subsided, and I felt nauseated and feverish, like I was going to throw up. I was drenched in sweat.

I turned the air conditioning on high. My hand trembled as I reached for the controls.

What just happened? "You lost control," I said aloud.

The light changed.

I crossed Magazine and headed down to Tchoupitoulas, like every other time I'd driven home from Paul's—automatic pilot taking over.

The last time I'd lost control, someone had died. It had been pretty stupid going to confront a killer: I'd told myself that a thousand times since then. What had I been thinking? I hadn't been armed with anything more dangerous than a tape recorder. I should have just gone to the police, even though all I had were suspicions. But no, I thought I could handle a killer without even telling anyone where I was going.

I remembered the roaring in my ears. Yes, he was trying to kill me—he had a knife—but there had to have been some other way to disarm him. I outweighed him by at least fifty pounds, but he was so much stronger than he'd looked. And his eyes—his eyes were so crazed when he came at me—wild and primal. He hadn't looked human anymore.

I'd seen those eyes many times in my dreams since then.

I closed my eyes, reliving the sound of the shattering of the glass as he went through the window. The glass exploded and sprayed everywhere. Later, I found splinters lodged in my hair. I'd hit him hard—a direct punch to the face with all of my weight behind me. I broke two knuckles in my right hand. He fell back and through the glass door as though it had offered no more resistance than a shower curtain. He seemed to go over the railing in slow motion. I would never forget the sound of him hitting the brick courtyard.

I was sweating again and struggling to catch my breath. I pulled over to the side of the road. I coughed, choked, and gagged.

Every time I'd relived this horror in my dreams,—waking up gasping and body shaking—Paul had been there, somehow waking up with me. He would put his strong arms around me, kiss me, talk me down from the emotional ledge and hold me until I could fall asleep again.

What the hell had I done? I pulled the car to the side of the road, turned the engine off, and got out.

There was a coffee shop on the corner. I walked unsteadily toward it. My lower back hurt, my stomach was churning, and my knees threatened to buckle as I walked. I stopped in front of the shop and tried to get control of my breathing. I used my shirtsleeves to wipe the sweat off my face. When I was done I saw my sleeves were soaked. *Nice,* I thought. Finally, everything in my body seemed to go back to normal.

As I climbed the steps, I heard my mother's voice in my head—and could almost smell the vodka on her breath: *You've got your father's temper, God help you.*

I'd been eight years old. My sister, who was six, was doing something. I don't remember what. But she was bothering me or wouldn't give me something I wanted, and she wouldn't relent. She was always doing that. She would want one of my toys and cry until my mother made me give it to her. Once the toy was securely in her fat little hands, she would give me a smug smile. It seemed like all she ever wanted to do was get me in trouble.

That day, my eight-year-old self decided that enough was, finally, enough. So I picked up the pewter replica of the Alamo off the coffee table and whacked her in the back of the head with it. I remembered how satisfying it felt; the thudding sound of pewter connecting with bone. Then there was blood everywhere. My sister screamed, loud enough for my mother to put down the vodka bottle and come running from the kitchen. I had to hold the white towel to her head as we headed to the emergency room. My mother babbled the entire time, "Remember, just remember to tell anyone she fell on the steps. We don't want any trouble—remember, she fell." And then she looked over at me, the Pall Mall hanging off her curled lip. "You've got your father's temper, God help you."

I ordered a cup of iced coffee and a muffin, grabbed a stack of napkins, and went back outside. I sat in a wicker chair facing the street. There were a couple of college-age kids sitting alone at various tables and pounding away at laptop computers propped up against worn backpacks.

The muffin tasted like sawdust, but I choked it down to get something in my stomach to settle it. I stared out at the street and watched the cars go by.

I grew up in fear of my father's temper. All three of us kids did. It got worse after my mother brought my baby brother home from the hospital. His crying always seemed to set Dad off, and the good days when Dad came home smiling and whistling became more and more rare. We learned to keep quiet when he was home—and not to raise our voices, never to say anything at all if possible. We watched what Dad wanted to watch on television. If Dad wanted to listen to the radio, we turned the television off. We didn't talk about school, and Dad never asked. Only Mom would talk and always in a low, quiet voice. When he walked in the door, she poured a beer for him from a bottle into a glass she'd had in the freezer all day and brought it to him when he sat in his reclining chair. It took Dad exactly thirty minutes to drink that beer, and when he finished it, dinner had better be on the table, goddamn it.

We tried to learn from our mistakes—any behavior that set him off was never repeated. But there was never any knowing *what* would set him off. Something mundane—some little thing that went on every day would suddenly, inexplicably, light the fuse.

He could be sitting in his reclining chair, his beer glass clutched in his right hand, laughing his head off at *Three's Company,* when all of a sudden his mood would turn. His face would harden, and his eyes would get the dangerous glitter in them. As the rage in him built, he would first talk in a low voice, so low it could barely be heard, and then the explosion came and he would start screaming.

Other times, you could tell it was coming from the moment he walked in the door from work. You could see him seething. He wouldn't say a word to anyone—this was usually when something happened at work to piss him off, and he'd had to hold it in all day—and then we were all completely silent. The only sound in the trailer was the canned laughter on the television as we all waited for the inevitable eruption of anger.

My brother and sister and I were very well-behaved when Dad was around. I think the last time he took a belt strap to me was when I was twelve. After that, I was too big for the belt—that's when he started punching. That was when he thought I was old enough to learn how to take a punch.

Nobody ever noticed. Teachers, other students, counselors at school—no one ever noticed. Maybe they chalked up the bruises to gym class or a fight that happened off-campus or something. Whatever they thought, they never said anything to me. Maybe they were waiting for me to say something.

It never occurred to me to tell anyone, partly because I grew up thinking everyone's parents acted like that. Later, when I knew better, I was too ashamed. Wasn't it bad enough we were trailer trash, that everyone knew we were poor and our clothes didn't fit right and my mother cut my hair with scissors as her cigarettes dropped hot ash on my shoulders? That other mothers had to smell the sour liquor on my mother at the Safeway. Why give them something else to laugh at us about?

I knew I had my father's temper. I felt it boiling inside of me whenever I heard kids at school whispering and giggling when I walked past. Sometimes they wouldn't bother to whisper. Sometimes I'd hear someone say, as I walked past their table in the cafeteria, something about my clothes or about seeing my mom weaving down the aisles in the Safeway as she put stuff in her cart. The rage would boil up then. I'd clench my fists and wanted to knock the smug smirks off their faces, pound them until I felt bones breaking. But I fought it down, struggled to control it.

What I really wanted to do was give in to the rage, let my vision go red and start screaming, throwing things, punching and kicking, let it take control and stop thinking so much, stop feeling so much, just let it go. But acting out wouldn't change anything. It would just make things so much worse.

So I never gave in to it. I just kept driving it deeper and deeper inside of me. Not even on the football field would I let it take over. I always kept cool on the field, never gave into any kind of emotion. Even when I scored a touchdown—my teammates jumping all over me in excitement, the band playing the fight song, the cheerleaders tumbling on the sideline, the fans screaming—I felt nothing. No elation. No joy. Giving into any kind of emotion was dangerous because it could turn without warning, just like in my dad. But I always knew it was there.

I'd have to apologize to Paul. There was no excuse for hurting him physically.

Paige was right. I was being an asshole. So Paul had a past. Big fucking deal. Everyone has a past. Everyone has secrets, things they don't talk about. So Paul made some wrestling videos and hadn't told me? So he'd posed naked? What did it matter?

It didn't matter. What mattered was I loved him.

Stupid jackass.

I left my coffee untouched and walked back to the car. I started it up and pulled out my cell phone. Loren answered on the second ring. "Found anything yet?" he asked.

"I haven't even had time to start," I said as I pulled out in front of a white Lexus. The driver, a perfectly coiffed bleached blond, flipped me the finger. I returned it with a smile.

"What did Paul say to you?" Loren asked.

I hesitated. "I…"

"Chanse, we are trying to save his life here, have you forgotten?" He exhaled. "All normal boundaries are off. I don't want to know anything intimate, for God's sake."

"He gave me another lead," I finally said. "I don't think it's very likely, but I'll check into it."

"Reasonable doubt, Chanse, it's all we need." Loren sounded more cheerful than he had earlier. "This isn't television. I don't need a confession from someone else, you know."

Maybe you don't, I thought. "I'll let you know if I turn up anything. How's the case looking?"

"The assistant D.A. wants to meet—probably wants to offer a plea bargain." He snorted. "Obviously, they think I graduated from law school yesterday."

"Maybe the case isn't that strong." Maybe it was just grasping at straws, but at this point anything would make me feel better.

"Well, they don't like not having the motive." Loren sighed. "That's in our favor."

"But when they find out about the wrestling stuff—"

"We don't have to tell them. Let's deal with that only if and when they do." Loren cut me off. "Look, I had to be in a meeting five minutes ago, so just find me something, okay? Anything. Reasonable doubt." He hung up.

I pulled into my driveway and waited for the gate to open. *No, I need to know. I have to know.*

Not guilty doesn't mean innocent; it means the state couldn't prove its case and nothing more than that. It doesn't mean the accused is cleared. That's why rich guilty people get away with it. They can hire a lawyer who can create reasonable doubt and say that's the same as innocence. It's up to the state to prove guilt.

But that wasn't good enough for me in this case. I had to find the person who killed Mark Williams. I had to prove it wasn't Paul. But I also knew if there was any chance for us, I had to know the truth.

I went into the house and immediately sat down to check my e-mail. Sure enough, Paul had forwarded the threatening message to me. *Maybe he wasn't that mad,* I thought as I opened the message. But there was nothing from Paul—no note, no nothing. It was just the forwarded e-mail.

I wanted to call him but knew it was best to wait a little while. Give him a chance to get over whatever he was feeling about me.

What if he never forgives me?

I couldn't think about that. He had to, that was all. I'd make it up to him somehow. *Focus on this e-mail, even if it proves to be a wild-goose chase. Reasonable doubt—remember that.* Getting Paul out of this jam was the most important thing, and I needed to focus on that.

I looked at the computer screen.

Well, for one thing, the guy who sent the e-mail was on a different Internet server than the one I ordinarily use. I made a note of the name, then pulled up Paul's Web site. I stared at the picture of him in the red Speedo for a minute. He looked great—he always looked great. He had his left thumb hooked in the waistband of the bikini, hiking it down just enough to reveal just a suggestion of trimmed black pubic hair. He had a lazy half-grin on his face.

I went to the links page, but the only one was to Full Nelson's home page.

Okay, then where would wrestlers go to meet each other? There has to be sites about gay wrestling, personal ads and all of that stuff on the Net. I mean, every other imaginable fetish had several sites. I typed "gay," "wrestling," and "personals" into my search engine, lit a cigarette, and waited.

So much for quitting. The cigarette felt perfectly natural

there, like I'd never stopped. Okay, granted, I'd been smokeless for only about five weeks. It was kind of like a controlled addiction. I'd sneak one whenever there was no chance in hell Paul would find out. Being with Paul had changed me. I hadn't minded letting go of the cigarettes and pot if it meant having him around. Oh, he'd never said anything about dumping me if I kept it up, but his disapproving silence whenever I'd light up around him spoke volumes. Once, I'd lit one after we'd come back from the gym dripping with sweat. He'd looked at me and said, "You know, you take better care of your car than your body." Shrugging, he added with an air of complete indifference, "And you can always get another car."

I'd taken another puff off the cigarette—I'd always enjoyed the after-workout cigarette the best, when the heart is pumping and the blood is full of oxygen—and put it out, as I watched him peel the sweaty clothes off and walk bare-assed toward the bathroom. When I'd joined him under the shower's hot water spray, he just smiled at me. "You know, kissing you after you've been smoking doesn't turn me on."

Statements like that made in that context will make you quit anything—or at least cut back.

But now I took another drag and enjoyed the exquisite feeling of the smoke filling my lungs and the delicious taste of the menthol in my mouth. The search engine had found thirty sites. I clicked on the first link and saw a white home page with a line drawing of two incredibly muscular men in bikinis and boots wrestling. The bikinis were tight, leaving no doubt as to the enormous size of the men's genitalia. The header line read WHERE REAL MEN MEET TO WRESTLE. I clicked the link to the personals, which brought up a search page. I typed in "New Orleans." The computer hummed as it brought up a list of wrestlers in the city as well as a tiny thumbnail photo of each guy. I scrolled through the page, recognizing some of the guys from the bars or the gym. About halfway down the page was Cody Dallas, with the same picture from Paul's own Web site. I clicked on the ad, and a profile popped up. A bunch of pictures of Paul posing and flexing in different bikinis ran along the left gutter. There was even a shot of him from behind in the red one, the Lycra hugging his hard bubble butt like sausage skin, the muscles in his back standing out as he flexed his arms.

Who wouldn't want to wrestle him? I swallowed and started reading the profile. *Who wouldn't want to fuck him?*

NAME: Paul. Makes wrestling videos as Cody Dallas for Full Nelson Productions.
AGE: 29
HEIGHT: 5' 9" WEIGHT: 185 HAIR: Brown
EYES: Brown
CHEST: 46 WAIST: 30 BICEPS: 18 QUADS: 26
LIKES: I like submission wrestling mostly; can do pro or pro/fantasy. Age and size unimportant, as long as you work out regularly and have some stamina. Not interested in guys who just want to roll around as a pretext to having sex—I like to compete. Wrestling is a great workout. Preferred gear: Speedos or jocks but pretty much open to whatever my opponent is comfortable with. Really enjoy the body contact, the feel of muscles straining, determining who the better man is. Willing to do erotic if chemistry is there—but don't expect it. Favorite holds are scissors, nelsons, camel clutches, backbreakers. Drop me a line with a shirtless pic and let's get it on.

I stared at it for a moment.

The cursor kept blinking, mocking me.

There was a blue link that read simply said E-MAIL THIS WRESTLER.

I took another breath. Erotic wrestling?

What the hell does that mean?

Sex wrestling, you idiot. Duh. Even an idiot could figure that out. What else could it mean?

So had he been 'erotic wrestling' after we'd started seeing each other? After we'd agreed to only see each other?

I lit another cigarette with shaking fingers.

I looked at the thumbnails, clicking on the one of Paul's rear view. It blew up into a full-page window. Paul was standing in what I recognized as his living room—it was hard to mistake the stained glass windows. His back was to the camera (and just who, I wondered, had taken these pictures anyway?), his lats fanned out to their full extent, making his waist look even tinier than usual. His ass looked incredible—round, hard, and inviting. I closed the window, and shut my eyes.

Think, Chanse, think.

If the guy who sent the e-mail wasn't just a voyeur, it was possible he cruised these kinds of sites. Therefore, didn't it make sense to list myself on a few of the sites and see what happened? I clicked on CREATE YOUR OWN LISTING.

Okay, it's a long shot, I thought as I typed up in my own ad. But other than getting a court order, which was an even bigger long shot, there was no way to find out this guy's name. I had to make this ad as appealing as Paul's to try to draw this guy out into the open. I might not have the mystique of being a video star, but my body was looking good, especially compared to some of the others ones I'd noticed on the New Orleans page.

NAME: *Chanse*
AGE: *29*
HEIGHT: *6' 4"* WEIGHT: *220* HAIR: *Blondish-brown*
EYES: *Gray*
CHEST: *48* WAIST: *33* BICEPS: *20* QUADS: *30*
LIKES: *New to wrestling. My boyfriend makes videos as Cody Dallas. He's a great teacher, but am looking for some other guys to wrestle as well to get more experience so I can get into the business. I love the body contact, I love to sweat, I get really turned on by wrestling. Will wrestle in anything, don't have mats but have space in my apartment. Interested in doing tag teams with partner eventually. Erotic is fine, but open to anything within reason. Former college athlete. Are you man enough to take me on? Let's see who the better man is.*

I hesitated, my finger on the mouse, poised to click send. Was that enough information? If the guy cruised these sites, mentioning Cody Dallas should flush him out—especially the part about being Cody's boyfriend. Getting in touch with me might give the guy the chance to get even with the guy who'd caused him to retire.

I clicked.

A window popped up: WOULD YOU KIKE TO POST SOME PICTURES WITH YOUR AD? ADS WITH PICTURES GET THE MOST RESPONSES.

Again, I hesitated. When Paul and I had gone to South Beach, we'd brought my digital camera. I didn't like the idea of posting pictures of myself on a Web site. What if someone I knew came across them somehow?

But if pictures were what it took…

I opened the folder with the pictures from South Beach and scrolled through the thumbnails. I clicked on one of me standing ankle deep in the water in my black squarecut with the white stripes up the side. The picture opened full-size. My arms were folded, my eyes squinting in the sun. My biceps looked huge, as did my legs and chest. I was wet from the water, beads of water glistening in the sun on my shoulders, chest, and arms. The squarecut was soaked and clinging to my privates. When I'd first seen the picture, I'd kind of been embarrassed, but Paul had loved it. "You look so hot," he'd grinned at me as we sat in front of the computer. "I'm getting pretty excited…"

I attached the picture, and started cruising through the others. I picked out three more, including one of me in the bathroom in my white briefs getting ready to shave. It was a side shot, and the angle of the camera and the way I was standing made my package look huge. It also made my ass look round and inviting.

I took a deep breath and closed my eyes.

I attached the pictures and clicked SEND.

A window opened. "Your ad will appear in the next couple of hours. Thanks for joining!"

Grimly, I pulled up another site. Might as well get listed on all of them.

CHAPTER NINE

After finishing with the Web sites, I decided to head down to the Quarter to talk to Dominique, find out her movements last night. The report I'd faxed her nailing Williams for the harassment couldn't have made her happy.

I tried calling Paul on my cell phone as I drove, but I got his voice mail.

Probably screening calls, I thought as I hung up before the beep and tossed my phone into the passenger seat. I couldn't blame him. Hell, I wouldn't want to talk to me either. *You really fucked up this time, buddy.*

I parked on Dauphine Street and stopped at Matassa's to buy a pack of cigarettes. Paul was probably never going to speak to me again, so it wasn't likely he'd smell smoke on my breath anytime soon. *Christ on the cross.*

I was on my second one when I turned onto St. Ann. There was someone standing in front of the gate to the Attitude PR office, smoking a cigarette. As I got closer I recognized the magazine editor. "Hi, Ghentry," I said when I got within hearing distance. "How you doing?"

He glared at me. "As good as can be expected, I guess." He ground out his cigarette under his shoe savagely. He shrugged. "Sorry, man. It's just—aw, fuck."

"It's not every day your boss gets murdered." I used my most sympathetic voice. "That's gotta be rough."

"Yeah." He shrugged, rolling his eyes. "I've never known anyone who was murdered before." He shook his head. "I still can't quite wrap my mind around it, you know?"

I put my hand on his shoulder. "You want to go get some coffee and talk?"

He looked at me funny. "Talk? About what?"

I shrugged. "What happened last night."

"Yeah, sure. Why not?"

We walked to the CC's on the corner of St. Philip and Royal. It wasn't very crowded, so we got our coffee and sat down at a table in the back. I pulled out my notebook and pen. "So, what happened yesterday?"

He looked at me funny. "What do you mean?"

"I'm looking into this." I looked at him. "The guy they've arrested is my boyfriend."

His eyes widened. "Are you fucking kidding me?"

I didn't answer.

He shook his head. "Man, oh, man…" He sighed. "I can tell you what I told the police."

"Okay."

"Let's see." He bit his lip. "It was a pretty normal day really. Julian was making sales calls, I was working on editing a couple of articles, and then around five the two of us ordered dinner. We asked Mark if he wanted anything, but he said he was going out to dinner later."

"Did he say with whom?"

"No, but he didn't have to. I figured he was going out with Ricky."

"Ricky?"

"Ricky Dahlgren, his boyfriend." He spelled the last name for me.

"He had a boyfriend?" This was the first I'd heard of this. Maybe Paul hadn't known about him. I felt a little bit of relief, a lifting of my spirits. If Mark had a boyfriend, then he and Paul probably hadn't been—

Chanse, you are *an asshole.*

"Yeah," he laughed. "I never understood what he saw in Ricky, though. What a jerk." I just raised my eyebrows. "I mean, Ricky was good-looking and all—nice body, all of that—but he was in his early twenties, and I don't think he'd been out very long."

"Why do you say that?"

He shrugged. "He was still really caught up in all that macho straight-boy bullshit, you know? Like, he'd say things like, 'I like watching hockey because of the fights'—you know, crazy shit like that. I got the sense he wasn't comfortable in his gay skin yet. And he was kind of mean to Mark."

"How so?"

"Well, I always got the sense Mark wasn't really happy with him. Mark always seemed really sad when he talked about him— and he never really talked about him very much. You know how boyfriends are—it's usually 'Ricky this' and 'Ricky that.' Not Mark. And for the most part, Ricky didn't have much to do with any of us. He'd drop in to see Mark, and if Mark wasn't there he'd hang out with us for a couple of minutes, say something really stupid like the hockey thing, and then would leave and not come back until Mark was there. And it's not like Mark wasn't a good-looking guy. He could have done a *lot* better than Ricky."

"So, you two ordered dinner?" I prodded.

"Yeah, from the Moon Wok." He took a drink of his coffee. "Then, around 5:30, Mark said he was going back to his apartment."

"That was in the old slave quarters in back, right?"

Ghentry nodded. "Then, about 6:30, Dominique called on a rampage...man, she was pissed off."

"Did she say why?" I'd sent her the fax around six.

"Not to me. She never would talk to anyone but Mark." He gave a weak smile. "She was furious, though—didn't seem to believe me when I said Mark wasn't in the office. She called both me and him some choice names. I was pretty upset when she finally hung up. Then, around seven, Ricky showed up."

"And how did he seem?"

"I don't know. I didn't talk to him." He shrugged. "I didn't actually see him—Zane did. He saw him go by the window...what did he say?" He frowned for a moment, then shook his head. "I don't remember exactly, but Zane didn't like Ricky at all, and he said some nasty things about him—you know, rolling his eyes and all."

"He didn't have to be buzzed in?"

"Nah. He knew the gate code. Then about half an hour later, that Paul guy—your boyfriend, I guess—came by looking for Mark. We sent him back, and then the next thing we knew the police were there." He shuddered.

"You didn't hear the gun shots?"

"No, the house is built pretty solid—brick. We hardly ever hear anything from the street or anything when we're in the office."

"Did you see Ricky leave?"

"No, but unless he came through the office on his way out, I probably wouldn't have." He sighed.

"So, anyone who knew the code could have gotten in without your knowing about it?"

"Mark could also buzz people in from his place."

Interesting. Paul's story began to make more sense. If he'd gone there to kill Mark, he wouldn't have gone in through the front and risked being seen by eyewitnesses who could put him there. And if people could have gotten in without going through the front, any number of people could have come and gone, including Ricky Dahlgren, without the people in the office knowing.

"What did you think of Mark?"

"He was a great guy." Ghentry looked down into his cup. "And smart. Very motivated. He was determined to make a success of the business, and we all worked really hard, you know?"

"So how did you come to work there?"

Ghentry sighed. "I was working part-time at an antique store on Magazine Street and did freelance writing work. I sent him a résumé. After about a month, he called and asked me to meet with him. We talked about writing and what he wanted to do with the magazine; how he wanted to eventually build it up and take it national—you know, like *Instinct* or *Genre*. He'd already made some changes—took it from black-and-white to full-color glossy, really improved the look of it. He didn't want it to be just another

New Orleans bar rag. He had read my writing in some of the other local papers, and he told me I was just the kind of writer he needed. He gave me a couple of assignments, and I did them over the next week before he asked me to meet with him again. I guess it was about late July when he offered me a part-time job. I was supposed to just write stuff for the magazine and do some stuff around the office."

"And how did that work out?"

"It was fun." He smiled. "We all loved our jobs. We always had a great time at work. Mark was very generous. He was always ordering lunch or dinner for us, and he was always very supportive and grateful for all the work we were doing. It was a pleasant change, you know what I mean?"

"Did you find him attractive?"

He stared at me. "Are you kidding? You met him, didn't you?"

I nodded. "But did you think he was attractive?"

He laughed. "How could anyone not? Those eyes, that face, that body! Hell, he was gorgeous...of course I was attracted to him. But he was way out of my league—wa-a-ay out of my league. Definitely too good for Ricky." He grinned at me. "You know what it is about Ricky? He's a gay geek." Ghentry laughed. "He doesn't know the difference between Whitney Houston and Mariah Carey, for God's sake. I saw him and Mark out one night at Oz, and the poor thing can't dance. He dances like a straight boy. Maybe once he's shaken off the straight-male conditioning—you know what I mean? I mean, he still talks about hunting and fishing, for God's sake."

I held my tongue. I've never understood the mentality that all gay man worship Liza, Judy, Barbra, and Bette; are good dancers, obsess about the Oscars, and always use the word "fabulous" whenever possible. Why couldn't a gay man be into hunting and fishing, or enjoy hockey for the fights? Hell, I'd been a college football player, and I never wore Speedos. Did that make me a failure as a gay man? "You said before they didn't seem happy."

"Well, Mark didn't seem to be...I tried to get him to talk to me a few times about Ricky, but he wouldn't say anything. I definitely got the sense there was something weird going on with them."

"Why?"

"I don't know, it's kind of hard to explain, it was just a feeling." Ghentry sighed. "Mark liked gay stuff, you know? He liked dressing nice, going dancing, that kind of stuff. I mean, he was all about supporting gay causes, like NO/AIDS and the Community Center. And he could be real queen sometimes...like, he'd dance in the office if he really liked the song playing on the radio, and that wasn't Ricky at all, so he never acted like that around him. He always butched it up when he was around."

"Anything else happen yesterday that seemed strange to you?"

"Well, yesterday was a strange day, you know? You came by in the afternoon. Julian and I were pretty happy Dominique hired you—what the bars are trying to do to her is awful. And Dominique wasn't the only call he got yesterday that was weird. This guy called a couple of times, and Mark wouldn't take the calls."

"Did you get the guy's name?"

"Ed Smith." He made a face. "Yeah, right. Like, I thought that was his name. But Mark wouldn't take the calls, and the guy was more and more pissed every time he called back."

"Do you know what he was calling about?"

He shook his head. "No, he just demanded to talk to Mark. It was, like, three different calls over the space of an hour. So, anyway, Mark just told us to take messages and then went back to the apartment."

"How did he seem?"

"Kind of nervous."

I made a note to see if the phone company had a record of the incoming calls. "Do you know why Paul Maxwell came to see him?"

"He told us he'd decided not to do the cover." Ghentry made a face. "Apparently, being on the cover was upsetting his boyfriend, so he wasn't doing to do it after all." He laughed. "That would be you, right?" He shrugged. "If you don't mind my saying so, I kind of thought you were being a bit possessive."

I bit my tongue and then said, "Did he seem upset about anything or angry?"

"No, he just seemed sad. He really wanted to do the cover." He glanced at his watch. "I really should get back. The phones have been crazy all day."

The sun had gone down a bit, and the afternoon shadows were getting long and cold. I shivered and wished I'd brought a jacket. "Do you know how I can get in touch with Ricky Dahlgren?"

He shrugged as he punched in a code at the gate. "I really don't know much about him. I've only seen him in passing and never really talked to him much. Zane would probably know."

We heard the loud voices as we climbed up the steps to the porch. One voice was louder than the other; deeper and more insistent. Ghentry made a face. "Great."

"What's going on?"

"Enrique Sanchez." He made a sound of disgust. "He's the concert promoter for the company. He books the acts and so on. He's an arrogant asshole." He opened the door, and the argument abruptly broke off. Julian was sitting at her desk, her mouth open and her arms crossed over her Lilith Fair sweatshirt. Zane was sitting at his desk, his face red. He looked like he was about to start crying at any minute. In the center of the room was a dark man about five foot ten and carrying about 200 pounds. He was wearing jeans about a size too small and a plaid flannel shirt. His hair was blue-black and slicked down. There were a couple of pinkish-red pimples spread over his face. Sadly, he looked like he was twenty-five, tops.

"Can I help you?" His smile was about as slick as his hair.

"I'd like to talk to Zane for a moment." I put my hands in my pockets, fixing him with an inexpressive stare.

He blinked and turned his head back to Zane. "Zane?"

Zane rose, wiping his hands on his jeans and taking a deep breath. "Let's go into Mark's office."

I followed him into the room and let out a low whistle. It was a shambles. Papers were scattered everywhere, the trash can and its contents spilled, drawers open. The computer was gone, a clean space in the center of the once-meticulous desk where it had once sat.

Zane sat down in Mark's chair and threw his arms out. "I'm surprised they didn't tear up the carpet."

I took a pile of disheveled papers out of a chair, placing them on a table and sitting down. "The police?"

He nodded. "They tore the place apart." He put his elbows down on the desk and put his face in his hands. "They fucking took Mark's computer! How the hell am I supposed to…" His voice died off in a strangled groan.

"You'll get it all back." I looked around the room. *What had the search warrant been for?* The case against Paul must not be very strong if they felt the need to search the office. With a twinge of hope, I put myself into cop mentality. You've got a shooter, fingerprints on the gun, gunpowder residue on the suspect's hands. Sure, there's no motive, but it literally was a smoking gun. But maybe the district attorney didn't think it was open and shut.

"All our financial records were in his computer." Zane looked at me. "How am I supposed to run the business without that?"

I stared at him. At best, he was maybe twenty-two. "I imagine it would be hard."

"I don't know what I'm going to do." He stared off into space, his eyes wet. "I can't run this company without Mark."

"How did you happen to go into business with him?"

"I met him last spring. At Oz. I was working as a bar back."

I looked at his thin arms. Oz's bar backs were known for being muscular. They had to be; they lugged tubs of ice and cases of liquor around. I couldn't imagine Zane carrying two cases of vodka on his shoulder. "Really?"

He nodded. "Yeah, but I never worked behind the bar. They always had me work the door."

That made sense. "So how did you meet?"

"He came in one night and started talking to me while I was working." He shrugged. "He was drinking water. I remember thinking he must be rolling or something, but he wasn't. He told me he wasn't much of a drinker. I don't know, I think at some point he told me he was the publisher of *Attitude*. I told him I'd always wanted to design a magazine, and he told me he wasn't very good at it, and why didn't I stop by his office?"

"You've done a good job." I didn't know if he had, but it never hurts to give compliments.

He smiled. "Thanks. I'd worked here for maybe a week or two when Mark's partner decided he wanted to close the business down."

"That sucks."

"Yeah, really. The last thing I wanted to do was go back to Oz to work, you know?" He rolled his eyes. "I'm not into that whole bar thing, you know? So, when Mark suggested we buy the business, I was all for it."

"How did you swing it?"

"My parents took out a loan for me." Zane stared out the window.

"How much did Mark put up?"

"Nothing." Zane twisted his class ring. "He has a trust fund he was going to come into on his next birthday, and then he was going to pay my parents back, but I was going to get fifty percent of the business for allowing us to keep it going."

A trust fund: It sounded like a scam to me. Mark gets Zane and his parents to put up the money to buy the business, which he then gets to run as if it's his. And somehow, I rather doubted Mark had told the Rathburns about his criminal conviction for fraud. "And where was the money coming from to run the business?"

"Well, we do pretty good with the ads from the magazine." Zane smiled. "And then there was the PR business. That was Mark's idea—to do PR and promote concerts."

"And how did all that work?"

"Dominique was paying us five grand a month for the PR, and we got to keep the door money from the shows we did there." He shrugged. "We were losing money on the shows, but they were getting our name out there. We were getting ready to branch out into other venues where we'd make more money." He sighed. "We were negotiating to do a show with Divas Three out at UNO." Divas Three was the latest rage in pop music—three black girls with exquisite harmonies who sang dance music and were being heralded as the new Supremes. "We'd have made a killing on that show."

"Can't you go ahead with it?"

"Not without Mark's computer." He drummed his fingers on the desk. "I don't even know how much money we have in the bank."

"So, you've only known Mark for a few months?"

"Yeah."

"Do you know anything about some phone calls Mark got that seemed to upset him yesterday?"

"No." He shrugged. "Mark got calls like that all the time. He always said it was the nature of the business, so I never thought much about it, to be honest." He sighed. "I don't deal with conflict well, so I was more than happy to let Mark handle that side of the business."

"And what can you tell me about his boyfriend, this Ricky Dahlgren?"

"Ricky." Zane made a face. "What a jerk. Good-looking, if you like that type." Obviously, from the look on his face, he didn't.

"You didn't care for him?"

"No. I didn't understand what Mark saw in him." Zane shrugged. "To each his own, I guess. Mark told me once that Ricky told him all he was to him was a big dick and a good massage. I don't know why anyone would put up with that."

"Do you have a number for him?"

He shuddered. "God, no. Why would I want his number?"

"And you were here last night?"

"Actually, no." He smiled. "I had a dinner date last night, so I left around seven to get ready for my date."

"Who was your date with?"

He tossed a copy of the magazine at me. The cover said JUNE. The guy on the cover was shirtless and pretty. "Danny DeMarco— that's him on the cover."

I whistled. "Nice."

"Well, we're just friends—for now." He winked at me. "We went to dinner at Père Antoine's and then I stopped by here around 9:30… and that's when I found out…" He closed his eyes and shuddered.

I closed my notebook. "Thanks. If I have any other questions..."

"Call me anytime."

I walked out of the office and stood on St. Ann. I flipped open my phone and called both Paul's home and cell phones. No answer on either.

I walked down to a flower shop on Decatur and ordered him a dozen roses. On the card I wrote "I'm sorry, so very sorry. Love, Chanse."

Everyone likes getting flowers, right?

My phone rang as I headed back up to Bourbon Street. "MacLeod."

"Hey Chanse. Loren here." I could hear voices in the background. "Can't talk for long...about to go into a conference, but I've got great news. They've dropped charges against Paul."

I let out a sigh of relief. "That's great. Why?"

"Because Paul has a brilliant attorney." I could hear the grin on his face. "The powder residue was on Paul's right hand."

I felt like the sun was coming up. "But Paul's left-handed!"

"Exactly. And they've traced the gun. You aren't going to believe this."

"Try me."

"It's registered to Judge Jerry Dahlgren."

Dahlgren.

"Isn't that the best news?" Loren chortled. "Judge Jerry fucking Dahlgren!"

"Thanks. I might be on to something here." I filled him in on what I'd found out about Ricky Dahlgren.

"Oh, man," Loren sighed. "Ricky Dahlgren is the judge's son, Chanse. This is getting really crazy."

"But this is all good news, right?"

"Maybe. I mean, they've dropped the charges—for now. But how hard do you think the police are going to investigate a judge's son? Especially Judge Dahlgren's son."

"What's the big deal?"

"Judge Dahlgren. Don't you ever read the newspapers?"

"No, not really." Paige always gave me shit about my lack of interest in current events.

"Judge Dahlgren is a racist, misogynist homophobe." Loren groaned. "He's going to be very embarrassed to find out his son is wanted for murdering his gay lover. He's going to look like a fool— and he's going to use every bit of influence he has to call off the dogs…and that's not good for Paul. Look, I've got to get into this meeting. I'll call you later, okay? We've got to handle the Dahlgrens with kid gloves, Chanse." He hung up.

I called Paige. "You busy?"

"Just getting ready to call it quits for the day." Her voice was cold. "I was going to call you."

"You were?"

"I talked to Paul a couple of hours ago." She exhaled. "Christ, Chanse, what the hell were you thinking?"

"I sent him flowers." It sounded lame to me now. "I've blown it, haven't I?"

"I think you're pretty close to it, yeah." She sighed. "The flowers are a nice touch. Paul loves you, and he wants this all to work out— but you scared him to death, Chanse."

"Oh…" I swallowed. "Wanna meet me for dinner at Snug Harbor?"

"Yeah, what the hell. What time?"

"Give me an hour." That should be plenty of time to check in with Dominique and ask her some questions.

"Okay." She hung up.

I dialed Paul again. Once again his voice mail picked up. I tried his cell phone, but he didn't answer that either.

I walked back up to Domino's.

CHAPTER TEN

I wasn't sure what to think as I walked down to the corner at Bourbon.

Dominique had known Mark Williams was partially involved in a conspiracy against her club. The harassment was costing her thousands of dollars a day as long as the club wasn't open. After she had received my fax, had she become frustrated when she couldn't get Williams on the phone and then come around the corner with murder on her mind? It wasn't beyond the realm of possibility—people killed every day for a lot less. I didn't know her well enough to make a decision on her guilt myself.

But the gun belonged to Judge Dahlgren. How could she have gotten it?

It was a relief knowing Paul wasn't the main suspect anymore. It was almost like I was floating rather than walking. Everything would work out for the best; I was sure of it now. Paul would forgive me. He'd have to understand it was the stress and pressure of his arrest that made me snap. We'd sit down and have a nice little chat about our pasts. It was high time we knew each other better anyway. I loved him, and no matter what secrets his past held, they didn't matter. We could work everything out. I would ask him point-blank about his money troubles, and if he needed help, I'd give it to him. The money I'd put up for his bail, well, I'd already written that off anyway, so I would loan more to him to get out of debt.

I smiled. No, fuck that. I would *give* it to him.

I walked into Domino's feeling much better than I had since yesterday morning, and I guess I walked into the middle of a celebration. Sly was opening a bottle of champagne, and several empties were sitting on the bar. The workmen and assorted other people were drinking, laughing, and chatting. The mood was happy and festive. Dominique herself was leaning against the bar, a glass of Wild Turkey in her hand, a big grin on her face.

"Chanse!" She motioned at Sly. "Pour him some champagne, Sly!' I took the plastic cup. "What's going on?"

"The liquor license finally came through this afternoon." She clinked her glass against my cup. "We can officially open this Friday."

"That's great." I sipped the champagne. It was cheap. "We need to talk; can you give me a few minutes?"

She looked around the room at her happy employees, then nodded. "Come up to my office."

Her office was on the second floor, with a window that looked out over the dance floor. It was utilitarian, with a few file cabinets shoved up against a wall, a large desk, and not much else other than a couple of chairs. Her desk was clear of clutter. A half-full coffeepot sat on top of one of the file cabinets. She took a seat behind the desk. "What's going on?"

"You don't seem to be mourning Mark Williams."

She made a sound of disgust. "Why would I mourn someone who tried to ruin me?" She sipped her whiskey. "That would be hypocritical, wouldn't it? I'm not sorry he's dead. Couldn't have happened to a nicer guy."

"You were pretty angry when you got my fax."

She raised a penciled eyebrow. "Who wouldn't have been? Someone I trusted implicitly, listened to…" Her voice trailed off. She shook her head. "I talked to my lawyer this morning. I'm thinking of suing Attitude PR for malicious activity." She gave me the shark-like smile again. "But I think there's a hell of a lot more to this than you found out…it's just the tip of the iceberg."

"Oh?"

"It doesn't make sense, Chanse." She drummed her long nails on her desk. "I believe he was involved, but I don't think he was the mastermind…" She stood up and walked over to the window, looking down on the darkened dance floor. "In your report, the only reason you could come up with for him doing it was to 'get me as a client.' Sorry, that just doesn't wash. He went to a lot of trouble for $500 a month."

I sat up. "Five hundred?"

She nodded.

I got out my notebook and flipped back through the pages. "Five *thousand* dollars a month is what you were paying Attitude PR, according to Zane Rathburn."

She looked at me for a moment, her mouth open, and then she started laughing. "Five thousand? Oh, please! I've been losing more than that every day this club has stayed closed! There's no way my investors would ever okay that!" She sat back down, crossing her legs and lighting a cigarette. She exhaled. "No, I was paying him $500 out of my own pocket. I also let them keep the door from when we did a concert here, but I kept the liquor sales."

"How well do you know Ricky Dahlgren?"

She sat up straighter. "Ricky? Why?"

"The gun that killed Mark was registered to his father."

She rubbed her eyes tiredly. After a few moments, she said, "Not well. I know he worked for Mark, and he was around from time to time, but that's about it." Her face hardened. "Why? What does this have to do with my club?"

"Well, nothing." I shrugged. "I'm checking into Mark's death, you know, just poking around. I'm a little curious." No sense in telling her that until just a little while ago my boyfriend was a prime suspect.

"That's not what I'm paying you for."

That came out of left field. "What?"

She looked at me as if I were stupid. "Like I said, Mark's just the tip of the iceberg. Someone else was behind all of this. I doubt he came up with all of this for 500 bucks a month. I still want you to find out who's trying to ruin me." She smoothed her hair. "I know, I sound like some conspiracy theory nut but…" She hesitated. "Does it make sense to you?"

"No." She was right. However starved for cash Attitude PR may have been, unless Mark was completely insane, going to all the trouble he had in order to keep a client paying him 500 bucks a month still didn't make sense. There had to be more. "You didn't know Mark before?"

"No. I told you. He just came by one day and offered his services. I liked him. He seemed to know what he was doing, and hell, for 500 bucks, like I said, I could pay him that out of my own pocket and not miss it, you know?"

"Let's talk about enemies, then."

"Enemies?" She looked at me like I was insane. "What enemies?"

I sighed. "Look, Dominique, if there's someone out there who is trying to ruin you, they have to have a reason."

"Mark thought it was the bars."

"But you told me you didn't think so." I sat back. "Maybe your ex-husband?"

"That's absurd."

"Amicable divorce?"

"I don't want to talk about Charlie."

"Can you at least tell me his name?"

She glared at me. "Charles Wyatt." She began tapping her nails on her desk again. "Are we finished here?"

"Just a few more questions." There's nothing like a client who doesn't tell you everything. "What did you do when you got the fax?"

She glowered. "I got mad. I tried calling Mark's cell phone, but he didn't answer, so I called the office number and talked to one of his flunkies." She smiled. "I gave him a piece of my mind. I was mad, so I decided to get the hell out of here and go get some dinner. It was about eight o'clock when I walked out." She folded her arms. "Are we done here? I have work to do."

I got up. "Sure." I walked out of her office, glancing at my watch as I went down the stairs. I had about twenty minutes before meeting Paige at Snug Harbor. The party was still going on in the front room. I stopped at the bar. "Hey, Sly."

Sly grinned at me. "More champagne, man?"

I shook my head. "Were you here last night?"

"I came in around four."

"Was Dominique here the whole time?"

He put his elbows down on the bar, looking off into space. "She was here when I got here—in her office. She was in there the whole time, then later on she went on."

"What time was that?"

"I'm not sure." He frowned. "Around eight, I think. She seemed in a rush."

"When did she come back?"

He shook his head. "I didn't see her come back." He shrugged.

"Thanks, man." I smiled at him, and walked back out onto Bourbon Street.

Snug Harbor is on Frenchmen Street in the Marigny, about nine blocks from Domino's. Parking down there is just as much a nightmare as it is in the Quarter, so it didn't make sense for me to move the car. I'd probably have a ticket when I came back, but it wouldn't be the first time. I tried calling Paul again as I walked but still just got his voice mail. I wondered if the flowers had been delivered.

Paige was waiting for me in the bar at Snug Harbor, which was a shock. Paige is always late, but she was puffing on a cigarette and had a lipstick-smeared glass of red wine on the table in front of her. She got up to hug me, then waved at the bartender. "Go ahead and put our order in." She grinned at me. "I ordered, since you always get the same thing."

Snug Harbor serves one of the best burgers in town, along with huge baked potatoes. I always got the same thing whenever I came in—a mushroom bacon cheeseburger with a baked potato buried in butter and cheese. "Thanks." I sat down. We were at one of the few restaurants in New Orleans where you can't smoke in the dining room, so we always ate in the bar. "Have you talked to Paul?"

She nodded. "He's really upset, poor thing." She took a drag on her cigarette. "Chanse, what were you thinking? He said you bruised him."

I looked down at the table. "I wasn't thinking." I toyed with a napkin. "Do you think he'll ever forgive me?"

She exhaled. "At some point. Do I need to give you the domestic violence lecture?"

"Uh-uh." I shook my head. I'd seen enough domestic violence when I'd been on the force. I knew the statistics, the patterns, everything. "Paige, I'd never hurt him."

"But you did," she said gently. She reached out and touched my hand. "What happened?"

"I lost my temper."

"Well, obviously, but that's not like you." She pulled her hand back and looked at me. "Is this because of Ryan?"

"You said you'd never bring him up again." My heart was pounding again.

"I think we need to talk about it. You've never told Paul, have you?"

The name echoed in my head.

"Isn't that the real reason you two have never talked about your pasts?"

"I...I don't want to talk about him."

"We have to, Chanse. You have to deal with it."

I'd met Ryan Colby my junior year at LSU. Fraternity Rush was always a nightmare for me. I was always on display: Beta Kappa's star football player. After my pledge semester, I'd learned very quickly why the brothers had taken someone from a small town in East Texas, who didn't wear Polo shirts and Tommy Hilfiger jeans. I was carted around by older brothers, introduced to pledges as "Chanse MacLeod—he's on the football team," and found myself discussing LSU's chances for the SEC championship with snobby young rich boys who'd never got closer to a football field than their seats in the stands, or when they tore down goalposts after we beat Ole Miss. My entire contribution to Beta Kappa consisted of being trotted out to meet alumni or prospective pledges.

I'd joined the house because they seemed to want me. Even during pledging, I was treated better than my pledge brothers, which, of course, didn't exactly endear me to my pledge brothers. During the "inspirational" activities (apparently, calling things "inspirational" rather than "hazing" made everything okay) I was never required to recite pledge lessons any more difficult than the Greek alphabet. No one ever gave me assignments to clean the grease trap in the kitchen. I never had to scrub urinals with a toothbrush and never had to streak on Sorority Row while screaming at the top of my lungs. My big brother, Scott Simons, was the president of the house. He came from a Mississippi family whose money and social status predated the War of 1812. That entire semester, I thought my exalted status was because of Scott. I wanted to be like Scott, just as I'd wanted to be like T.J. in high school. Scott was short, maybe five foot seven, with a lean little body and blond hair. He was very in demand for sex from little sisters and sorority girls, so he actually had very little time for me except on Big Brother Night, when he'd forced me to drink a bottle of tequila, and Initiation Night, when we'd shared a bottle of champagne before he went looking for that night's piece of ass.

I'd joined Beta Kappa for two reasons. I wanted to belong to something that would accept me. I was also trying to bury my needs and desires for other men. I figured joining a fraternity, in addition to the macho camaraderie of the football team, would "straighten" me out.

I'd gotten back to the house after football practice the first night of rush my junior year, tired as hell. We'd already played two games, and were undefeated; ranked in the top ten in all the polls and a heavy favorite to win the Southeastern Conference. We were a long shot for the national championship, but the entire state was already talking in those terms. The city of Baton Rouge was covered in purple and gold. I'd scored a touchdown in each of the first games, and pro scouts were coming to the games. But my body was tired and battered, and the last thing in the world I wanted to do was put on my phony frat boy smile and talk football with a bunch of spoiled, rich prospective pledges.

The night's theme was Casino Night, and again, rather than involving me as a dealer or anything, all I needed to do was to show up. As I stood in my room, I thought about just wearing my game jersey and being done with it. Sullenly, I put on a tank top and jeans and walked into the party room. I was given a name tag and went to stand by myself in a corner and wait.

"Are you one of the brothers?" came a voice from behind me.

I turned and found myself looking up into the green eyes of a strange man. He looked really young, maybe in his mid teens, but he was long and lanky with strong muscles and big legs. He had short dark hair, and a gorgeous smile—but it was the eyes that got to me. "I'm Chanse MacLeod," I said, sticking out my hand and shaking his.

The moment our hands touched, I felt a stirring in my groin.

"Ryan Colby." He had a Georgia accent.

"Looking to pledge?"

He looked around the room. The brothers who were dealing at the tables or working the roulette wheels were all dressed in black jacket and ties and had those stupid green visors on. Little sisters were circulating. Their job at rush was to sell the house by looking as sexy as possible and being flirty, implying that they were the house whores. Paige was doing her job admirably in a tight black leather skirt, her big breasts barely restrained in a tight red tube top under an open white blouse. "I'm not sure." He smiled at me again. "Maybe."

I immediately went into the house spiel: "It's like having eighty best friends. We have really well-connected alumni who can help get you a job when you graduate. We have a lot of fun."

It sounded just as stupid coming out of my mouth as it did when I heard the others saying it.

"Cool. Can you show me around?"

So for the first (and last) time in my career as a Greek, I took a prospective on a tour of the house, talking the usual mindless fraternity truisms as if I were a used-car salesman who'd landed a gullible one. All the while I was trying to make him flash that smile again, trying to get glimpses of his butt in his jeans, trying to figure out what his chest and stomach looked like under his shirt.

He was a business major on a tennis scholarship from Valdosta, Georgia. He dreamed of someday qualifying to play at the U.S. Open but didn't think he'd make it that far. He loved exercise; he loved being good at tennis.

Never once did he mention a girlfriend.

He'd pledged, and it seemed he was always stopping by my room for advice, or my thoughts on scholarship athletics, school, or the fraternity itself.

I lay awake at night, wondering what his lips would feel like, how he would feel lying next to me in my bed.

I was thrilled when he picked me for his big brother.

"Do you think he's gay?" I asked Paige over a greasy pizza one night at her apartment.

She shrugged. "Hard to say, but he's never made any attempts to get laid at any parties."

Big Brother Night was one of those nights where things really did sink to an *Animal House* level. The objective of the evening was not only to let the pledge know who his big brother is but also to get the pledge as fucked up as humanly possible. The evening started with the pledges, dressed in jackets and ties, being herded into the chapter room and blindfolded and then led into the party room. They were lined up, faces against the wall, and a bottle was placed in each pledge's hands: his "family beer." Mine was Olde English 800. Then, at a signal, they were required to drink it down. As each "family beer" was a quart bottle and the pledge was blindfolded, he would feel as if he were on an endless quest. When the bottle was empty, the pledge had to put it upside down on top of his head, and then he was allowed to remove his blindfold and turn around to face his big brother.

Ryan's face and hair were drenched with beer when he turned around and smiled at me before belching.

The fun and games last all night, but it only took about an hour before I could get Ryan out of there without really being missed.

By then everyone was incredibly drunk, chugging contests and drinking games going on, and the floor was covered with about an inch deep pool of sticky beer. Once we were alone in my room, I sat him down on my bed. His eyes were kind of glassy. As I rolled a joint, I asked him, "Do you need to throw up?"

He nodded. I led him over to the window, and opened it. All the beer he'd been forced to drink came up quickly in a foamy froth. "Thanks," he said, wiping his mouth on his sleeve.

I lit the joint and tossed him a pair of sweats. His suit was soaked through in places. "You might as well change."

He smiled at me, his face pale, as he stood up and unbuttoned his shirt.

I watched as he neatly folded the shirt. His torso was tan and muscular, sinewy but not thick. There was a patch of hair in the center of his chest that trailed down to his navel and beyond.

Next came the pants. He was wearing white underwear with a gold stripe around the waistband. His legs were thick, muscular, and hairy. He pulled the sweats on hurriedly. I offered him the joint, but he shook his head and smiled. "It'll just make me sick…I don't think I'm done throwing up yet."

I nodded.

He sat back down on the bed as I took another hit. "Thanks for taking me as your little brother."

I stubbed the joint out. I was pleasantly high. "No prob."

"Chanse…" he started, then flushed bright red. "Can I ask you something?"

"Sure."

"If I was gay, what would happen to me around here?"

My jaw dropped. "You're gay?" I asked, my heart jumping.

He couldn't look at me. "I…I'm not sure. I mean, I've slept with girls and liked it, you know, but there are some guys…" His face reddened. "Please don't tell anyone."

It took all of my courage, but I got up and sat beside him on the bed. "It'll be our little secret."

And I kissed him.

"Paul isn't Ryan, you know," Paige said as our waitress arrived with our dinner. "And Ryan wasn't a bad guy either. He did love you."

"He had a funny way of showing it." I mashed my baked potato into an orangey-yellow mass.

"So he couldn't handle it." Paige moaned as she took a bite of her burger. "This is almost orgasmic." She looked me in the eyes and continued. "You guys were just kids then, Chanse. You loved him and he left you, and ever since then you've closed yourself off from everyone, really. You haven't had any kind of relationship with any-one—not even friendship—with anyone other than Blaine and me since then."

I couldn't argue with her. She was right. "But I've already blown it with Paul."

"You haven't," she insisted. She reached over and touched my hand. "Look, it's not too late to patch things up. The two of you need to talk. You need to tell him about Ryan. Tell him everything, Chanse."

"What did he say to you?"

"Just that you bruised him. That you lost your temper." She sighed. "He's afraid you don't love him anymore."

"Of course I do."

"Well, he doesn't know that. I mean, look at how you reacted to all this wrestling stuff."

"I was a jerk."

"Stop calling and go over there. Let your guard down once and for all, okay?"

"Yeah." I finished my burger. "Look, I need you to do me a favor."

"Sure."

"I need you to find out whatever you can about Charlie Wyatt, an Atlanta lawyer. He's Dominique's ex-husband, and I also need you to find out everything you can about a Ricky Dahlgren." Paige has access that I don't have to newspaper archives, and even though she complains about it, she likes to help me out when she can.

"Ricky Dahlgren?" Her eyebrows went up. "Why?"

"He was Mark Williams's boyfriend, and he was there that night."

"That isn't possible," Paige replied. "There's no way he was Mark's boyfriend, no way."

"Why do you say that?"

"I know Ricky Dahlgren." She laughed. "I dated his older brother a couple of times, and I met the whole family. Ricky's not gay."

"Paige, several people have told me Ricky was Mark's boyfriend."

"Hmm." She scratched her head. "Well, I would have thought if any of the Dahlgren kids were gay, it was the sister. That's a dyke if I've ever met one. But okay."

She took one last bite of her potato. "Go on, go see Paul and work this out, okay?"

I started to get out my wallet, but she waved me off. "This is on me."

She never treats if she can possibly help it. I smiled at her. "Thanks, Paige, for everything."

"Get out of here." She lit another cigarette. "I'll e-mail you what I find out tomorrow."

CHAPTER ELEVEN

I didn't call and tell him I was on my way. I told myself I just wanted to surprise him. I was afraid he'd leave if he knew I was coming—or worse yet, tell me not to come at all. I did have a bright-orange parking ticket tucked neatly under one of my windshield wipers when I got back to the car. I put it in the glove compartment. It had gotten colder while Paige and I were having dinner, so I started the car and turned on the heater. I sat there for a while, rubbing my arms for warmth while the engine got hot.

Ryan Colby.

I shivered.

We'd been inseparable after Big Brother Night. I remembered the following morning, waking up with him in my arms. I hadn't gotten drunk, but he had a hell of hangover. We'd started kissing, bad morning breath and all, all over again. I couldn't believe I was so lucky. This was what I'd wanted with T.J., with some of the guys I'd meet when I snuck down to New Orleans on a weekend. The trick was to spend as much time together as possible without raising suspicion among the rest of the brothers. Being his big brother helped somewhat, as it was a kind of mentoring thing. Maybe we were closer than most pledges were with their big brothers, but no one seemed to notice—not that the rest of the brothers were paying much attention. They were all busy studying, getting drunk, smoking pot, snorting coke and trying to get laid. It didn't hurt that we were both scholarship athletes, either. After all, we were jocks, and jocks couldn't be fags, right? Sometimes those stereotypes work in your favor. Besides, we were the only real jocks in the house. It was only natural we'd become friends. His explanation for spending so much time at the house was his roommate in the dorms was a complete asshole. Nobody really questioned him. Spending so much time at the house was a point in his favor as a pledge, and no one really fucked with him much. The brothers believed Beta Kappa was the center of the universe. Being the football star's little brother helped—nobody wanted to piss me off. I was easily the biggest guy in the house, and there were all my so-called buddies on the football team.

He'd come by to study as soon as I was home from practice. If we could wait until after eleven, we were pretty safe from being intruded on. Most everyone was either studying or locked down in a room getting wasted by then. Those were quiet hours, when no one was supposed to be loud or bother anyone. I'd bolt and lock the door— earlier than eleven, it would seem odd. He would come up behind me and put his arms around me and start kissing me on the neck, while I reached back with my hands and undid his pants. We always waited until we got down on the bed before finishing undressing each other.

It was the first time in my life I remember being happy.

Like a lovesick schoolgirl, I thought about him all the time. I wouldn't have been surprised to find myself doodling hearts during class with his name in them. Even if I had wanted to, I couldn't have stopped thinking about him. One minute, I'd be sitting there in class, taking notes as the professor droned on. Then my mind would be gone...and in my head I'd see him lying naked in my bed, that beautiful joyful smile on his face. I'd get hard right there in the class, squirming in my seat, as I remembered the taste of his mouth, the suppleness of his muscles, the softness of his skin. It even happened at football practice. A practice coach yelled at me for the first time since I'd first strapped on pads in junior high school. "MacLeod!" he'd screamed at me. "Get your fucking head into this practice or get the hell off my practice field!" I'd been startled, some of my teammates gaping at me in shock. I was always focused and disciplined at practice.

Until then.

I lived for those nights when he came by the house, or when we'd meet up at Paige's apartment. Paige had always been my cover at the house—everyone thought we were dating. Every once in a while she'd get really wasted at a party and sleep with one of the other brothers. This was a pain in the ass, and I always lectured her about it. The brother would always be terrified, and there would be mini-drama at the house, until I finally got drunk privately with the brother and renewed the bonds of brotherhood with him. Besides, as one said in relief afterward, "brothers can't let bitches come in between them."

God, it was all so fucking stupid.

Probably the most stupid thing I did was assume Ryan would be protected from the malicious tongues of the brothers because he was my little brother. It never occurred to me that Ryan didn't have a 'girlfriend' like me. In the minds of the troglodytes of Beta Kappa, tennis wasn't a real sport like football. If I paid more attention, I might have been able to head things off before they boiled over—but I was a football player, by God, and not a regular student, and I'd underestimated a couple of things. If I resented being the trained display seal of Beta Kappa, some of the brothers resented that I never went to meetings and blew off initiation ceremonies without repercussions. But since they couldn't say anything about me to anyone—I was sacrosanct—they decided to get at me through Ryan.

I never saw it coming.

On Initiation Night, we were all dressed in our best clothes for the ritual. After it was over, the champagne corks were popped and the keg tapped. The girls started arriving, all the little sisters and sorority girls who liked to party. I was proud of Ryan. He was the only initiate who took the house oaths without stumbling over words, whose voice rang out proud and true.

I was in my room, loading my bong, when Paige swept in, making me jump and almost spill the bong water. "Christ, Paige," I griped.

"Big trouble, Kemo Sabe," she said, nabbing the bong from me and taking a big hit.

"What big trouble?" I took the bong from her and lit up.

She coughed, expelling a cloud of smoke with each hack. "You'd just better thank God I'm a better little sister in this fucking place than you're a brother, okay?"

"What are you talking about?" I asked between my own coughs. The pot was harsh, rough on my throat and lungs. I made a mental note to complain to the house vice president, who was my supplier.

"Some of the brothers have started wondering about Ryan."

I stopped, my lighter poised to flick. "Wondering what about Ryan?"

"Why he hasn't gotten laid all semester." She took the bong from me and took another hit. She coughed and smiled. "Oh, much better now, much better. They are starting to wonder if he even likes girls, if you catch my drift."

I went cold. "Oh, no."

"It gets better. They've even decided to sick Pauline Jaworski on him." She grinned at me. "The pigs. Since she's a sure thing…"

I felt sick to my stomach. Pauline Jaworski was a loudmouthed drunk from Chicago. She was a pudgy little thing with big breasts and thick thighs and a tiny waist whom the brothers privately referred to as a "house utility." She'd fucked any number of the brothers. She had no idea she was a joke around the house, or if she did, she didn't care. She'd joined up as a little sister when she was a freshman, and now she was a senior. House lore was she'd once been gangbanged by an entire pledge class. She'd once given another brother a yeast infection in his throat. But she still came around, flashing her cleavage and flirting at rush, following up on the promise of things to come during the semester.

"Jon Shelby asked her to find out, and I quote, 'if Ryan Colby's a queer.'"

"Oh, man, oh, man." My head was pounding with fear. "How'd you find out?"

"Poor dumb Pauline." Paige had been at a preparty at another little sister's while the ceremonies were going on. "You know how she is...she kept hinting to me that something was up but wouldn't tell me what." Paige smiled grimly. "So I pumped a couple of tequila shots into her, and she spilled all in the car on the way over here."

"We've got to tell Ryan—warn him!"

"I'll go find him." She took another hit and then walked over to the door just as someone knocked. "Who is it?" she sang out.

"Ryan."

She let him in, giving him a big hug and kiss for the benefit of the people milling around in the hallway.

"Ryan, we've, um, we've—um, we've got a bit of a problem," I said, filling him on what Paige had just told me.

He looked at me with those big green eyes, his smile fading. "What should I do?"

"You're going to have to..." I closed my eyes. "You're going to have to do it."

"You want me to do this?" He stared at me, his face working through a range of expressions, the vein in his neck throbbing. "And if I won't?"

"Darling, you have to," Paige said, taking another hit off the bong and reloading it. "These guys will make your life a living hell. Trust me on this. At the Phi house they caught one of the brothers with another guy..." She sighed. "Trust me, you don't want to know."

I'd heard about this, but never the full story. Rumor on Greek Row was the Phi's had kicked him out of the house after beating him so badly he needed hospitalization.

"But..." He looked at me. "But I'm a brother now."

"No one can find out." I couldn't believe he didn't understand how serious this was.

"I'm not afraid." His chin went up. "Let them do their worst. I'm not sleeping with Pauline." He laughed. "And what will me not wanting to sleep with her prove? She's just a house whore."

"Ryan..."

He looked from me to Paige and then back to me again. "This

isn't about me really, is it?" Neither one of us said anything. "This is about you."

"No, it isn't." I couldn't look at him.

"If they think I'm a fag, before long they might think the big football stud is too."

"Ryan, please." I looked at him. "I'd lose my scholarship."

"So lose it! So what?"

"What am I supposed to do, go back to Cottonwood Falls?" I shook my head. Just the thought made me sick to my stomach. I was never, ever going back there. "This is all I have, Ryan—please."

He laughed, an unpleasant sound completely devoid of mirth. "Aren't you tired of being afraid?"

I didn't answer.

He walked over to the door, unbolted it, and walked out.

I never left my room that night. As usual, the brothers left me alone. They were too busy getting drunk. I could hear the music blaring in the party room, and could look out my window and see them dancing. The house was a cacophony of stereos and loud voices and the occasional shriek. Paige stayed with me all night, occasionally running down to refill our cups at the keg. We sat there, drinking beer, smoking pot, and listening to old Fleetwood Mac albums. Every time she came back, she would give me an update.

"Everyone's talking about Ryan and Pauline... He was grabbing her boobs on the dance floor... No one has ever seen him this drunk before... I heard one brother say Ryan had been a wimp pledge but now that he's a brother he's a real stud the house can be proud of... He grabbed Gail Nakamura's ass... He's sitting in a corner with Pauline on his lap, making out... He's gone with Pauline into Jim Froelich's room and locked the door...but the curtains are open and guys are out there watching...

I kept hoping he'd come back.

He fucked Pauline that night. It was all over the house the next morning as I picked my way through the wreckage left from the party to make myself breakfast. I was scrambling eggs when Jon Shelby came into the kitchen. "Hey, MacLeod man, that little brother of yours is some big stud." He was a good-looking boy usually, but this morning in his shorts with sleep snot still in his eyes and his hair sticking up in all directions, he looked comical.

"Is he now?"

"Man, he fucked the shit out of the house utility last night." He laughed. "Man, we gave him the wrong nickname. We should have called him 'Horsedick.'"

It took all of my control not to kill him.

I never saw Ryan again.

Over the Christmas break I got a letter.

Dear Chanse:

I wanted to thank you for a wonderful semester. For the first time in my life, I understood what all the fuss about love was all about. I do love you, I want you to understand that. This hasn't been easy for me, but I feel that it's for the best.

I've decided not to come back to LSU. I am going to take this semester off and work on my tennis some more, and then I am going to transfer to the University of Georgia. Athens is a lot closer to home than Baton Rouge, and it's a lot more liberal city than Baton Rouge...and Atlanta is just down the road. There's a strong gay community there, and that's what I need to be around now. I've told my parents, and they've been incredibly loving and supportive, which is part of the reason I've decided to transfer so I can be closer to home.

I don't want you to think I'm an asshole, Chanse, but I can't be happy there with you, having to hide who I am from everyone all of the time. I don't care if people hate me for being myself; I'd rather that than have eighty so-called "best friends" whom I can't be honest with. That's not brotherhood, that's not friendship, that's nothing but dishonesty.

I can't tell you how much it hurt me to hear you tell me to have sex with that poor girl. The only reason I stuck it out with Beta Kappa was to be with you...and it wasn't possible any other way. I have a sister who's a little sister at Alpha Tau Omega in Tuscaloosa, and just the thought that some of the brothers there might think of her as 'the house utility', some stupid whore who is only there for their pleasure, to do their bidding, makes me burn with rage...

Pauline may be many things, but she's a human being. And human beings deserve better than that. I deserve better than that.

I felt so bad for her, lying there underneath me in the bed, pretending that she couldn't hear Jon Shelby and all of those assholes out there watching through the window...and she asked me to tell her that I loved her, Chanse. That was all she wanted...and my heart broke for her. All I could think was she just wants to be loved, that she's lonely, and all she was to me was a way to prove to the brothers that I wasn't gay. She deserves better than that. I deserve better than that.

Please take care of yourself and know you'll always have a place in my heart.

Love, Ryan

I remained a coward the entire time I was at LSU, although after that next semester I moved out of the Beta Kappa house and stopped going to any events. I was still in the closet at the New Orleans P.D., but I was openly gay in my private life, hitting the nearby bars and picking up guys. I'd lived in the Quarter then. I lost myself in my time off in alcohol and Ecstasy.

One night during Southern Decadence, I walked into the Parade. It was packed full of hot guys. And dancing on the stage, wearing nothing more than a pair of white jeans cut off short enough to embarrass Daisy Duke, was my Beta Kappa big brother himself, Scott Simons. I pushed my way through the dance floor and grabbed his leg. His eyes, glazed with whatever drug he was on, lit up when he saw me. He jumped down, threw his sweaty arms around me, and planted a trembling wet kiss on my lips. Later, in my apartment, fucking him, I pondered the irony of fraternity incest. I'd fucked both my big and little brothers.

Shortly after that, I left the force and came out once and for all.

But I never allowed anyone inside the walls around my heart until Paul.

I parked across the street from Paul's house. Maybe I should have stopped at home and gotten Ryan's letter for Paul to read. Hell, there was time for that later, right?

His car was parked right in front and all of his lights were on. He must have gone to get it after I'd left. He was definitely at home.

What the hell, I thought, as I lit another cigarette. Smoking was the least thing we had to worry about right now, and he'd have to understand I had to smoke during this conversation. Hell yes, it was a crutch, but at least I knew that. I got out of the car and leaned back against it, watching his windows.

Nothing was moving up there.

Maybe he was just watching television.

I tossed the cigarette into the street and walked up the driveway. I paused at the foot of the wooden stairs and looked down into the flower bed.

Right off the paved walkway was a footprint in the soft dirt.

Quit delaying and get up there, I said to myself as I knelt down to get a closer look at the footprint. It was from a normal-size foot, probably about a ten and a half, but what was unusual was that it was several inches deep. The ground was soft but dry, so whoever left it had to be pretty heavy. The tread looked to be from a sneaker. I looked around the bed and couldn't see another one. I stepped up onto the front step and looked at it again. It was just off to the side of the stairs. I'd missed the walk and put my right foot into the flower bed myself a couple of times when I'd come down in a hurry.

I shrugged. Probably from a gardener or something. I started climbing the steps, my heart pounding in my ears. My palms were sweating. *Almost like walking the last mile,* I thought and laughed out loud. Don't be stupid—everything's going to work out just fine.

My heart stopped briefly when I reached the top of the stairs.

In front of the door sat a green glass vase with bullet-headed roses and baby's breath. He'd either not answered the door or not taken them into the house.

Not a good sign.

Of course, he could just not be at home. But Paul would never leave all the lights on. *We all have to do our part to conserve energy,* his voice echoed in my head. He'd lectured me about it all the time. He used to walk around behind me, shutting off lights in my apartment when I left a room. And his car was sitting right there on the street.

I knocked on the window pane set in the door. "Paul?" I could hear the television in the background. I leaned over the railing and tried to see in through the living room windows, but the stained glass was too dark. "Paul?" I called again, reaching into my pocket for my keys. *Sure, it's an invasion of privacy,* I thought as I went through them to find his apartment key. But he'd given me the key of his own free will, hadn't he? Hadn't he given me a key to let myself in? It was rationalizing, but I didn't care. Something was wrong, something seemed off.

The deadbolt turned, and with a start I realized I'd locked it.

Paul never in a million years would leave his door unlocked.

This was not good, not good at all. The hair on my forearms stood up.

I unlocked the door and stepped inside. It was freezing in there, as if the air conditioner was set on fifty or something. I could hear it running. "Paul?" I called out again, louder, over the television. I could hear canned laughter. It was one of those stupid sitcoms where the husband was a fat loser pig of a man with a gorgeous, sexy, and intelligent wife.

Which happens all the time in real life, right?

I stepped into the living room. I could sense the stillness beneath the sound of the television. No sign of life anywhere, everything in its place as usual, nothing out of the ordinary…but the print over the fireplace was gone.

"Weird," I said aloud, and turned to look for the other print. My blood ran cold.

It was leaning against the wall.

Paul's head had been completely blacked out with such angry strokes that in a couple of places the pen had pierced the print.

"PAUL!" I screamed, running into the bedroom.

The room was empty, but the bedclothes were rumpled. There was a wet stain in the center of the bedspread. I walked over to it, careful not to touch or disturb anything. My stomach quaking, I leaned over and sniffed the spot, then touched it with my finger.

It was semen.

I stumbled back out of the living room, my heart pounding, my head screaming *Crime scene, Crime scene—don't touch anything. Get out of here...*

I pulled out my cell phone when I got to the kitchen, fumbling through the speed dial till I found the one for Venus Casanova.

That was when I noticed a reddish-brown puddle on the linoleum.

Blood.

Oh, sweet Jesus.

Paul's blood.

I shivered, staring at the pool of blood.

"Casanova," she answered.

"Venus, this is Chanse MacLeod. You need to get over to Paul Maxwell's apartment."

"Why? What's going on?"

"I don't know." I tried to catch my breath. "But I think something's happened to him."

"Go outside and wait for the squad car. I'm on my way." She hung up.

I looked back into the living room at the print.

Paul's head, completely blacked out.

A pool of sperm on his bed.

A puddle of blood in the kitchen.

I walked out and sat on the top step and started shaking. I tried to light a cigarette. It took me a couple of tries. I stared up at the stars in the cloudless sky. I took deep breaths. "Logical explanation—there has to be a logical explanation," I kept saying like a litany. "He's okay—nothing's happened to him."

And then I started to cry.

CHAPTER TWELVE

Fortunately, for patrol cop Sean Mallory, it's against the law to strike a police officer. Within a few minutes of meeting him, I was tempted to knock out a few of his teeth.

I was sitting on the bottom step of Paul's staircase smoking my third cigarette when the patrol car came swooping up, sirens blaring and lights flashing. You'd think this would bring the neighbors to their windows to see what was happening, but twenty years of an ever-increasing crime rate has deadened New Orleanians to the sound of police sirens. Two cops got out and approached me. One was an older black man with gray at his temples and in his mustache and a bit of a belly. "What seems to be the problem?" he asked.

I gave it to them as briefly as possible, and the black cop, whose name was Stallings, went up to poke around in Paul's apartment, leaving me down with Sean Mallory, his partner.

"You know we can't file a missing persons report for twenty-four hours," he said in a thick parish accent. He was a little under six feet tall and couldn't weigh more than 150 pounds, and even that had to be mostly bone. He had short red hair, very pale skin covered with greenish-tan freckles, and crooked teeth. Acne scars pitted his left cheek, and a couple of large pimples were scattered across his forehead. His thin lips were chapped. His uniform hung on him like a tent. He didn't look any older than fifteen.

"Yes, I know." I decided against telling him I was an ex-cop.

"Maybe your friend"—extra emphasis on 'friend'—"just went away for a while. Did you check to see if he took any clothes or a suitcase?" He was smirking at me, which was when I started wondering how my fist would feel against his mouth.

"And he just happened to leave a puddle of blood in his kitchen before he left." I lit another cigarette. "And blacked out his face in a picture. And jacked off on his bed, for good measure."

"Queers do funny things sometimes." The cop smirked. "Who knows why they do what they do?" His tone was condescending. He obviously had been picked on a lot in high school and had got even with the world by becoming a cop—the kind who wishes it were still okay to beat confessions out of suspects. He got off on the power the uniform conveyed. By the time he was thirty his file would be filled with allegations of excessive force and civilian complaints. No doubt he'd be bounced from the force after shooting a suspect in "self-defense."

"Yeah, right," I muttered.

I heard the heavy footsteps of Officer Stallings coming down the stairs behind me, so I stood up. Immediately, Mallory's attitude shifted and his facial expression changed. "What's up, Ted?"

"It's definitely blood." He scratched his head. "I think we'd better call in the Lab."

Mallory didn't like the idea and was about to say something when Venus Casanova's white SUV pulled up. She got out and walked up the driveway with an air of authority Mallory lacked. "Thanks, guys," she said, dismissing them with a wave of her hand. "What did you find?"

"There's blood on the kitchen floor, all right," Stallings replied. "And there is a print in the living room with the face blacked out. And what appears to be sperm on the bed."

She nodded and motioned to me. "Come with me."

I followed her up the stairs. Venus is tall, an inch or two over six feet, and always wears heels to add a few more inches. She carries herself with an air of regal authority that demands respect, which she accepts as a matter of course. She played scholarship basketball at LSU and has kept her long frame in excellent shape since. The calves beneath her long skirt were muscular. She is not a woman to fuck with. She looked like she could kick your ass with one hand while talking on the phone.

She motioned for me to stay outside on the porch while she walked in and headed for the drying blood. She knelt down and stared at it for a few minutes, then looked around the rest of the kitchen. I stood there finishing my cigarette, while she went into the living room. A few minutes later, she came back out. "Okay, it looks odd, but there could be any explanation. He could have cut himself and called an ambulance."

"And only bled on the floor." I flicked the butt into the driveway. "And cleaned up the rest of the kitchen while he waited. And for good measure, blacked out his own face in a print, and took the other one to the hospital with him just in case. Maybe he fell off the bed when he was beating off?"

"Don't be a smart-ass, MacLeod. I've had a long day, okay? The lab will be here in a minute——I just called in for them." She folded her arms. "Did you check to see if his suitcases were here? If any of his clothes were missing or anything?"

"No. Once I found the blood I got out of there." I shrugged. "Besides, his car is still here."

"Couldn't he have taken a cab? To the airport?"

"Venus, you've seen the place." I leaned back against the railing. "The fucking place is spotless-no dust anywhere. He wouldn't have gone anywhere without cleaning up the blood, if he had cut himself. And there is a print missing."

"He could have gotten rid of it since you were here last, couldn't he?"

"What about the other one? With the blacked-out face?"

"He could have done that himself. There's really not a lot to go on here."

"But you went ahead and called in the lab——" I cut myself off in mid sentence. She wasn't looking at me and was avoiding my eyes. That was not like her. Venus was a great cop, one of the best on the force. She didn't bullshit, she didn't play politics, she spoke her mind, regardless of how much shit it might bring down on her from above. "Venus, why were the charges against Paul dropped?"

"The powder residue…" She still wouldn't look at me.

"Yeah, Loren told me about that." Something was starting to stink. "Just because it was on the wrong hand, the D.A. decided to drop charges? It was a slam dunk and you know it—he easily could be ambidextrous. It's flimsy, Venus, very flimsy. What the hell is going on?"

"I'm not at liberty to say."

"You do think something's happened to him, don't you?"

She bit her lower lip before saying, "It wouldn't surprise me, and that's all I can say." She reached out and touched my arm. "Look, Chanse, go check his closet and see if any clothes are missing, and give a statement to Stallings, okay? And then forget about this."

"I can't, Venus. You know that," I replied. My heart was starting to pound. "He's my lover, for Christ's sake."

"Stay out of it, Chanse. Let us do our jobs."

"Yeah, whatever." I felt my temper start to rise, and I swallowed to fight it down. I walked back into the bedroom and, using a paper towel, opened the closet door. His clothes were organized by color and style—sweaters, dress shirts, T-shirts, jeans, dress slacks. I swallowed, I couldn't tell if anything was missing, but his suitcases were still in the closet. Unless he'd put clothes in garbage bags, he hadn't taken anything with him.

I finished giving Stallings my statement right after the lab arrived, promised to come down and sign it in the morning, and got into my car. I lit another cigarette, sat there for a moment, then began pounding on the steering wheel until my hands hurt.

Something was very wrong.

I started up the car and drove the few blocks over to Paige's. She lived in a carriage house behind a big yellow mansion on State Street. Her car was parked on the street. I parked behind her and got out. As I approached, I could hear a Cher CD blaring from inside. I pounded on the door. A few moments later the door swung open. She was wearing a sweatshirt with Tennessee Williams's face on it and a pajama bottoms. Her hair was messy, her eyes bloodshot. I could smell the delightful odor of marijuana. "What?"

I pushed in past her and turned down the volume on the stereo. "Paul's missing."

"What?" She slammed the door behind her. Her computer was on, and I could see she was working on her romance novel. An open bottle of wine sat on the desk beside a full glass, and her pipe, which was still smoking a little. Paige always like to get a mild wine-pot buzz going when she worked on the book she hoped would get her out of the reporter business forever. "What do you mean?"

"After dinner I went to see him." I picked up the pipe and took a hit. "When I got there, all the lights were on, but he wasn't there. His car was out in front. I pounded on the door and then let myself in with my key."

After I finished catching her up, she picked up her glass and downed the wine in one swallow. "Jesus fucking Christ, Chanse." She sat down on the couch and motioned for me to hand her the pipe. She took a hit and refilled it from a Ziploc bag. "Well, it might not be anything."

"Come on, Paige." I started pacing. "Do you really think Paul would leave blood on the floor? You know how anal he is about that apartment."

She shrugged. "Chanse, look at what's happened to him in the last twenty-four hours, okay? He's arrested for murdering a friend. He gets out on bail, you two have a fight, and you end up hurting him. He might have felt the need to get away for a while. It's understandable." She sighed.

"And the prints?"

"Yeah, well, that's a stretch, I admit. He was pretty damned proud of those prints."

"And what about Venus asking me to stay out of it? She wasn't telling me everything."

"That's hardly fair." Paige took another hit and offered me the pipe. "Here, have another hit and mellow, dude. Sit down, you're working my nerves."

I obliged.

"Venus isn't going to tell you jack shit about her investigation, Chanse. You aren't a cop anymore. She isn't going to risk it."

"Well, don't you think it's fucking weird they dropped the charges so fast?"

"Yeah, I do." Paige ran a hand through her unruly hair, messing it up even more. "Now that they have, I can say it: I was scared. I didn't think he did it, but it looked pretty airtight to me. They must have found something pretty definitive, you know? That and the powder residue being on the wrong hand." She lit a cigarette and coughed. "We really should quit smoking, you know."

"Yeah." I lit one.

"Okay, let's go over this whole thing and see what we're missing." She got a steno pad off her coffee table and plucked a pencil from behind her ear. "First of all, Mark Williams was murdered between six and eight o'clock last night. Paul finds the body, picks up the gun and it goes off. The police come and arrest him."

"Make a time line." I pulled my tattered little notebook out of my pants pocket. "Okay, at six Williams leaves his office and goes back to his apartment. A little while later, Ghentry sees Ricky Dahlgren go back there and doesn't see him come back out. Also, at 5:30, I faxed Dominique my report nailing Williams for harassing her."

"Do we know where she was?"

"She called for Williams at six, in a rage, and stormed out of her club about eight. The bartender was pretty definite about that, but he also didn't see her come back. Paul said he got to Mark's around seven, and he was already dead."

"Looks like Ricky Dahlgren is the man of the hour—that and the gun was his father's." Paige stared down at her pad. "You know, it makes sense, Chanse. They dropped the charges against Paul because they think Ricky Dahlgren is the killer." She whistled. "Man, this comes at a really shitty time for Judge Dahlgren."

"Why?"

She glared at me. "You know, you could at least fucking pretend that you read the paper for my articles, you know." She got up and threw the day's paper at me. On the front page was a headline: JURY SELECTION BEGINS FOR SANTINI TRIAL. "He's hearing the Santini case."

I read the article. Marco Santini was up on several charges, including racketeering and murder-for-hire. He was described as a local business entrepreneur.

"Local business entrepreneur?"

"Newspaper euphemism for mob ties."

My head started to hurt. "Ruth Solomon told me Dominique's ex-husband was a mob lawyer in Atlanta."

"This Charlie Wyatt guy you wanted me to check out?" The color drained out of her face. "Oh, God." She grabbed the pipe and took another long, slow hit. "Chanse, what if Paul saw something he shouldn't have?"

"That doesn't make sense, Paige." I shook my head. "Ricky Dahlgren went back there, he had his father's gun. He killed Mark for whatever reason. Maybe they had a fight—I don't know. The mob couldn't be involved in this."

"It might not make sense to us now, but we don't know everything." Paige rubbed her chin. "Dominique's ex-husband is a mob lawyer. Dominique hires Mark Williams. Mark Williams is killed by Ricky Dahlgren, whose father just happens to be presiding over the biggest mob trial in decades here...how did Dominique just happen to hire Mark?"

"She says he dropped by one day and offered his services. He knew she was having trouble with VCC complaints and her licenses." I shrugged. "It sounded weird to me when she told me, but now that we know Williams was behind her trouble—"

"Yeah, but there wasn't a guarantee she was going to hire him, so why bother? It doesn't make any sense. I mean, the $500 she was paying him seems hardly worth the risk."

"Zane claimed it was $5,000—and that was the operating fund for the company, really, so the money was coming in." I wracked my brain. A ghost of an idea was floating on the outer rims of my awareness, and I tried to grab on to it. "So, if Dominique is telling the truth and she wasn't paying him that much, where was the money coming from? Maybe someone was paying him to sabotage her."

"Who?"

"The ex-husband—Charlie Wyatt." That made some sort of sense. "And maybe Wyatt was paying him to spy on her too." I shook my head. "No. That doesn't explain Ricky Dahlgren."

None of it made any sense. I got up. "I'm going to head home." The pot had made tired. I hadn't slept well, and the day had been an emotional roller coaster.

"You okay to drive?" Paige stood up. "You can crash here if you want."

"No. I want to go home." I didn't want to tell her I was hoping Paul might call.

If he could.

I kissed her cheek and gave her a big hug. She walked me to the door and stroked my arm. "I'm sure he's okay, Chanse," she said quietly.

I just nodded and walked back to my car. I sat for a minute before wiping the tears out of my eyes and drove off. Paul would be okay, I figured. I was just emotionally raw and exhausted and needed to get home and into bed.

The traffic on St. Charles was pretty sparse, which was why I spotted the car following me.

I'd noticed it vaguely when I pulled out from the curb—about half a block down the street: a big, dark Oldsmobile-size car. The headlights came on when I pulled out and headed up State Street. I didn't think anything about it when it also turned onto St. Charles, but when I reached the light at Jefferson and it stopped several car lengths behind me, my mind came wide awake. I stared at it in my rearview mirror, but it was far enough back I couldn't get any idea of its color or shape. I also couldn't tell if the driver was alone. But a chill went down my spine. When the light changed, I floored it. It kept pace behind me.

As I passed Valmont, another car turned after I went past, getting between us and going slow. The other car swung around it, just missing a parked car.

Think, Chanse, think.

The light coming up at Napoleon was red, and I slammed on my breaks and managed to come to a stop before rear-ending a battered pickup truck.

The big car slowed and stopped at the same distance behind me. I grabbed my cell phone and dialed Paige. "What?"

"I'm being followed," I said, staring in the rearview mirror at the headlights behind me.

"Oh, God, what do you want me to do?"

"When I hang up, call Venus. Tell her I'm heading home...and I'd greatly appreciate it if a squad car was waiting at my house, or if they can pick up the tail on the way."

Just at that moment, I heard the shriek of a siren behind me. I looked into the rearview mirror and saw the approaching flashing lights coming. The big car suddenly turned right and disappeared down a side street. It was a dark-blue or black Pontiac. The squad car made a U-turn through the neutral ground and sped off back the other way. I let out my breath. The light changed. "They're gone for now."

"Be fucking careful!" She hung up.

I made it home without spotting the other car, but the adrenaline spike had my eyes wide open. As I turned into my driveway, I noticed a package resting against my front door. I parked the car and walked around to the front, just getting past the automatic gate as it slid shut. I looked around Camp Street but didn't see any cars. I scanned Coliseum Square, but none of the cars parked around the park looked out of place.

I walked through the front gate and up the cracked and tilted sidewalk to the steps.

What if it's a bomb?

I stopped.

"Get a grip," I said out loud. I climbed the steps and picked it up. It was addressed to me, and the return address said FULL NELSON PRODUCTIONS.

Paul's videos.

"Fucking idiot," I said as I unlocked the front door. I closed it behind me, locking the dead bolt and putting the chain on. This just made me feel better. Like most front doors in New Orleans, half of it was glass. Some security, right?

I turned on the light and picked up the remote as I sat on the couch. A rerun of *Roseanne* was on. I tore up the package and shook out four videos: *Musclestud Challenge 12; Gods of the Ring 8; Musclestud Erotic Challenge; Jocks 15.* I took *Musclestud Erotic Challenge* out of its sleeve.

The label on front said the match was between Cody Dallas and Joe Bob Jones.

I put the tape into the VCR.

The video started with the title, then the word FEATURING before it showed a still photo of Paul. He was smiling at the camera, his arms folded and muscles bulging. CODY DALLAS appeared at the bottom of the screen, and then it morphed into another picture, of a smiling young boy in an open sleeveless red and black flannel shirt and a cowboy hat. His chest looked huge, as were the arms hanging at his side. JOE BOB JONES scrolled across the bottom before the screen faded to black.

The next shot showed a room with a wall-to-wall mat on the floor. The camera focused in on two bottles of baby oil, then switched over to a shot of Paul, who was sitting on the floor wearing nothing more than a black jock. He was stretching, and the camera zoomed in on his crotch. He continued stretching and showing off his muscles, while pretending the camera wasn't there. The camera panned to a door swinging open as Joe Bob sauntered in wearing a cowboy hat, the same flannel shirt from the picture, and baggy jeans that didn't disguise how big his legs were. He stood watching Paul stretching for a minute, then took off his shirt.

I gasped.

Joe Bob was huge. He was built like someone you'd see on the cover of *Muscle & Fitness*. His muscles were huge and perfectly defined, striations popping out in each one of them with even the slightest movement he made. He undid his pants, and the baggy denim dropped away to show that his legs were perfectly in proportion to the rest of his body. He was darkly tanned, and as he stood there in his red jock, loosening up, I thought, *Paul, honey, you are going to get your ass kicked.*

Joe Bob took his hat off, and I got a good look at his face. He looked like he was maybe nineteen, and had a kind of an "aw, shucks" look to him—like a simple, sweet muscle boy from some rural area who had no clue how good he looked. Of course his name would be Joe Bob.

They shook hands and started wrestling, and I could see immediately that I had been wrong about the outcome. Paul was a good wrestler, and Joe Bob didn't know anything—that was obvious after just a few seconds. He was just big and strong, whereas Paul was quick and skilled. Joe Bob might get a momentary advantage, but Paul would swiftly reverse out of it and get Joe Bob down.

I found myself getting aroused.

Wrestling was a lot more sexual than I'd thought. I'd never really paid much attention to it—there hadn't been a wrestling team at Cottonwood Wells High, so I'd only gotten brief glimpses of matches while watching the Olympics. Or the pro stuff, which was always so silly I'd never bothered with it. The Beta Kappas who'd been into the pro stuff were jerks. I'd watched some of the TV shows with Paul, but really hadn't paid a lot of attention. It just seemed stupid to me.

But seeing two guys with great bodies who were wearing nothing but jockstraps as they wrestled—one trying to establish dominance over the other—was very sexually arousing. Their bodies came into almost constant close contact—especially their crotches when they would get locked in some hold where one was lying on top of the other.

Paul finally pinned Joe Bob, and they lay on the mat side by side, laughing and joking and trying to catch their breaths. Both bodies were bathed in sweat. Then Joe Bob picked up a bottle of oil and squirted Paul. Paul got the other bottle and squirted Joe Bob back. Soon they facing each other on their knees and rubbing the oil in with steady, measured strokes. The camera focused on their soaked jocks, lingering as each of them began to stiffen.

And then they were rolling and slipping and sliding over the mats, the slick oil making it harder to hold on to each other.

Then somehow the jocks came off, and you knew for sure that both were erect.

I picked up the remote and hit fast-forward.

The images flew past. The two of them laughing and rolling around naked, grabbing at each other and slipping and sliding.

Then Paul got on top of Joe Bob and kissed him.

Joe Bob slid down on Paul's body, and took him in his mouth.

I hit the stop button and sat there for a moment.

I was turned on, but Paul's voice echoed in my head.

I never had sex on camera.

Another lie.

I got up and walked back to the bedroom.

All my energy drained out of me, and I was asleep the minute I hit the bed

CHAPTER THIRTEEN

I was startled out of a deep sleep by some noise I couldn't identify at about seven in the morning.

I blinked the sleep out of my eyes as the early-morning sun was streaming through the iron bars on my bedroom window. I kept listening in the silence. Cars were going past on Camp Street, and a dog was barking in Coliseum Square, but that was it. I wasn't sure what it had been—just something out of the ordinary that had jarred my mind into consciousness without warning. As I waited, I reflexively reached my right arm across the bed. Then, as my questing hand continued to find nothing but pillow and comforter, I remembered the bed was empty and closed my eyes again. Paul wasn't there, and I didn't know where he was.

We'd usually spent every night together, unless he had an early shift. Every morning we'd set the alarm for nine and wake up, our bodies in a tangled mess of arms, legs, quilt, and sheets. Paul never woke easily. He'd moan and beg for at least five minutes, opening his eyes pleadingly and giving me a shy grin as I disentangled from the soothing warmth of his body and the bedclothes. I always let him have his extra time while I brushed my teeth, washed my face, and started coffee. Some mornings, if I woke up clearheaded, I'd make him breakfast and bring it to him in bed. He never failed to be delighted, especially if it was pancakes. On those mornings it was easy to see what kind of little boy he'd been. I loved bringing that out in him. He'd eat and then get up, and we'd go to the gym to work out.

But this morning I was alone.

I didn't hear the sound again, so I swung my legs off the bed and got up. Sometime during the night I'd managed to get my shirt off and thrown it on the floor, but I didn't remember doing it. I still had on my jeans, and walked into the kitchen and started coffee. I checked in the living room, and nothing looked out of the ordinary. Probably had just been something outside, just the neighbor's dog.

I looked like hell in the bathroom mirror as I brushed my teeth, but I felt better. Somehow, I'd managed to sleep deeply and restfully. The stress of the last day or so seemed under control. All I'd needed, I told myself as I washed my face, was a good night's sleep.

I showered, shaved and got dressed. I'd skip the gym this morning, figuring maybe I'd try to get down there in the afternoon. I walked into the living room and booted up my computer.

Paul's videotapes were still lying on the coffee table. I walked over and picked up one of them: *Gods of the Ring 8*. I looked at the label: *Cody Dallas vs. Ronny Marshall*. I set it back down. I sat down on the couch and picked up the remote, turning on the television and hitting play.

I sat there, sipping my coffee and watching my boyfriend have sex with another man.

When the credits rolled, I hit rewind, feeling like the biggest jerk on the planet.

He hadn't been my boyfriend when he made these videos. And who was I to judge him anyway?

Paige was right. Again.

It hadn't been cool of Paul to lie to me, but I'd really left him no choice.

Yeah, like he was going to tell me he'd done porn after I'd freaked about him posing shirtless on a magazine cover? *I* would have lied. The truth was I was overly jealous in an incredibly self-absorbed, ugly way. I hadn't questioned it when Paul lost interest in going out dancing, even though he'd loved it and looked forward every week to Saturday night. I just assumed he preferred our alone time more, but he'd been tired of me getting jealous every time someone smiled at him. Rather than calling me on it, he'd taken the easier way out. He'd always been willing to sacrifice something he loved to keep me happy.

He'd loved flying, being in a different city every night, but he'd also given that up to be ground-based and with me every night. God, was I a piece of work. I'd been completely oblivious while I suffocated him, but in spite of the fact that I was a jealous, untrusting ass, he'd loved me anyway, done everything he could to make me happy and keep the peace. Every time I got jealous when someone smiled or touched him, I was basically saying to him, *You don't love me, and you're going to leave me as soon as you find something better.* I hadn't been able to accept his unconditional love for what it was. We'd never really talked about anything.

Why hadn't I realized all of this before?

And now he was gone, I didn't know where. When he came back, I'd make it all up to him. I would tell him about T.J. and Ryan, why it was so hard for me. I'd never be jealous again, I vowed. I'd focus on making him happy for a change. And if he wanted to keep making these tapes, I wouldn't complain. Just no more sex on camera. That wasn't too much to ask.

The blood in the kitchen was easy enough to explain. He could have slipped, hit his head, and called an ambulance. Sadly, even the prints could be explained. The argument had started with me noticing for the first time the model was him. After I left, he could have gotten rid of the one and, in an emotional rage of some kind, blacked out his face in the other one. It was all very logically explained—even the sperm spot on his bed. It wasn't like him—at least not like the Paul I knew. But I didn't know him as well as I should, and that was partly my own fault. I'd never taken the time to get to know him. All I'd really allowed him to be was my good-looking boyfriend.

So why *had* Venus jumped into action the instant I called her?

The patrol cop's attitude, which had pissed me off so much the night before, was the proper reaction...nothing could be done for twenty-four hours. The reason for that rule is simple: Why go to all the trouble of filling out a report when the person could have just wandered off for a while and might still turn up? Venus had also jumped jurisdictions—Uptown wasn't her turf. Of course, Paul was a suspect in an ongoing investigation of hers, but why hadn't the Uptown detective pool shown up? Venus had to have called them off on her way and taken over jurisdiction.

Had Venus thought Paul would leave town?

Or did she think something was going to happen to him?

No proof, Chanse, no proof, I reassured myself, heading over to my computer. I logged onto the Internet and pulled up my e-mails. *Stop imagining things and focus on the facts.*

I was shocked to see I had thirty-eight new messages. The header line of almost every one of them said things like "I saw you" (on this Web site) or "You have e-mail from" (this person). And they almost all had attachments. I started reading.

> *My God, are you hot... I'd love to wrestle you sometime... I am coming to New Orleans in a couple of months and would like a match... What do you get into? I like to... I'm not into oil myself but would be willing to try it with you... Do you ever get to Dallas? We'd be a good match... Have you ever tried being a heel?*

The pictures were a mixed bag: older guys, younger guys, overweight guys, guys with incredible bodies. Some guys were naked; others were wearing thongs, jocks, bikinis, or underwear. Some photos were headless and out of focus; others showed the guy's face and looked professionally done, in black-and-white with artistic poses and shadings. Yet others were taken in front of mirrors with digital cameras so that the reflecting flash obscured the face.

There were about three left when I hit pay dirt.

> *Hey, Chanse:*
> *So you're the reason Paul retired from the business? He's a great guy. We made a video together once. I think it was called* Jocks 15. *How's he doing? Haven't heard from him in a while.*

I'll be in New Orleans for Halloween...maybe we could all get together for dinner or drinks or some wrestling...:) Hit me back with an e-mail and let me know what you think...and tell Paul to e-mail me.

Jude

I downloaded his picture and whistled. Jude was in his late twenties, with the look of a nice farm boy. Dark-blond hair, blue eyes, and a strong-looking face with dimples. He was wearing a pair of loose-fitting jeans. He had his fists in his pockets, which pulled the jeans down far enough to show his tan line and the deep-cut lines from his hips heading gradually toward each other inside his pants. The big muscles in his arms bulged. It might have been the way the jeans were cut and hanging on him, but he looked fully qualified to be a porn star. His head was tilted to one side, a piece of straw jutting out of his mouth as he grinned at the camera, one of his eyes closed in a wink.

My computer dinged and an instant message opened on my screen.

Wrestlejude: "Chanse? How you doing?"

I looked at the return address on the e-mail. Yep: Wrestlejude.

Chansemac: "Hey, Jude—just read your e-mail...thanks for the pic."

Wrestlejude: "The ones of the site of you are hot, man. Got any others? Nudes?"

Chansemac: LOL. "No nudes, sorry."

Wrestlejude: "I'll send some of me...just a sec, okay? Don't go away, okay?"

Chansemac: "Okay."

While I waited, I did a search for Judge Dahlgren and found one, a *Times-Picayune* profile.

Judge Ronald Dahlgren was a native of New Orleans, born in Uptown, and had gone to Vanderbilt and Tulane Law. He had married Miss Lois Winston of Mobile right out of law school. He had joined a large firm and become active in politics, working for several local and state campaigns. The candidates he'd supported had one thing in common: conservatism. He was a deacon of his church. He worked hard, earning a reputation as a fierce litigator while also rising in state politics. He had been appointed to the local U.S. district judgeship by a conservative politician as a thank-you for all of his political help, presumably to steer the court in a conservative direction. He had three children: two sons, Darcy and Richard, and a daughter, Laura. He always gave out the maximum sentence permitted by law. Some critics felt he wasn't impartial; he always favored the prosecution in his rulings.

Not surprising he owns a gun, I thought. *He probably belongs to the NRA.*

My computer dinged.

Wrestlejude: "Sent. Hope you like…"

I unzipped the file he sent me and started opening pictures of Jude naked from every possible angle. Nothing was left to the imagination. He was definitely a well-put-together man.

Chansemac: "WOW. Thanks…where you at?"

Wrestlejude: "I live in Dallas. Coming in for Halloween, would be great to hook up with you guys…"

Chansemac: "Sounds great, man. Did you know Paul in Dallas?"

Wrestlejude: "Yeah, Paul was the one who turned me on to wrestling. LOL. It's all his fault!"

Chansemac: "LOL. Know what you mean…"

Wrestlejude: "I'd always wanted to do it—you know, try it out, but was always afraid if I said anything people would think I was weird…"

The way I would have if Paul told me.

Chansemac: "Yeah, who knew? How'd you two meet?"

Wrestlejude: "He was in the Dallas chat room one night…hey, would you mind if I called?"

Chansemac: "No…my number is 504-555-8153."

Wrestlejude: "Give me a sec…I have to sign off to call."

The phone rang maybe a minute later. The caller I.D. read MUELLER, JUDE with a Dallas number. I answered, "Hello?"

"Hey, man, how you doing?" His voice was deep, melodious but playful.

"Good."

"It's great to talk to you." He laughed. "Hell, I've heard so much about you, it's kind of like I already know you, man."

Wish I could say the same, I thought, laughing into the phone and saying, "Good things, I hope."

"Oh, yeah, man. Paul thinks you're the second coming of Christ. I keep telling him, 'Come on, nobody's perfect,' and he always says 'Chanse is.'"

I didn't respond. I couldn't.

But Jude apparently liked to talk, so he didn't notice and just went on. "Paul's a great guy. That night in the chat room I read his profile and it says right there, plain as day, he's into wrestling, so I sent him a message and we started chatting. I ended up inviting him over, and it was so much fun, and he was such a great guy! He showed me all kinds of stuff."

"Really?" I swallowed.

"He taught me how to wrestle! Like he's teaching you!" He laughed. "I was lucky he was the first wrestler I met, man—you too."

"Why?"

"Hasn't Paul warned you about the freaks and liars?"

Freaks and liars? "Um, no."

"That's weird…he warned me right off." He sounded puzzled. "I mean, he had to know the freaks and weirdos would come out of the woodwork when you posted your profile."

"He—he doesn't know." It wasn't a lie. And it fit in perfectly.

Jude laughed long and hard. "That's pretty ballsy, man, especially when you named him in your profile! He's probably already gotten a couple of e-mails from guys he knows who saw it. I know I did!" He got serious. "Oh, man, I hope I didn't get you in trouble."

"Um, it's okay," I said, thinking fast. "He's out of town and won't have access to his e-mails for a while. I'll tell him before." I swallowed. "What about these freaks and weirdos?"

He sighed. "Wrestling is so much fun, and there are so many cool guys into it—but not everyone is…you're going to meet up with the lunatic fringe sooner rather than later, especially with those pictures posted."

"Lunatic fringe?" I prompted.

"The liars. The freaks. The guys who don't show. The guys who send you a picture of themselves when they had hair and teeth. The guys who send you a skinny pic. The guys who talk all big and then never show up. The guys who send other people's pictures—that's happened to both me and Paul, and it'll happen to you, too. The ones who you meet and are frickin' crazy. The ones who decide after one match you're their boyfriend. The stalkers…there's this one guy in Mississippi who scares the shit out of me."

"I can't imagine why Paul didn't tell me about this guy."

"Paul always laughed it off, but I think he was scared of the guy—and not in a wrestling sense, if you know what I mean. Paul could take care of himself wrestling, man. He's one of the best. He only lost a match when he wanted to." Jude paused, then added, "This guy was totally obsessed with Paul. He used to e-mail him pictures all the time, offer to pay him to wrestle him, stuff like that."

"Offered to pay him?"

Jude laughed again. "Dude, when people offer money or to pay your airfare to come wrestle, the alarm bells need to go off. There's something wrong with that person—no social skills, really ugly or something, or just plain crazy."

"Which was this guy?"

"Crazy."

"How do you know."

"I met him." I could practically see Jude shiver. "He came to Dallas specifically to wrestle me. He got in touch with me, and he seemed cool, you know. We talked via e-mail and on the phone a couple of times. He didn't like that I wouldn't let him stay at my house—I could tell he wasn't happy about that, but hell, I don't invite anyone I don't know to stay in my house—and at that time, you know, Paul was just laughing it all off. Paul went out of town that weekend. Later, I realized he left town on purpose."

My heart was pounding so hard I could barely think. Paul hadn't been exaggerating: He did have a stalker.

I wanted to punch myself.

"So, anyway, this guy shows up, right? I mean, he was okay-looking and all, but he was white. I've never seen anyone so white, like he never saw the sun or something, and his eyes were blue but kind of pinkish-looking, too—you know what I mean? He had a nice body and all, and right away he starts bitching about how much the hotel room is costing, you know? Jesus!"

"Sounds like a jerk."

"I should have told him to leave then, but no, I figure he came all the way in from Mississippi, so I should wrestle him, right? So we go into my mat room and we change into bikinis, and all of his skin is pale like that, fish-belly white— it was really kind of gross, you know? I've never seen anyone that white. And we start wrestling, and you know, he's not a bad wrestler. Then I start to realize he gets off on pain, not wrestling, and not just getting it, either."

"Oh."

"That's pretty scary, you know, when you realize you're wrestling someone who's really into pain, you know? He would get me into a hold and try to hurt me, and I was getting madder and madder, and then he really pissed me off, so I jerked out of the hold, and my elbow caught him square in the mouth..."

"What did he do?"

"He backed off for a bit and put his hand up to his mouth, and when he took it away he just fucking grinned at me. His mouth was bleeding, man. His teeth were covered in blood, and it was dripping out the side of his mouth, and he just fucking grinned at me and says, 'That's how you like it? Me too.'"

"Oh, my God." This guy had been stalking Paul? Why hadn't he told me?

"I told him to get in the bathroom and we'd put some ice in it, apologizing, but he wasn't interested—he wanted to keep fighting."

"What did you do?"

"I told him we had to stop and take care of his mouth, or he had to leave." He laughed. "And he fucking freaked, man. He started ranting and raving and screaming at me, saying he was going to have me arrested for assaulting him, or he was going to sue me. And I said if he didn't get dressed and leave, I'd call the cops, and he just kept screaming—then he just got real calm. He picked up a towel and wiped his mouth, put on his clothes, and left. But before he walked out my front door, he turns back to me and says, 'Be seeing ya.' I locked the door the minute it closed."

"Where in Mississippi was this guy from?."

"Some little town on the coast—Louis Bay?"

Bay St. Louis was an hour and half away.

"Yeah, watch out for that one—Chris Fowler. If you ever hear from him, don't answer," Jude said. "So, what are you up to today?"

The switch was jarring. "Well, I have to go to work in a bit," I said, needing to get off the phone as quickly as I could.

"I'm off today," he practically purred into the phone. "I wish you were here so we could wrestle."

"Well, you'll be in town soon enough."

"Yeah, I'm just laying here in bed naked...wishing you were here. What are you wearing?"

"Jeans and a T-shirt," I replied without thinking.

"Take 'em off."

"What?"

His voice was low and seductive. "I'm lying here naked with a hard-on. Why don't you join me here on the bed?"

I didn't respond.

"Afraid you'll lose, big guy?" he taunted.

I looked up at my computer screen. His picture, stark naked, grinned at me.

"No," I said. "I'm not afraid."

"You should be," he whispered. "You might have thirty pounds on me, but I've taken apart bigger guys than you."

I didn't know what to say. I knew I should get off the phone, but I couldn't just hang up.

He laughed. "You've never done a phone match, have you?"

"Um, no."

"Okay, never mind then. I'll just pop in a video." He yawned. "Okay, man, I'm glad we met. I can't wait till we meet in person and I am gonna kick your ass."

"Bring it on," I said. It seemed like the right thing to say.

"I will. My love to Paul." He hung up.

I sat there, staring at the phone receiver for a moment, then set it down. I got out my atlas. I'd never been to Bay St. Louis. My landlady had a beach house there she escaped to in the summer to get away from the city's stifling heat. I flipped pages to the map of Louisiana, which showed most of the Mississippi Gulf Coast, too, and traced I-10 out of New Orleans with my finger past Slidell. Bay St. Louis was on U.S. Highway 90, just past Waveland and before Pass Christian. I closed the atlas and went back to my computer.

Jude's naked body was still on the screen, winking at me, holding his hard-on in his right hand. I stared at him for a minute before closing the windows. *Thank God Paul stopped making videos,* I thought. *Guys like Jude and Joe Bob would be way too tempting.* Hell, I'd be tempted to cheat, too, if I was rolling around in a Speedo with them. I logged back onto the Internet and pulled up the phone directory for Bay St. Louis, and plugged in "Chris Fowler" into the search engine. After a few moments a window opened.

FOWLER, CHRISTOPHER. 1736 FOREST ROAD. 555-9078.

I mapped out directions from my house to his, then printed them out. It was a long shot, but what else did I have to do? It couldn't hurt to check him out.

My phone rang. "MacLeod."

"Hey, Chanse, it's Venus." She sounded tired. "I'm not sure how to tell you this, but the sperm on the bed and the blood in the kitchen—they didn't match up. They came from two different people." She sighed. "I've put out an all-points on Paul. I also checked with his employer, and he didn't fly out anywhere."

My heart sank. "So you think it was foul play."

"It looks like it. I'm sorry." She cleared her throat. "Can you meet me somewhere this afternoon? I don't want to talk on the phone."

I looked at my watch. It was close to nine. I added up the time in my head. I could probably be back from Bay St. Louis no later than two. "Say about three? At Goodfriends Bar?"

"Yeah." She hung up.

I got my keys and headed out the door.

CHAPTER FOURTEEN

I-10 East was packed, but traffic was still zipping along at seventy miles an hour.

When I got the chance, I pulled over into the middle lane and settled into the flow. The sun was bright, the sky was blue, and NPR was playing Rachmaninoff. *This might be a wild-goose chase,* I thought, rolling down the window and letting fresh air in. *But where could he be?* He didn't have any other friends in New Orleans I knew of—but then I hadn't known about Mark Williams either. He never talked about his job or his coworkers, so it was possible he was close enough to one of them to "hide out" with at their place for a while. But surely he would have taken his car...and that didn't explain what I'd found in his apartment. This stalker was the only possible lead I had, and I'm not a patient person.

It was disconcerting to think how little I knew of Paul's life. Just a few days earlier, if someone had asked, I would have said that I knew him inside and out. But now I hadn't the slightest idea of where he would have gone voluntarily.

The car's transmission groaned as I urged it to climb the high bridge over the industrial canal connecting Lake Pontchartrain to the river. "Come on," I said out loud, pushing the gas pedal to the floor and listening to the engine whine. Cars and trucks zipped past me, making the car rock in their wind wake. The speedometer needle began slipping down below seventy miles per hour. I began to sweat. "Come on, come on, come on." I envisioned the car stalling on the span's rise and starting to roll backward into the oncoming traffic. Finally, I reached the top and let out a sigh as I started down the other side. I should have taken the car in right away, but I hate mechanics. Who knows if they're telling the truth?

The traffic thinned as I got closer to the city limits, heading out past Jazzland Amusement Park for the lake bridge to Slidell. Slidell is one of those outlying small cities most New Orleanians think of contemptuously as the "burbs," with its neon signs, motel chains, and fast-food hell. There was an outlet mall just off the second Slidell exit, which was the only thing that ever dragged the nice Uptown ladies out this far, though none would admit it. Paige loved to shop there, but I'd never bothered. I hate to shop anyway, and outlet shopping wasn't enough of a savings to drag me out of the city proper.

A few miles past Slidell the countryside changed as the ground got higher. Instead of swamp and marsh, the earth solidified with massive pine trees reaching for the sky. The highway cut through some hillsides and rose and fell with others. I'd driven through here at night once. It was creepy, the huge trees blocking out any light on either side. I always wondered if I was going to have a UFO sighting. There were several places that looked like the cover of that old Time-Life book about alien contact. I kept waiting for a silvery being with slit-like black eyes to attach itself to the side of my car and look through the windshield at me.

As I drove toward the state line, I went over my phone call with Jude again. He seemed nice enough, and like he was telling the truth. There was no reason for him to lie to me about this Chris Fowler. If he'd been harassing Paul for a while, it stood to reason he might have escalated. I wondered what exactly he had said or done...and if Paul had ever thought about telling me. He could very well be harmless, but I'd brought my gun just in case. If the guy was crazy and some-how had managed to abduct Paul, I was ready. Never again would I go face a possible suspect without my gun. It was cool enough that wearing a jacket to hide my shoulder holster wouldn't look strange.

I passed the WELCOME TO MISSISSIPPI sign and the tourist wel-come center. Once over the state line, the cars became spare. Instead of nice, new-looking cars, the vehicles I passed were dilapidated pickup trucks. I never felt completely comfortable in Mississippi; almost like I have a big neon sign on my car flashing FAG. Sure, I knew the image of the uneducated redneck Mississippi bigot was a stereotype, just like the mincing makeup-wearing queen, but it didn't make me feel any safer.

I got off I-10 at the 607, then a few minutes later switched to U.S. Highway 90, which took me into Waveland and finally Bay St. Louis at about the time I lost connection to the NPR station. I searched through the stations and finally found a strong signal playing Johnny Cash's "Ring of Fire." One of my best-kept secrets was my liking of country music, especially the classics. Paige liked jazz and blues, and Paul was primarily into dance music, that techno stuff with the driving bass line you usually hear only in gay bars. He called it "Ecstasy music" and, while listening in my apartment, would indicate what exactly each change in the music signified while making dinner.

"Here's where you put your arms up in the air and say 'whooo,'" he'd demonstrate, a big grin on his face as he moved his feet back and forth with the bass line. We'd done Ecstasy together during Decadence. I hadn't done it since the notorious summer after I left the force, when every night had seemed like a weekend. Every Friday and Saturday night, I took Ecstasy and walked around with a big stupid grin on my face. I later called it my summer of drugs.

I'd never done Ecstasy and gone dancing, though. Dancing was never one of my favorite things to do. I always felt awkward and goofy on the dance floor, but Paul danced with such abandonment that I enjoyed just kind of moving from side to side and watching him. "I can't believe you've never danced on X before," he said as we both took our pills and washed them down with water. "You're going to have so much fun, baby!" He grabbed me by the hand and dragged me out into the midst of the packed dance floor. I stood still and watched him start moving. I started dancing, too, feeling awkward, stupid, and out of place, as I got bumped from opposite sides. We just kept dancing, until my awkwardness just dropped away. I began to sense the music, feel it in my soul and in my feet, and I started moving like I'd never moved before. It was fun; everything was fun...the music was incredible, like nothing I'd ever heard before, and then Paul had started tapping my chest, and it felt amazingly good. I tucked my water bottle into my back pocket—as Paul had done—and pulled my shirt off and tucked it through a belt loop, where it swung into my leg every once in a while as I moved. Another song started, one I recognized, and it was like it was playing just for us, and I felt the sound coming up and out of my mouth before I could even think about it. "Whooooo..." Paul just gave me a big grin and joined me. We grabbed each other's hands and held them up over the crowd, waving them back and forth, grinning like morons at each other. We'd stood on the Oz dance floor, moving and dancing and grinning and touching and kissing, surrounded wall-to-wall by musclemen drenched in sweat and having the time of their lives. I just followed Paul's lead, moving my arms and dancing, sometimes just touching him because he was so damned pretty, because everyone was pretty, the whole world was pretty...

That had been the only night in the past two months we'd gone out dancing, and the only reason we'd gone was because some friends of Paul had come into town for the weekend. We were supposed to meet them that night at Oz, but we never did. Thinking back, I smiled, remembering the joy on Paul's face that night on the dance floor, how many times he had just grabbed me and held on to me with all his strength, and then would look up and say, "I love you, Chanse."

I love you, Chanse.

My stomach growled just as I pulled into Waveland. It could have been any generic Southern town with a highway through it. The road was lined with fast-food and chain stores of every type, gas stations, the obligatory mall, and Wal-Mart. When I saw the golden arches, I put on my turn signal and slowed down.

When I got down to twenty miles per hour, the car began to hiccup and lurch. I immediately shifted into neutral, and the car stopped its gasping and rolled into the parking lot for the McDonald's, barely making it up the slight incline and almost coming to a stop. I shifted back into drive but the car simply stalled. I put it back into neutral, restarted the car, revved the engine a few times, then put it into drive. The transmission groaned, then caught with a lurch, and I guided the car into a parking spot.

I turned it off. *Stupid, stupid, stupid,* I berated myself. I should have borrowed Paige's car. I should have taken Paul's. I should have fucking rented one. I should have taken the fucking thing into the garage instead of putting it off. It would be my luck to have it break down completely out here in the middle of nowhere, stranding me in Mississippi of all places. It usually ran just fine, but whenever I had to go out on the highway, getting it up to a speed over fifty, it would have trouble downshifting when I was slowing down. Once it had stalled on the St. Charles Avenue exit ramp. It had taken me several minutes to get it started and going again, with cars honking behind me and traffic blocked all the way back to the highway as everyone on the ramp missed several light changes because of me.

I got out of the car and locked it. Pulling my cell phone out, I called Paige. "Tourneur."

"Hey, Paige, I may need your help. Are you tied up there all day?"

"I've got a zillion things to do, but since I'm wonderful, it shouldn't be a problem getting it all done in a hurry if I need to." She laughed. "I am so underpaid. What's up?"

"I'm checking into this guy who was sending Paul the e-mails."

"What did you find?"

She listened to my recap of the morning and then exploded. "Jesus H. Christ, will you have a priest give that car the last rites and put a bullet through it's engine already? Put it out of its misery! And me out of mine!"

"Well, it'll probably be okay—it usually is after it cools down a bit."

"You're fucking crazy. I can't believe you—what if this guy is a wacko? No one would have known where you were. You'd just vanish like Paul. Christ, I need a cigarette." Paige had almost quit her job when *The Times-Picayune* had gone smoke-free.

"I'll be fine, Paige. I've got my gun this time." Paige had ripped me up one side and down the other after I'd almost been killed. The main thing she'd harped on was I hadn't even taken my gun with me. She claimed she never went anywhere without hers, although I seriously doubted she went on dates with it tucked into her purse next to her makeup and wallet. "And that's why I'm calling— so someone does know where I am."

"If you haven't called me by five, I'm calling Venus. What's this guy's address?"

I read it to her off the directions I'd printed out. She repeated it as she wrote it down. "Oh, guess what?"

I hated when she did that. "What?"

"Did you know Ricky Dahlgren had applied for a private .eye license?" Paige could get anyone to talk to her, tell her things they wouldn't tell anyone else. None of Paige's sources ever asked her for money. They just liked her, so they helped her out. She could establish rapport with a stranger faster than anyone I'd ever seen in my life. If she'd been a cop, she'd have solved every case thrown her way. She'd convince everyone to confess, and if they didn't, they weren't guilty, most likely. I never questioned where she got her information. The most important thing was that her information was always right. "He'd applied several times for a job with the FBI."

"No shit." I leaned against my car and lit a cigarette. "Any idea why the Feds didn't want him?"

"None. He apparently just wasn't Feeb material."

"Interesting."

"Isn't it though? Okay, gotta get back to this work bullshit. If I haven't heard from you by five—"

"You're calling Venus. Got it."

"And if the car stalls—"

"I'll call."

"And if doesn't, fucking take it into the shop!"

"When I get back, I will."

"*If* you make it back…" On that cheery note, she hung up.

I went inside the McDonald's, ordered a Quarter Pounder with cheese meal, and sat down. I decided not to try a cover story when I got to Fowler's house. I'd just tell him enough of the truth and see how he'd react. It was one of those times I really missed the badge. Even as a cop, he didn't have to talk to me, but the badge often intimidated people into talking. Part of police routine is to convince people that if they didn't talk, they'd look guilty, as if they had something to hide.

The car started fine and rode all the way into Bay St. Louis without a stutter. Even when I stopped at an intersection, it purred like new. I kept making turns, finding myself driving down beautiful streets lined with pine trees drenched in Spanish moss. The large Victorian-style houses all had lush green lawns. All the driveways were long, and the fences were painted white. I made another turn and found myself on a more densely wooded street. The houses were almost invisible behind their screen of pine trees. I drove for a while, watching the mailboxes. The road curved to the right, and the plain black mailbox with white letters almost jumped out at me on the left: FOWLER.

I turned into the driveway. The massive yard was almost completely covered in brown pine needles and massive pinecones. A once-white birdbath sat forlornly out in the center, surrounded by weed-choked white gravel. I stopped the car about twenty yards from the garage door and shut the engine off. The house had one story and was brick with a slate roof. There was a paved sidewalk leading from the driveway to the front porch, which was supported by brick columns. The flower beds were overgrown. The cement porch was bare, except for scattered browned pine needles. Blinds were closed on the louvered windows all along the front of the house. I slipped my gun into the holster and slid out of the car.

The quiet bothered me. There was the usual sounds of crickets and other insects, despite it being late in the year, and a dog was barking somewhere in the distance. But there was silence from the house. Usually, when you come up a house's front walk you can hear the muted sounds of life inside. People always listened to either music or the television loud enough to be heard outside. But there was no noise coming from inside the house. If I'd come all this way and he wasn't home…I looked at my watch. It never even dawned on me he could be at work.

Well, if he's at work, I can always get into the house and have a look around.

Sure, it was breaking and entering, but I hadn't seen another car or any sign of life since I'd turned onto Forest Road. There wasn't a security sign in the window or planted in the flower beds, so I was probably safe from setting off an alarm. And if Fowler had a home security system, it undoubtedly would be the kind that made noise—most people preferred to scare their burglars off rather than take the chance the cops will respond in time to a silent alarm. I rang the doorbell while looking around. Where would a spare key be hidden?

To my surprise, I heard footsteps approaching and the door opened a crack. "What do you want?" a very soft, masculine voice asked.

"I'm looking for Chris Fowler."

"Why?"

"Are you Chris Fowler?"

"Why are you looking for him?"

I pulled my badge out of my back pocket and showed it to him. "My name is Chanse MacLeod. I'm a private investigator out of New Orleans, and I need to speak to Chris Fowler."

"What about?" The door opened wider, and I got a glimpse of a man wearing a white velour robe that dropped to his knees.

"Are you Chris Fowler?"

"What's this about?"

"It's about Cody Dallas."

He was silent for a moment, and then he opened the door and took a few steps back inside the house. "I'm Chris Fowler. Come in."

I stepped through the screen door into a darkened living room. The only light was leaking through the closed blinds, but it was enough to see the place was a pigsty. Empty soda cans, crumpled bags of chips, and greasy pizza boxes were scattered throughout the room, covering tables, chairs, and the floor. Newspapers and magazines were liberally thrown into the mix. I saw a cat moving across the back of a couch, and another one sitting on top of the television. The entire place reeked of stale air and cat urine.

He turned on a lamp next to the sofa and moved a pile of newspapers crowned by a Kentucky Fried chicken box off a chair. "Have a seat, Mr. Uh…uh…."

"MacLeod." I tried not to step on anything as I made my way over to the chair. The pale light from the bulb, glowing through a red shade, showed that everything was covered with dust and cat hair. I sat down and looked at him, holding out my hand, "Chanse MacLeod."

He moved into the light and I suppressed a gasp, hoping my face stayed blank. Jude hadn't been lying when he said Chris Fowler was white. I'd never seen anyone so white in my life. His milky skin was almost translucent. You could see all the little blue veins in his neck and on his face. His pale blue eyes were red around the edges, and the eyelids looked pale enough to see through. His lashes and eyebrows were also white, and his scalp showed pinkish beneath the parted white hair. He shook my hand with a strong grip. "Chris Fowler." He sat down on the sofa, arranging the robe. His calves were the same white, covered with sparse white hairs. But they were thick, muscular, and defined. "Now, what's this about Cody Dallas? I don't know if I can help you. I've never met him."

"But you know of him? And you've corresponded with him online?"

"Well, yes." He smiled. His gums were pink, his teeth a little yellowed. "I'm a big fan of his." He gestured to the wall behind him. "As you can see."

I followed his hand and saw a full-size framed print, full-color, of Paul. It was the same shot in the red bikini from his Web site. I swallowed and turned back to him. "Yes. But some of the e-mails were of a threatening nature…"

He laughed. It wasn't a pleasant sound. It was high-pitched, like a whinnying frightened horse. "You're not a wrestler, are you?"

"No, I'm not. What does that have to do with anything?"

"It has everything to do with it." He laughed again, and I wished he'd stop. "Wrestling is a game boys play with each other. That's all. It's all about bravado and being butch. We threaten each other."

"I don't follow." Maybe he *was* crazy. "Threats made in *fun?*"

"It's all harmless fun. If you meet someone online you get along with, you threaten each other. It's part of the getting to know someone." He leaned forward. "You exchange e-mails with someone from a site, or you meet someone in a chat room. You talk about what kind of wrestling you like, what kind of scenarios you're into, and if you both like the same thing, you talk about it…and hopefully someday you'll actually get to meet the person and do it. Sometimes you never meet them. But you threaten each other—'when we wrestle I'm gonna kick your ass'—you know, stuff like that." He waved his hand. "That's all it was."

I remember Jude taunting me on the phone: *You afraid you're going to get your ass kicked?* "Isn't it possible to go too far?"

"I suppose." He frowned. "Has something happened to Cody? Is that why you're here? And you think—"

"I'm just following up on your e-mails, that's all, Mr. Fowler."

"Chris. So something has happened to Cody?"

"Have you ever met someone you felt might be dangerous?"

"No."

"And your e-mails were all just meant as fun?"

"Yes." He stood up. "I'm sorry, but I have to excuse myself. I have to be somewhere in a little bit. Are you going to tell me about Cody?"

"It's nothing serious, Chris. Just looking into a few things."

"Well, if there's anything I can do, just let me know. Or if you think of any other questions, here." He tore off a piece of a Burger King bag and scribbled his phone number on it. "Feel free to call anytime."

"I'll do that." I shook his hand and walked out the door. I could feel him watching me all the way back to the car. Once I was safely inside, I looked back and waved. I put the car in reverse and backed down the driveway.

He seems okay, almost normal, I thought as I started down Forest Road, retracing my steps out of Bay St. Louis. I lit a cigarette. Maybe he'd seen the whole thing as a game, and Paul and Jude both just misconstrued his meaning. Maybe he was into pain—just because Jude wasn't didn't make him a crazed stalker. And it's not like I knew Jude at all.

But I still didn't have the slightest idea of where Paul was.

CHAPTER FIFTEEN

The car ran perfectly all the way back to New Orleans, thank God. I stopped at my usual garage on Camp Street. They weren't sure if they could get to it until the next day, as always. I could practically see the dollar signs in the mechanic's eyes when I said "transmission trouble."

I flagged a cab and went down to the Quarter to meet Venus.

I got there fifteen minutes early, but she was already there, toying with the straw in her vodka tonic. There were only three or four other people in the bar, all clustered around one corner where the bartender was talking to them. Venus had grabbed a table in the opposite corner. I got a Coke and walked back to her. "Hey, Venus," I said, pulling up a barstool. "What's up?"

She looked at the door, then back at me. "We never had this conversation, okay?"

I stared at her. "What's with the cloak-and-dagger bullshit?"

She looked at me. Her eyes were bloodshot. She looked tired. Everything about her seemed to sag, as if it took every bit of strength in her to remain erect. "I don't feel comfortable talking in a place this public."

"Let's go up to the balcony, then." I got up. She followed me up the stairs and down to a secluded bench in a far corner of the balcony on the Dauphine Street side. The bench was barely visible from the street.

She took a big sip of her drink. "Chanse, I am talking to you as a friend here—not as a cop, okay? I'm trusting you as a friend. If anyone finds out I talked to you, I could lose my job."

Jesus Christ. "Venus, I won't say anything to anyone."

"I must be crazy doing this." She sighed, leaning back against the bench. "But I know you well enough to know you'll keep bulldozing around, and I don't think I could live with myself if I let you get killed."

That got my full attention. "What are you talking about?" I enunciated each syllable. The Quarter Pounder was no longer resting easy.

"You need to back off from the Williams case."

I exhaled, and pulled out a cigarette, lighting it. "Venus, I don't give a rat's ass about who killed Williams. I just want to find my boyfriend—that's all I care about."

"Give me one of those." She grabbed the pack out of my hand and lit one.

I stared at her as she exhaled. I'd never seen her smoke. "Since when—"

"I quit ten years ago. Every now and again I have one. Sue me." She glared at me as she took another slow sensual drag. "You have to stop looking for Paul."

"Look, Venus, I get that you don't want me to—"

She grabbed my arm so tight it hurt, the long nails digging into my skin. "Chanse, shut up for a minute and listen to me." She took a third and final hit from the cigarette before tossing it over the railing into the street. "Nasty things, really." She turned to me. "The Williams case isn't mine anymore, just so you know."

"What?" The hairs on the back of my neck stood straight up as my mind tried to wrap itself around this.

She nodded and whispered, "That's right. Something stunk to high heaven on this one from the beginning. Everything was wrong, you know? The crime scene just didn't feel right to me—you know what I mean?" She held up a hand to stop me from speaking. "I know it sounds crazy, but it's a feeling I had, an instinct—and my instincts are rarely wrong." She smiled grimly. "I didn't get to where I am today without having good instincts."

I knew what she meant. Training can only take you so far. The best cops always seemed to have this sixth sense about their work. "What seemed off to you?"

She sighed. "I couldn't put my finger on it, you know? I mean, first of all, Paul called it in—but it was the *second* call we got. A squad car was already on its way over when he called it in. That didn't sit right with me, you know? The first phone call came from a pay phone, and it just reported a gunshot and gave the address, then the caller hung up." She rubbed her eyes. "I didn't think Paul shot Williams, but the evidence was strong. Fingerprints on the gun—but there were *two* sets. The second set didn't match up to anything in the computer."

"Two sets of fingerprints." My mind was racing. "So obviously, the other set belonged to the killer."

"Well, they didn't belong to Judge Dahlgren. Once we knew who the gun was registered to, we checked on that." Venus sighed. "I was against booking him, but my lieutenant overruled me." She shrugged. "I mean, the evidence was strong—the powder residue, his fingerprints—but I thought Williams had been dead for a while before Paul showed up."

I got up and walked over to the railing, leaning against it. I was getting a little angry. It almost sounded like they'd been railroading Paul. "That's bullshit, Venus. He shouldn't have been charged."

"I know." She wouldn't look at me. "I argued with my lieutenant. McKeithen is a damned good lawyer. Once he sunk his teeth into the evidence, none of it would have gotten past a motion to dismiss—especially after I got a good look at the powder-residue test results." She exhaled. "I interrogated him...once I saw the residue was on his right hand, I knew he wasn't the shooter." She shook her head. "I'd noticed he was left-handed—because I am too. Sure, he could have been ambidextrous but—"

"So he spent the night in jail for nothing. That is such bullshit!"

"I'm sorry, Chanse, it wasn't my call." She held her hands up. "Once I saw that, I called the D.A....and while I'm on the phone trying to get him released, the U. S. Attorney and some Feds show up."

"Feds?" *Oh Christ, oh Christ, oh Christ...*

"They take the case away from us completely, and they tell us Paul wasn't the shooter. Well, I'd already figured that much already, right? They ask a bunch of questions about Ricky Dahlgren—"

"Ricky Dahlgren?" I interrupted. "Him again." I sat back down on the bench beside her. "Come on, Venus, I don't give a fuck who his dad is. His name keeps popping up every fucking time I turn around."

"So the marshals ask all these questions about him, right? And the murder weapon belongs to his dad, right?" She shook her head. "I'm thinking they're trying to pull some fast one, right? You know how things work around here." She ran her hands over her hair. "I mean, we should be pulling him in for questioning—but when I bring it up, they clam up."

"They didn't say anything else?"

"Nothing. That was it. Wouldn't answer any of my other questions. They just left after warning me to keep my nose out of the case. So the D.A. put together the paperwork to drop the charges against Paul." She finished her drink and toasted me with the empty cup. "And then a few hours later, Paul disappears."

"That's why you showed up in a hurry when I called." My heart was pounding.

"I was afraid something might happen to him—another hunch, for what it's worth." She shook her head.

"What are you thinking?"

She balled up her fists. "I don't know. I was worried, and I didn't know anything. Maybe we should have put him in protective custody, or at least assign a detail to keep an eye on him. My lieutenant refused, just based on a hunch." She swallowed. "I'm sorry, Chanse."

"Where do you think he is?" My heart was throbbing so hard, it was a struggle to keep breathing normally.

"Look, I don't know anything for a fact, okay? But the Feds and the U.S. Attorney? That usually means the mob. Add in Ricky

Dahlgren…and you've got the Santini crime family. No one has seen or heard from Ricky since Zane saw him going back to the slave quarter Monday night."

"He's disappeared?"

"The Santinis might have put out a hit on him, to teach Judge Dahlgren a lesson. Maybe Mark Williams got in the way. And then Paul—"

"Walks into the middle of everything." I finished for her. I felt sick. Lunch was going to come back up if I wasn't careful. I sucked on an ice cube for a minute. "But what about Ricky's body? If they hit him back there—"

"Maybe they're holding him as leverage—I don't know. But Paul didn't know anything about it—anything. Talk about being in the wrong place at the wrong time." Venus patted my leg. "I interrogated him for hours. But it's possible he did see *something* and didn't realize it was important. I don't know—you know how that goes. Then again, he might not have seen anything. But the killer didn't know that…if it was the mob, he might been considered a…" She swallowed. "A loose end."

The world seemed to have stopped. The sun was still shining, the wind still blowing, but everything else was suspended in that moment. All I could hear was the beat of my heart in my ears, the sound of my lungs filling with air. I didn't want to say it but had to. "You think Paul's dead, don't you?"

"They'd have no reason to leave him alive. I'm sorry, Chanse." She took a deep breath. "I called his parents. They haven't heard from him. I talked to his coworkers. Nothing. Do you know of anywhere else he might be?"

She was wrong. I knew it as surely as I knew I was still alive. "He could be holed up in a hotel somewhere."

"No activity on his credit cards for the last couple of days other than a dinner on Sunday night."

We'd gone out to Bravo on St. Charles that night. He'd been tired, a long day of delays and canceled flights at the airport, and I hadn't been in the mood to cook either.

That couldn't have been our last night together.

No.

"Are you okay?" Venus asked.

"I'm fine, really."

"Do you want me to call someone?" She gave me a half-smile. "You don't look so good."

"No, really, I'm fine. I'm okay." I sat there, unable to move. All I could hear was the sound echoing through my head, over and over again. *He's dead, dead, dead...* I was vaguely aware of Venus getting up, excusing herself, asking me again if I was okay. I waved her off and sat there, the ice in my Coke melting.

Paul couldn't be dead. Venus is wrong.

No body, no death.

"It's just a theory," I said aloud. "She doesn't have any proof."

My mind didn't seem to be functioning. It just felt right to keep sitting there, with the sound of the cars going by below me. Despite the sun, I felt cold, as if my blood weren't flowing anymore. I heard the music coming from the bar and knew someone was playing the piano on the second floor. Someone came out and sat on the stoop of the house across the street. I was dimly aware of a ringing sound.

My cell phone. "MacLeod," I answered. My voice came out as a hoarse gasp.

"Chanse?" It was Paige. "Are you all right?"

"Yeah." The spell was sort of broken, but my mind was numb, not capable of making connections and thought. "I made it back okay. I'm in the Quarter. At Goodfriends."

"So this lead turned out to be nothing??"

"Yeah, I guess." I shook my head, trying to jump-start my brain.

"Are you sure you're fine? You sound funny."

"No, I'm fine." I stood up. My head swam a little bit at first, then everything seemed to come into focus. "Really. What's up?"

"I just wanted to let you know I found some interesting stuff. I'm going to be leaving here in about an hour. Want me to come by your place and bring dinner?"

Food of any kind sounded disgusting. I couldn't possibly eat anything. "Sure."

"Okay, I'll be there around five." She hung up.

I walked out of Goodfriends and headed up St. Ann. *Zane...* Zane had seen Ricky going back there. *It couldn't be mob-related—it couldn't be.* It didn't make sense. A lover's quarrel of some sort had gone wrong and Ricky had fled. The Feds were trying to cover it all up for the Judge's sake. That made more sense...I had to talk to Zane, find out more about Mark and Ricky.

I looked through the gate. Attitude PR's office looked deserted. The lights were off. The shutters were closed and latched. Several boxes full of crumpled paper and garbage were sitting on the porch. I rang the buzzer. No one answered. I pressed again. "Come on, come on..." He had to be there. "Come on, Zane. Damn it, answer!"

"Hey, Chanse." I looked up and saw Ghentry. I plastered a phony smile on my face. He'd just stepped out of the Hit Parade, the little gay boutique on the corner. He had a bag in his hand and a bottle of diet Pepsi in the other. He had a sad look on his face as he walked up to me.

"'Fraid nobody's home—not now, not ever." He shrugged, his dilapidated glasses sliding down on his nose. He lit a cigarette.

"Why? What happened?"

"Zane called me last night and said he was shutting the business down. He dropped off my last paycheck at my house last night." He sighed. "I knew that job was too good to last."

"Did Zane say why he was closing it down?"

"Apparently, Monday afternoon Mark emptied the accounts."

"Really?" *Interesting.*

He nodded. "There's no money left. Mark cleaned the business out..." He raised his eyebrows. "Zane said he couldn't handle it without Mark anyway. The only real money coming in was from the PR stuff, and that was Mark's gig. He sounded pretty upset. Can't say as I blame him." Ghentry took a long pull on his cigarette and shrugged. "I took that check straight to the bank this morning and cashed it." He held up the bag. "Since I'm unemployed again, I thought I'd treat myself to something new. Who knows when I'll be able to buy anything ever again."

"Mark stole the money?" Why not? He'd been convicted of credit card fraud. Why wouldn't he steal money from his business partner? "Do you know how much it was?"

"Zane said it was about twenty grand, give or take."

So, Monday afternoon, Mark embezzled $20,000. I stared at the office door for a moment. It sounded like he'd been getting ready to skip town the day he was killed.

And it also gave Zane a motive—one that didn't involve the mob. A surge of energy shot through my body. Venus was wrong. Paul was alive.

I turned back to Ghentry. "Does your code still work on the gate?"

"I imagine it does. I could try it." He stepped up to the keypad and punched in four numbers. There was a buzz, and he pulled the gate open. "Why do you want to go in there? It's all locked up. Zane even brought all my stuff from my desk with him. I wasn't really happy about that, you know—I don't like people going through my stuff. Some of it was personal, you know, but I kind of got the impression he wanted everything out of there, like he was skipping out on the rent or something." He frowned. "That didn't seem like him, but..." He shrugged. "I never would have thought Mark would have stolen money either. Just goes to show ya, you know? You can't trust anyone."

"Yeah." I gave him a smile. "Do you mind coming in with me?" I didn't want to be accused later of planting evidence.

"Got nothing else to do." He gave a half-laugh. "Besides find another job...not that I want to deal with that. Christ, I hate looking for work."

I stepped through the gate, and climbed the steps. I knelt down beside one of the boxes and started digging through the crumpled paper. There was a computer keyboard buried in there and old copies of the magazine. I found myself looking down into the face of the guy Zane said he'd had the date with the night of the murder.

I pulled out my notepad and flipped through it. Danny DeMarco. I turned to Ghentry. "You know this guy?"

"Danny? Sure." He grinned. "It was really sad the way Zane mooned over that guy. I mean, anyone could see he was straight."

"But didn't Zane have a date with him that night?"

"I wouldn't exactly call it a date." Ghentry winked at me. "Zane might have considered it a date, but it wasn't, not by a long shot. I mean, Julian knew Danny's girlfriend, and she was always telling Zane Danny was straight, but he just kept insisting…"

"Uh-huh." I flipped back a couple of pages. "This Ed Smith person who kept calling for Mark Monday—he'd called before?"

"Not that I know of." Ghentry sat down on the steps. "I never talked to him before."

I wondered if Venus had pulled the phone records for the office. I dug through the box some more, but without knowing exactly what to look for, none of it seemed useful. I stood up and walked over to the corner of the house, looking down the path to the slave quarter where Mark was murdered. It had two stories, with a gallery running along the upper level. And to the right, on the other side of the brick wall, was another slave quarter with an adjacent balcony. It would be easy enough to cross from one to the other…but surely the police had thought of that.

But they'd had a suspect with powder residue, who had been holding on to the murder weapon. They'd had no reason to think someone might have gone over the balconies into the next yard. It would have been easy enough for Ricky to shoot Mark and climb over.

It would be equally easy for a hit man to carry Ricky's body off that way as well.

Don't even think about that.

"Who lives next door?"

Ghentry shrugged. "Don't know."

"Where does Zane live?"

"Somewhere around here—I never knew for sure. It's not like he ever invited anyone over or anything."

"You said when we talked last that you didn't like Ricky Dahlgren." An idea was struggling to form in my head.

"No, like I said, he was a gay geek."

"Because he didn't know things gays would know, right?"

"Yeah." His face was puzzled. "What is all this about?"

"Why did you think he was dating Mark?"

"Well, because…" He stopped. "Come to think of it, Mark never really talked much about Ricky."

"Did you ever see them kiss? Be affectionate to each other?"

He shook his head. "No. I mean, they hugged and kissed each other on the cheek to say hello but other than that…" His voice trailed off.

"So why did you think they were lovers?"

"Because Zane said so. Zane talked about them all the time." He scratched his head. "It was always Zane saying something. But he never said anything in front of Mark. That's weird, isn't it?"

And Zane was the only person who saw Ricky the day of the murder.

Ghentry followed me as I walked around the house to the back courtyard. There was a door with steps in the rear of the house. "Where does that door lead?"

"Mark's office." I thought back to my interview with him that afternoon. I hadn't paid much attention at the time, but yes, I had seen a door on the back wall of his office.

My head was spinning. "Do you have Zane's phone number?"

"Yeah." He got out his cell phone and scrolled through his stored numbers. "Here it is. You want me to call him?"

I got out my notebook and wrote the number down. "Was that a cell or apartment number?"

"Home number. Let me find his cell."

I wrote that number down and grinned at Ghentry. "Thanks, man, you've been a huge help." I started to walk away, then stopped. "Do you remember exactly what it was Zane said when he saw Ricky on his way back?"

"He made a face." Ghentry closed his eyes, thinking. "And a noise, you know, like *pfui*. Julian asked him what was wrong, and he said, 'I just hate that Ricky.' I said something like 'What brought that on?' And Zane said, 'He's on his way back there—I saw him in the window' and went back to work."

I walked back to the street before I dialed Zane's home number. I got the voice mail there and on his cell phone. I left a message on both, asking him to call me. Zane was the only witness who could place Ricky at the murder site—if Ricky was the killer—that didn't bode well for Zane.

I glanced at my watch. Twenty till five. There were no cabs to be seen. Fuck, it figured. I walked on down to Dauphine. Finally, I hailed an oncoming United cab. Luckily, the cabbie wasn't talkative. He was older and listening to a country station: Martina McBride's "Independence Day." I hummed along in my head.

I was onto something, I could feel it. But who to tell? Venus was off the case. I couldn't go to the Feds without letting them know Venus had talked to me. Fuck. There had to be some way around this. Of course, Venus and I could always pretend as if she'd never told me anything, so it would make sense for me to call her.

I can be a good liar, but lying to the cops always makes me nervous. I'd talk to Paige...she had a really devious mind. I could trust her not to fuck over Venus. They were friends.

I closed my eyes. *Venus*. I heard her voice saying, *He's probably dead, Chanse. They don't leave loose ends.*

She was wrong. I knew it. Mark's murder had nothing to do with the Santini trial. Yes, there were some coincidences—Dominique's ex, the Judge—but I was sure. Ricky had killed Mark, which meant Paul had to be alive somewhere.

Paige was sitting on my front steps with a greasy brown paper bag when I got out of the cab. I gave her a quick hug and kiss. I could smell the fried shrimp. "Po' boys?"

"Of course." I held the door open for her before I followed her in, and quickly shut, locked, and chained the door.

She stared at me. "What are you doing?"

I sat down. "You wouldn't believe what I found out."

She handed me my sandwich and a bottle of Dr. Pepper. "I found out some things too. You want me to go first?"

"Yeah." I took a bite of my sandwich. I decided not to tell her Venus's theory that Paul was dead. No sense in upsetting her. *No body, no death.*

"The Dahlgren family has been getting death threats. Not just the judge, but the whole family's been threatened." She smiled at me. "I got that straight from the woman herself, Lois Dahlgren. That's why Ricky was carrying the judge's gun."

Death threats? "Why didn't they have protection?" The po' boy was heavenly.

"Judge Dahlgren refused it, said it would be giving into fear."

"Pretty ballsy to risk your family like that."

"That's Judge Dahlgren for you. Your turn."

The great thing about Paige is she can be trusted. I swore her to secrecy, then filled her in on everything Venus told me, watching her eyes grow wider and her face get paler. "Chanse, then that means that Paul's—" She broke off, putting her sandwich down.

"Don't say it. It's not possible."

"Chanse, you have to—"

"No, I don't." My voice shook. "I'm convinced Ricky killed Mark. Venus is wrong. We'll find him, Paige. He's alive, I know it."

She bit her lip. "Okay." She wiped at her eyes and pulled herself together. She sat up straighter. I smiled to myself. I could always count on Paige to show her steel backbone. "So, you think there might be more to this Zane than you thought?"

"If he found out Mark cleaned out the accounts on Monday, it sure gives him a hell of a motive, doesn't it? It can't hurt to do some research." I crumpled up my sandwich wrapper and put it back in the bag. Paige pulled out a baggie of pot from her purse and got my pipe from under the couch. As she loaded, I went over to my computer and woke it up.

I had left Jude's pictures up. I tried to close them before she saw them, to no avail.

She whistled from behind me, pot smoke drifting around my head. "Who's that?"

"One of Paul's wrestling buddies—the one who turned me onto

Chris Fowler." I finished closing the pictures and logged onto the Internet.

"Nice."

"Yeah."

Paige's phone rang, and she answered. She walked away out of earshot while I finished saving and closing Jude's pictures. I was vaguely aware of murmuring, then the sound of her snapping her phone closed. "Chanse?"

"Yeah?"

She put her hand on my shoulder. "That was Paul's mom. Um, they are on their way over here."

CHAPTER SIXTEEN

This wasn't exactly how I'd envisioned meeting Paul's parents.

We'd talked about it a few times. I'd even talked to his mother about it on the phone—either Paul and I going out there or them coming to New Orleans. Something always managed to come up, though. We'd been invited out there for Thanksgiving, and I'd already bought the plane tickets, but that was still a few months away. I'd liked Mrs. Maxwell from talking to her on the phone. She seemed like a really sweet woman, and Paul adored his dad. I'd been a little nervous about meeting them, but Paul was sure they'd like me. "How could they not?" he'd say with that big grin of his. "What's not to love?"

However I'd imagined it, it hadn't been like this.

"Um, this place reeks of pot," Paige said, walking over to a window and sliding it up.

I walked into the kitchen and got out a can of room deodorizer, spraying it liberally throughout the living room. I got out a couple of sticks of strawberry incense, lighting them and sticking them into holders I'd scattered around the apartment. The heavy thick scent filled the room.

"That's better." Paige nodded.

"What are we going to tell them? Why are they here, anyway?"

"I called them." Paige wouldn't look at me. "Look, it was possible he'd gone home to them, wasn't it? And if he's missing, they have a right to know. If it were my kid, I'd want to know." She swallowed. "Besides, they already knew—Venus had called them. When I talked to them, they were getting ready to head for the airport."

A car door slammed outside. I sat back down in my chair and took some deep breaths. I heard footsteps coming up the walk. My doorbell rang, and Paige answered it. "Mr. and Mrs. Maxwell?"

"You must be Paige," a woman's voice said, and I could see Paige being hugged. Paige stepped back after a moment, and the couple walked into my living room. The woman was short, a little over five feet tall. She was wearing a worn-looking pair of jeans underneath a red cable-knit sweater. Her hair was curly like Paul's, thick and wavy but sprinkled with gray. She was a little overweight, but it suited her. Her face was round and full and free of wrinkles. Her eyes were brown. Paul got his eyes from his father.

Ian Maxwell was almost as tall as me, with a strong, heavy build that could easily be mistaken for fat—but the size was deceptive. I got the sense of coiled strength in reserve. Paul looked more like his father with the same blue eyes, the same cleft in the chin, and the same dimples in his tanned ,worn cheeks. Ian's hair was reddish and thinning on the top. He strode across the room with his hand out. "Chanse! We meet at last!" He grabbed my hand in a death grip.

I swear I felt bones crack.

"Hello, Mr. Maxwell," I managed to get out, shaking my hand a bit when he let go.

"Call me Ian," he said as his wife grabbed me into a stranglehold of a hug. She smelled faintly of Chanel. "And this is Fee."

"Oh, Chanse." Fee Maxwell smiled up at me with Paul's smile. It was uncanny. "You're everything Paul said, everything I imagined."

"Anybody want something to drink?" Paige flawlessly slipped into hostess mode, with a note in her voice I'd never heard before.

"We're fine," Ian answered for both of them. They both sat on the couch. "Now what the hell is going on with our boy?"

I looked at Paige, who gave me a weak smile. "Um, we're trying to find him."

"That's just not like Paul," Fee said, her jaw set. "That's why we decided to come out here after that nice policewoman called, Paige. Paul just doesn't run off without telling anyone where he's going."

Paige sat down in the reclining chair. "I'm not really sure there's anything you can do here."

Fee reached out and patted Paige with a small, plump hand. The only ring on her hand was her wedding ring. Her nails were short and rough, as if she'd been biting them. "Of course not, dear. We didn't think that, but we figured we needed to be here if something was going on with our son. When we talked, I could tell in your voice you were worried, honey."

Paige swallowed and looked over at me. I shrugged and nodded. She cleared her throat. "What I'm going to tell you isn't going to be easy to hear."

Fee affected an Irish brogue. "Ah, that's all right, lassie. We Irish have been enduring whatever the Good Lord's thrown at us for centuries now." She smiled, but her lips were white. She reached up, clasping the medal of St. Mary hanging around her neck, and her other hand snaked into Ian's, and he squeezed it. They leaned into each other, an almost imperceptible shift in how they were sitting, as Paige started to talk.

What must it have been like to have them for parents? I thought as Paige talked, unable to take my eyes off them. Paul adored them, called them every other day without fail. I knew they owned an Irish pub in Albuquerque, which Ian ran while Fee kept the books. All of their kids had helped out around the pub growing up, earning spending money by moving cases of liquor and carting kegs. "It was hard work, but it was fun," Paul told me one night when we were lying in bed curled around each other. "Mom and Dad were the best bosses. All their employees loved them and stayed with them for years—were like a part of the family." I imagined what it was like growing up a loving household of parents who worked and played hard, together with three other boys and a sister very close in age, caring, loving, and enjoying life.

It hadn't been like that in my house growing up. The loose Catholicism Paul followed was patterned on his parents' faith. In my family, the Bible was the law, the words that came out of the preacher's mouth on Sunday jewels of faith to live by. My dad's mother was a fanatic who had quoted Bible verses to prove her point and had always tried to affect the image of the righteous woman who was saved. But my dad's temper had come from her. She would switch from a laughing, relaxed woman into a raving lunatic with the bat of an eye. She frequently berated my mother for letting my sister wear makeup and skirts shorter than those approved of by the Church of Christ. "You let her dress like a whore, and she'll become one," she would say. My mother would just smile and say nothing, which was the safest course with grandma. My sister would flush red—it had to suck, having your grandmother say you looked like a whore. She would lecture me on the sin of pride as well as the loose morality of non–Church of Christ high-school harlots, who would try to lure me into the sins of the flesh. There were times I wanted to tell her the girls were the last thing she needed to worry about.

Fee was saying something to me I didn't hear. "I'm sorry?"

"I said, we'd checked with his brothers and his sister, and they haven't heard from him either." She sounded confused. "Paul wouldn't just go run off like that and not tell us—he wouldn't do that. I don't understand why he didn't call me when he got home from that jail."

"With all due respect, Fee, it couldn't have been easy to call to tell you he'd been arrested for murder," Paige said.

"If one of my children thought they couldn't call and tell me anything, then I've failed as a mother," Fee replied, her jaw jutting out just a bit. "And believe you me, I told that nice policewoman a thing or two when she called me."

I couldn't help but grin. "Like what?"

"Like Paul wouldn't have killed Mark. That's just ridiculous."

She mentioned him casually, as though she knew him. "Did you know Mark Williams?"

She turned to me with a smile. "Of course we did, Chanse. Paul brought him home for Christmas one year. The poor thing had no family. Paul was very fond of Mark, and Mark of Paul. We liked him—he was very nice."

"Paul always brought his friends home to meet us," Ian said. "We didn't like all of them, of course, but they were nice boys for the most part."

"Did you know about the—" I hesitated.

Fee sighed. "About the videos? Yes, we did. We didn't approve— he was our baby, of course—but it was his life to live as he saw it, not ours. I thought he'd regret it one day, and I was right. After he met you, he was sorry he'd made them."

"He was?"

"When he met you, dear. He didn't know how to tell you about them—he agonized over it, I can tell you that." Fee shook her head. "I kept telling him—Chanse loves you, it won't matter. But he worried and worried. I told him you'd find out sooner or later, and the later it was the worse it would be."

I swallowed. "Yeah, well. Is anyone thirsty?" No one was, so I excused myself and walked into the kitchen for a Dr. Pepper. *Paul was right to be worried about telling me,* I thought as I popped the tab and took a drink. And she was right; the later it was, the harder and rougher it had been for both of us.

I walked back into the living room just as Fee and Ian stood up. "We'd best be getting back to the hotel. We're staying at the Pontchartrain if you need us for anything."

They hugged us both at the door, and Fee whispered in my ear, "Everything will be all right, dear. You'll see." And then I shut the door behind them.

Paige was already reaching for the pipe. "Nice people."

"Yeah, well, they raised a good son." My voice cracked a bit, and I turned away from her. I sat back down in front of my computer. It was time to face facts. I took a deep breath. "Paige, you don't think Paul's dead, do you?"

She was holding in smoke, and starting waving at me. She blew the smoke out, coughed and choked, and said, "Jesus, don't say shit to me like that!" She reached for my Dr. Pepper, and downed at least half of the can before rubbing her eyes. "Whew. Okay. We can't rule out the possibility he is."

"Yeah." I looked down at my hands. "But wouldn't I..." I stopped. It would sound stupid.

"What?"

"Never mind, it was stupid." My entire body seemed to relax, letting go of a tension I hadn't even been aware of until it was gone. It was like every muscle in my body had been coiled, ready to pounce. I took a deep, cleansing breath, and then another.

"Chanse, I won't think you're stupid, okay?"

"Wouldn't I sense it?" I said it in a low voice, refusing to meet her eyes. There was a very interesting spot on the hardwood floor holding my attention. "I mean, if you love someone, don't you know when they're dead?"

"Oh, Chanse." Her voice broke. "You...you..." She got up and walked over to me, sliding her arms around my shoulders, tears starting to fall. "You hopeless romantic!"

After a moment I put my arms around her. Paige was soft and warm and comforting and human. My body continued to relax even more, and when tears started welling up in my eyes, I let them come. I'd never really experienced what it was like to let go. Crying had only made my dad angrier and increased the chance of a beating. I had learned at an early age that men don't cry. I hadn't cried when I read Ryan's letter. I hadn't cried when I graduated from high school. I hadn't cried for anything in my life. But now I let myself go and cried for Paul. I cried for the look on his face the last time I saw him. I cried for the empty bed I'd woken up in that morning. I cried for the things I'd said, the things I'd thought, the way I'd messed everything up.

And then, finally, they stopped. I wiped my cheeks dry.

Paige leaned away from me. "It helps sometimes, doesn't it?" She wiped away her own tears. "I never understood why men won't cry."

"It's not manly," I said, wiping my nose, and laughed. After a moment, she started laughing, too. Finally I took a hit off the pipe and blew out smoke. "All right, let's get to work, okay?"

"Okay." She kissed the top of my head. "We're going to find him, honey."

"We have to operate on the assumption he's alive, until we know otherwise," I reasoned. "We'd never forgive ourselves if we didn't do everything we could to find him and he was somewhere out there needing help."

"Damned right." Paige reached past me to the keyboard and pulled up Paul's Internet server. "Let's start by checking his e-mail."

"How? We don't know his password."

She gave me a look. "I bet you I can get it the first try."

"I'll take that bet." She moved the curser to the sign in window and typed in Paul's account number. She went down to the password line and typed six letters quickly and hit enter. The welcome screen popped up.

"I should have bet money," Paige grumbled.

"How did you do that?"

She laughed. "Do you know him at all? His password is 'chanse.'"

Apparently, I don't know him at all, I thought, fighting back the tears threatening to start again. Paige pulled up his mail folder. There were over a hundred new mail messages, and she moved the cursor down, scrolling through them. "Do you recognize any of these return addresses?"

"That's Jude," I said as she highlighted an e-mail with YOU SLY PUSS as the header. "Judewrestle."

"Doesn't look promising. Should we read them?"

"No," I said. I didn't see any new ones from Chris Fowler, or anything that looked like it could be threatening. There was a lot of spam, but that was nothing new.

"So who do you think killed Mark?" Paige asked. "Zane or Ricky?"

"I don't care," I said, logging out of the system. "All I want to do is find Paul." I logged into my own Internet account. "Okay, Zane, let's see what we can find out about you." I went to the reverse directory and typed in Zane's name and phone number and got the listing: RATHBURN, ZANE; 1206 DAUPHINE STREET; NEW ORLEANS, LA 70116.

"What are you doing?" Paige asked, passing me the pipe.

"Getting some information." I moved to a search engine that brought up past addresses, and put in Zane's name and address. It was expensive—ten dollars charged to my credit card per search—but it was worth it. This site also gave you the Social Security number. Once you have that, you can find out anything about anyone. Credit reports, financial records, military history, criminal records, marriage history—pretty much everything except sexual history.

"If you don't care about the killer, why look up all this stuff?"

"Just curious," I said, staring at the screen and waiting for the report to come back.

"Didn't you say he was just a kid."

The report scrolled onto the screen. I started writing down Zane's Social Security number when Paige said, "That's weird. I thought you said he was a kid."

I looked back at the screen. She was pointing at the line above the Dauphine Street address. I stared. That didn't make any sense: According to the report, Zane's last known address prior to Dauphine Street was on Robert E. Lee—but it showed he'd stopped living there five years earlier. He'd told me he was from Houma, but that address was nowhere in the report. Besides all the addresses being in New Orleans, they went back fifty-three years. "I swear to God, Paige, he couldn't be more than twenty-three, tops."

"The site must have made a mistake. There must be another Zane Rathburn."

I pointed to the Social Security numbers next to the addresses. "With the same Social Security number?"

I went to another site that searched for death certificates and entered Zane's Social Security number. Sure enough, one popped up for a Zane Rathburn who'd been seventy-four when he died five years ago. I then went to a credit report site, plugged in the Social Security number, and brought up a credit report that showed no activity for five years. Three credit cards—Visa, a MasterCard, and Discover—had all been issued to Zane Rathburn during the past summer.

"Identity theft of a dead man." Paige whistled. "I'm calling Venus."

"Don't!" I was surfing to another site. "Not yet—let me check one more thing." The directory for Houma came up. I typed in "Rathburn." No matches found.

"Why not?" Paige went back and sat on the couch, her phone still in her hand. "Come on. You'd still think she was in charge of the investigation, right? Who else would you call? Let her decide what to do with the information."

"The priority is finding Paul, Paige." I went to another site.

"Chanse, listen to me."

Her tone was strange, so I turned to look at her. She licked her top lip. "Don't you think it's weird that Zane didn't exist anywhere until he turned up in New Orleans last spring?"

"Yes." I spun around in my chair. "It doesn't look good for him. And he was the only person to see Ricky the day of the murder. Yes, we need to tell Venus all this—if she doesn't already know. But my priority is Paul."

"What does Zane have to do with finding Paul?"

I took a deep breath. "What if Paul knew something, or saw something, not realizing it? You know, like Venus's theory about the mob hit? The only person he'd be a threat to is the killer...that's why I want to find Zane."

"So you think Zane has him somewhere?"

"Maybe!"

"Chanse." Her eyes were wet, and I looked away from her. "You aren't facing reality. Look at me." I turned my head back. "Unless Paul went away on his own, he's dead. If Zane killed Ricky and Mark, then he killed Paul. If it was a mob hit, the same thing."

"No, Paige." Even as I said it, the reality was settling in over my mind. I was finding it hard to breathe. The room swam in my vision, and I opened my mouth but nothing came out.

Paul was dead. I knew it. I'd known the moment Venus had told me about the Feds taking the case away from her. I'd just refused to accept it.

My computer dinged.

Wrestlejude: "Hey, stud, how you doing?"

I stared at the computer. The cursor blinked at me. I wiped at my eyes.

Wrestlejude: "You there?"

I swallowed and typed. "Hey there."

Wrestlejude: "Dude, can I call you?"

Chansemac: "Now's not a really good time."

The last thing I wanted to do was have another phone sex come-on. I swallowed again. Paige came up behind me and started rubbing my shoulders. I reached up with my left hand and squeezed it, not saying anything.

Wrestlejude: "Dude, I don't want to have phone sex. Is everything okay with Paul?"

"Who's that?" Paige asked. "You've had phone sex with this guy?"

"No, he's a friend of Paul's—the one who told me about Chris Fowler."

Chansemac: "I told you he's out of town. I haven't heard from him. Why?"

Wrestlejude: "I got this weird e-mail from him today. Can I call you?"

Hope dawned. "Paige, do you see that? He got an e-mail from Paul today!"

Chansemac: "Yes, call me. Do you need the number again?"

Wrestlejude: "LOL. No, I made sure I kept your number, hot stuff!"

"Hot stuff?" Paige asked.

"I'll tell you later." The phone was ringing. "Hello?" I answered.

"Hey, stud." Maybe it was just the way he always talked, but he seemed to just purr. "You haven't talked to Paul?"

"No, I haven't."

"Well, he sent me this weird e-mail. Hang on a second." I

heard him rattling papers, moving stuff around. "I went ahead and printed it out. Here it is." He started reading: "'Hey, Jude, hope all is well. I had to get away from New Orleans for a while. Chanse was kind of being a jerk, so I left, you know, to get my head together—like that time I left Jeff, remember? So the next time you talk to Chanse, tell him I'm okay, but don't tell him where I am. Love, Paul.'"

"How did he know we'd talked?" The hairs on the back of my neck stood up, despite the fact my heart was soaring. *Paul is alive!*

"Well—I know I promised you I wouldn't say anything to him, but I e-mailed him after we talked," Jude rushed on. "Don't be mad, but I wanted to let him know we'd talked and things were cool—and to apologize for any trouble I might have caused, you know, when I sent the earlier e-mail about seeing your listing on the site?"

"What time was the e-mail sent?"

"Two o'clock this afternoon."

I wanted to scream at the top of my lungs: *He's alive!* "Cool."

"But Chanse—you don't get it. There has to be something wrong."

"Why do you say that?"

"Okay, give me a minute, okay?" He took a deep breath. "Paul never left Jeff that I know of." Jeff had been the doctor Paul had lived with for five years. "They never fought, man—it was sickening. I mean, they just didn't fight, and Paul never left Jeff until they broke up, you know? And their breakup was amicable. They both just moved on."

"Well, it's possible he just thought you knew about it, right?"

"Paul also never signs his e-mails 'love.' He just doesn't do that. He signs with little X's and O's—you know, hugs and kisses?"

That was true. On the rare occasions when Paul e-mailed me, he always signed with a row of them across the bottom before his name. "I'm sure everything's okay, Jude. But would you mind forwarding the e-mail to me?"

"Yeah, sure." He sighed. "You're probably right—it's nothing, but still, man, it's fucking weird." He hung up.

Paige sat back on the couch. "So Paul's alive? He sent this guy an e-mail?"

"Yeah." I was grinning from ear to ear. "He's alive and he's safe, and he just went away on his own."

"Then who beat off on his bed?" She crossed her arms. "This e-mail was weird, wasn't it? This Wrestlejude thought it was weird, right? Why?"

I gave her Jude's reasons and shrugged. "So it's different."

"Chanse." Paige lit a cigarette. "I don't think it's weird that Paul would e-mail this guy instead of you; if he went away to think about things, you'd be the last person he'd want to contact." She held up her hand. "Don't interrupt—I'm sorry, but you know I'm right. Why would Paul e-mail this guy instead of *me*?"

"What?"

"Chanse, I know you find this hard to believe, but Paul and I are *friends*." Paige shrugged. "We've talked a lot. We've hung out and had fun together, even when you weren't there. And you know if Paul is anything, he's thorough. Almost obsessive."

"So?" I shrugged.

"Suppose Paul wanted to let you know he was okay and just needed space—wouldn't it make more sense for him to e-mail me?" Paige rolled her eyes. "Come on—he gives the message to someone you've never met, have only talked to once? How did he know Jude would tell you?"

"Maybe he trusts Jude?"

"It's just not Paul." Paige walked over to me and knelt in front of me. "Look, honey, I know you want to believe he's still alive. Trust me, I do too. I'm still holding out hope—but we can't grasp at straws either. Paul might not have sent that e-mail."

"Then who did?" I turned back to the computer and pulled up my e-mail folder. The forwarded e-mail from Jude was there. I opened it and read it quickly. It was exactly what Jude had read to me, and the time it was sent was in the upper right-hand corner.

"Paul never left Jeff," Paige said after scanning it quickly. "Jude was right about that."

"How do you know that?"

"Paul and I talked about Jeff. They were still friends, you know."

I hadn't known. "They still talked?"

"About once a week." Paige stared at the screen. "Paul told me part of the reason their relationship didn't work was because they never fought. They just kept drifting apart until it was like they were just roommates. I wonder if Paul could have been trying to tell us something?"

"I thought Paul didn't send this." I couldn't keep the nasty note out of my voice.

She glanced at me, then said through gritted teeth, "Operating on the assumption Paul sent this, maybe he was being coerced. So he was trying to get a message to us through Jude. Maybe it didn't make sense to Jude because the message was meant for us, not him."

I looked at the screen. There it was at the bottom: "Love, Paul." No X's, no O's. "Maybe he was trying to tell me he loved me—Jude would be sure to notice he signed it love."

She patted my leg. "Maybe. But this stuff about Jeff...I wonder. Pull up the Dallas phone directory." I obliged. She reached over me and typed Jeff's name into the search window. The listing popped up. She flipped open her phone and dialed. She tapped her foot while it rang. "Damn it, I've got the machine...um, hello, Jeff, this is Paige, a friend of Paul's in New Orleans. Would you mind giving me a call when you get this?" She left her number and hung up. "All right, I'm going to run. I've got some things to do before I call it a night." She opened her purse and handed me a file folder. "I printed out everything I could find on Lexis-Nexus on Charles Wyatt. I couldn't find anything on that Ed Smith."

"Thanks." I put the folder down on my desk and walked her out to her car.

Before she left, she rolled the car window down. "Honey, I know you don't want to hear this—but you have to prepare for the possibility—"

"You're right. I don't want to hear it."

She started the car and drove off. I walked back into my apartment. No, as long as I refused to believe it, he was alive. It wasn't rational, I knew that, but I believed it in my heart.

My phone started ringing. I picked it up. "MacLeod."

"Mr. MacLeod, this is Lois Dahlgren. Do you have some free time tomorrow morning?" Her voice was soft. "I'd like to talk to you about my son."

CHAPTER SEVENTEEN

My appointment with Mrs. Dahlgren was for noon, so I set my alarm for eight and went to bed around midnight.

She hadn't been forthcoming with much information and had evaded all of my questions—"I prefer to discuss this in person, Mr. MacLeod" was all she would say. After I got off the phone with her, my mind was fried, so I smoked some more pot and idly watched television. I looked through the folder on Wyatt that Paige left, but all I got from it was the certainty he was, indeed, a mob lawyer.

I did some meditation exercises to clear my mind and release some of tension. I needed to relax and somehow managed it. When I went to bed, at first I couldn't get past its empty feel and had to clear my mind again. Eventually, I fell into a dreamless sleep.

I woke a few minutes before the alarm, showered and made coffee before calling the mechanic. They hadn't gotten to it yet, which figured. I made a rental-car reservation and called a cab to go pick it up. A half hour later I was heading home in a nice metallic- blue Toyota something-or-another with a CD player. I still had a few hours before I had to head out to Metairie, so I decided to hit the gym.

I'd gotten so used to going with Paul, it felt strange walking through the doors of Bodytech by myself. Alan Gardner, who owned and ran the place, was working at the front desk as usual. He was a good-looking guy with big front teeth that gave him a kind of chipmunk look, but it worked for him. "Morning, Chanse," he said as I handed him my membership card. "Where's Paul? Out of town?"

"At his parents'," I said without even thinking twice. Alan was a notorious gossip. "Telephone, telegram, tell-Alan" was the joke around the gym.

"Kind of a shock about Mark Williams, huh?"

I had started to turn away from the counter, but turned back. "Did you know him?"

"He used to work out here." Alan leaned on the counter. "He asked me to pose for the cover of *Attitude* once." He laughed. "Like Greg would have ever allowed me to do that!" Greg Buchmaier was Alan's life partner.

"I only met him once," I replied. "Did you like him?"

"Ah, he was okay." Alan waved a hand dismissively, "He was nice, you know, but always kind of smarmy."

"Smarmy?"

"Oily. Slick. The kind of guy who thinks everyone has to like him, so he'll say what he thinks you want to hear. You know what I mean?"

"Yeah." Maybe Alan liked to gossip, but he was an excellent judge of character. He'd managed to sum up exactly how I'd felt about Mark after meeting him. I couldn't have put it better myself.

"When he started up that PR business, he was always after me to hire him." Alan got himself a protein drink out of the cooler. "I just didn't see how he could help me, and I told him so, but he just wouldn't take no for an answer." He twisted off the top and tossed it in a trash can. "Guess I don't have to worry about that anymore. Shame."

"Yeah." I picked up my bag and headed for the locker room. There were about ten people working out, more women than men, which was typical for this time of day. The guy doing squats on the Smith Machine looked slightly familiar. I tried to place where I'd seen him before as I put my bag into a locker. It was a fun little exercise I liked to play from time to time: You live in New Orleans long enough, you see people all the time that you've seen before, so you try to place them. Did he work at my favorite coffee shop? Had I seen him in a bar sometime? Was he a waiter somewhere I'd eaten lately?

When I walked out of the locker room, he was standing by a weight machine and drinking out of a bottle of water. He was a little shorter than me and was wearing New Orleans Hornets basketball shorts that hung down loosely to just past his knees. A white tank top fit snugly over a muscular tanned torso. His hair was short and dark. He nodded at me when he saw me looking. I nodded back and walked over to the curl bars.

I was halfway through my first set of preacher curls when I remembered where'd I'd seen him.

Danny DeMarco: Zane's dinner date the night Mark was killed.

I finished my set and walked over to him. He let out a loud gasp as he finished his set and stood there, panting for a moment. "Hey," he finally said, reaching for his water bottle.

"You're Danny DeMarco, right?"

He nodded, holding the bottle. "Yeah, so?"

"I'm Chanse MacLeod. Have you got a minute?" I held out my hand, which he shook for a second. His hands were warm and sweaty.

"Yeah, I'm done for today. What?" He looked at me warily. His eyes were large and brown. "I'm not gay, if that's what you're looking for."

"No." He was in his early twenties. Why do guys that age always think people are hitting on them?

"You had dinner with Zane Rathburn the other night."

"Yeah. So? You a cop?" He looked me up and down.

"No, I'm a private eye."

He shrugged. "Look, I told the cops already—he met me at the Moon Wok around seven. We had dinner, and he left around 9:30. I walked to my car and went home. I haven't seen or talked to him since."

"Why did you have dinner with him?"

"We're friends." He shrugged. "I met him when I posed for the magazine cover. He was nice, so we had dinner a couple of times."

"Did you know Mark Williams?"

"That's who asked me to pose for the cover." He wiped his forehead with a towel. "I said sure, went over to their office, and posed. It took maybe an hour. I talked to Zane a little bit, and I was going to get something to eat, and he was hungry, so we went together. He called me and invited me to dinner another time—this was the third time we'd had dinner. No biggie."

"What did you think of Mark?"

"Nice guy." He made a face. "Not like some of the guys around here—you know what I mean? He was gay, but he knew I was straight and respected that. Nice. You wouldn't believe some of the guys around here." He shuddered. "I don't mind if they look, you know, but it pisses me off when they follow me into the locker room or watch me shower—stuff like that." He took another swig of water.

Nice. "What about Zane?"

"Ah, Zane knew better than to try anything." Danny grinned. "He was pretty cool. He just wanted some advice about working out, asked me about my girlfriend, how school was going—nice guy, like I said."

"You didn't sense he had a crush or anything?"

He looked at me like I was crazy. "If Zane had a crush on anyone, it was Mark."

"Why would you say that?"

"He was always watching him when he didn't think anyone was watching." Danny grinned. "Anything else? I need to get going or I'll be late to class."

"Nah. Thanks."

I went back over to the preacher-curl bench and launched into a second set, trying to put everything out of my mind, but my thoughts kept wandering back to Paul. I finished my workout and showered at the gym. As I soaped up my body, the hot water coursing over me, I thought about what Danny'd said. It didn't really make much of a difference if Zane had a crush on Mark—although it would explain why he didn't like Ricky. I doubted it had been enough to drive Zane to kill Mark. I'd already planned to stop by Zane's after seeing Mrs. Dahlgren. Ricky, though, seemed to be the key to everything. Mark had taken $20,000 out of the bank and within a few hours was dead.

Where is the money?

Venus surely would have said something to me about it if the police had found it,

The Dahlgrens lived in old Metairie. Old Metairie was one of the original suburbs of the city, until New Orleans had kept growing out in that direction, eventually surrounding it and absorbing it. There was a distinct difference between old Metairie and Metairie proper. Old Metairie had money: old houses and beautiful streets lined with swamp oaks. I got off the highway at the City Park exit and turned back under I-10, heading onto Old Metairie Road.

The Dahlgren house was a replica of an old plantation house. The red-brick house had a wide veranda supported by marble columns and a large expanse of perfectly coiffed emerald-green grass in front. The only thing missing was a cotton field stretching into the distance behind it. I pulled into the driveway, noting that the three cars in front of mine were all Mercedes. I walked up the brick walk, climbed the steps, and rang the bell next to the oak front door. I heard footsteps, then the door opened.

"Mr. MacLeod?" It was a young black woman wearing a maid's uniform, complete with white apron.

"Yes."

She held the door open for me, then quickly shut it without a sound. "Mrs. Dahlgren is waiting for you in the breakfast room." She indicated a door right off the hallway.

I walked under a massive chandelier and past a wide hanging stair. A huge portrait of a woman dressed in eighteenth-century costume hung on the yellow wall just above the curved stairway. I walked through the doorway and stepped back into time at least a century.

The small room was completely furnished with well-polished

antiques. A huge grandfather clock was pushed up against one wall. There was a small mahogany table with a lace tablecloth in the center of the room. Huge mirrors set in gilt frames hung opposite each other on the walls. The one window was deep inset with a blue velvet pillow covering the window seat. It matched the curtains that hung on either side.

The woman seated there set down her copy of *Architectural Digest* and stood up, then walked toward me with her arm outstretched. Lois Dahlgren was not tall, but her slender, straight body gave the illusion of more height. She was wearing a white silk blouse with black slacks over matching pumps. The pearl necklace hanging around her neck matched the pearls at both ears. Her silvery hair was swept back into a French braid hanging down her back. Her makeup was perfectly applied, although the skin around her eyes looked a little too tight. The deep sockets of her bluish-gray eyes were a dead giveaway that she'd had her eyes done more than once. Still, she walked with the air of confidence only money and privilege can give someone. She extended her right hand to me, and I could see a huge ruby inset with diamonds that dwarfed her ring finger. "Mr. MacLeod, thank you for joining me. Can I offer you tea? Coffee?" I shook her limp hand for a moment, just a quick pump. The skin felt delicate, hot and papery. Her nails were long, with French tips

"Coffee."

She smiled, and walked over to the table. She poured me a cup of dark black coffee from a silver coffee pot. "Cream? Sugar?"

"Both, please."

"Ah." She nodded, adding cream from a silver creamer and a couple of lumps of sugar into the delicate cup of bone china. She set it down, then poured a cup for herself. "Please, Mr. MacLeod, have a seat." Her voice still retained its Mobile accent, and I noted little lines around the bright red lips.

I pulled out a chair and sat down. She sat directly across the table from me. I smiled and took a sip of the coffee. I set it back down in its matching saucer. She was watching me, her eyes slightly narrowed. I cleared my throat. "Frankly, Mrs. Dahlgren, I don't know why I'm here."

"Don't you, Mr. MacLeod?" Ice dangled from each word.

"No."

"You don't know where my son is, do you?"

"No." I stared at her. *What the hell?*

She stared back into my eyes for a minute, then sat back with a sigh, her face relaxing. She exhaled. "I didn't think so." She picked up her cup. I noticed her hand was shaking a bit. "It was a long shot, but…" She reached for a silver cigarette case. "Do you mind if I smoke?"

"No."

She lit one and inhaled deeply. She flicked ash into a crystal ashtray.

"Mrs. Dahlgren, why am I here?"

She took a deep breath. "My son is missing, Mr. MacLeod. We last heard from him on Friday morning." Her free hand started toying with her pearls. "He was going to Houston to visit a friend from college, and he never arrived."

"Why would you think I'd know where he was?" I took another drink of the jet fuel–strength coffee. "Besides, he was seen in the Quarter on Monday night."

"That's a lie," she said softly. She tugged on the pearls, twisting them around her hand. "If he were still in town, he would have called or come home one night."

She sounded just like Mrs. Maxwell talking about Paul. "No offense, Mrs. Dahlgren, but maybe—"

"Oh, he thought he was keeping secrets from me, but I knew what he was up to." She went on, "I knew all about his lover in the Quarter. New Orleans is a very small town, you know. Maybe I should have said something to him about it, but I thought he'd tell me when he was ready. And whenever he was staying down there, he always called and checked in. He knew how important it was to me."

"Why would you think I'd know anything?"

"You're a private eye, aren't you? You've been nosing into things down there. I thought maybe you'd have heard something you hadn't shared with the police." She poured herself another cup of coffee. Some splashed out into the saucer. "You have to understand, Mr. MacLeod, what things have been like around here since this stupid trial fell onto my husband's caseload." She sipped the coffee. "The threats, the phone calls…Ricky knew how important it was to me for him to check in. But not a word since he walked out of the house Friday morning."

"Have you called the police?"

"Of course." She looked at me as if I were stupid. "And the marshals. And…nothing." She rubbed her eyes. "I was hoping you might have…might have found something."

"Why are you so certain Ricky wasn't in the Quarter on Monday night?"

She paused for a moment, her throat working, no words coming out. "He wasn't staying where he usually stayed when he didn't come home."

"How do you know that?"

"My husband might not have wanted marshals to protect us, but I did." Her eyes flashed. "I called that U. S. Attorney myself. I told him since the Judge had said no, he couldn't know about it. It's all well and good for him to not want to 'live in fear' but I wasn't about to risk *my* children's lives for *his* principles."

"So marshals have been following him around?" This put a whole new face on everything. If Ricky had indeed shot Mark, the marshals could easily have been witnesses.

"They lost him on Friday morning." She swallowed. "I don't know how it could have happened, but they did. They put out a bulletin on his SUV, but it wasn't spotted anywhere between here and Houston…and then he never showed up." She got up and walked over to the window. "I know they all think he's dead, that those awful mobsters got him somehow. But I'd know, wouldn't I? If my child were dead, wouldn't I…wouldn't I sense it?"

I had a strong sense of déjà vu.

My own words to Paige just last night.

There was a huge lump in my throat. I gripped the side of the table to steady myself. "But the Judge's gun was found at the murder site."

"Ricky never had that gun." Mrs. Dahlgren turned back to me from the window. "That particular gun was kept in a case to which only the Judge and I had keys."

"Then how…" My mind was spinning. Was this Metairie matron confessing to me?

"I loaned that gun to my son's lover." She shrugged. "Yes, the marshals were keeping an eye on him and all, but I felt more comfortable with everyone carrying a gun, just to be on the safe side. I've got one in my purse, a nice little pearl-handled revolver."

"So you gave the gun to Mark?" I shook my head a little. If Mark had the gun, that cleared Ricky for sure. But what could Paul have known that would have put Mark's life in danger?

"Mark?" Mrs. Dahlgren eyes opened wide and her forehead creased. "Mark who? And why would I give a gun to him?"

"Mark Williams. You said you gave the gun to Ricky's lover—"

"And you think…" She stared at me as though I'd lost my mind. "My son wasn't gay, Mr. MacLeod."

"I don't care if you're in denial. Who'd you give the gun to?"

"I would have known if he were gay." She kept blinking. "He would have told me."

"Some people don't feel comfortable coming out to their parents." *Christ, bitch, focus!* "Who'd you give the gun to?"

"It's because the Judge is a conservative, isn't it?" Her lips narrowed. "That makes me so angry! Just because you're a conservative, people just assume you're racist, homophobic—all of that! Ricky could have told us if he were gay!"

"We're getting a little off point here…"

But Mrs. Dahlgren was off and running. "We are not homophobic!" She walked over to a photograph on the mantle and picked it up. "Our daughter is a lesbian, and we love her and her partner just as much as our other children!" She shoved the picture at me as if to prove her point.

Score one for Paige, I thought as I took the picture from Mrs. Dahlgren. I held it as she continued on her rant. I figured she was probably doing that to take her mind off her son. I looked down at the picture. It was a professionally done portrait, with the family all dressed to the teeth. Sitting in the center of the picture were two women in their early thirties holding hands. One had short, close-cropped blond hair and was wearing a black tux with a white shirt underneath. She had Mrs. Dahlgren's eyes. The other woman was wearing a nice beige pantsuit, her dark hair cut in a mullet. Behind them, each with a hand on the shoulder seated in front of them, were the proud parents. The Judge was also in a tux and was a handsome older man. Mrs. Dahlgren was wearing a peach silk gown and the same pearls she currently had on; she was smiling at the camera. To her left was a tall man, also in his early thirties with blond hair. He also looked like Mrs. Dahlgren. In front of him was a slender woman. His hand was on her shoulder: obviously his wife.

Next to the Judge was a handsome young man with short, dark hair and deep dimples. *He looks familiar,* I thought, staring at him. It had to be Ricky, but where had I seen him before? I kept staring at him and searching my brain—Ricky, who'd applied for a private eye license, who'd applied several times for a job with the Feds. Ricky, who his mother swore wasn't gay.

I looked at her. She'd stopped talking. "All right, Mrs. Dahlgren. I understand."

"Besides…" She sat back down, her entire body seeming to collapse on itself. "If he was seeing Mark Williams, the Feds would have known. They reported everything he was doing to me. How do you think I found out about his lover?"

"Who was his lover, Mrs. Dahlgren?" I asked.

And as my mind wrapped itself around the question, Ghentry's voice played in my head.

I never saw them touch or anything… Ricky was a gay geek… He said the grossest things, like he liked to watch hockey for the fights… Ricky was the straightest gay guy I ever met… I saw Ricky and Mark at Oz and he couldn't dance… He danced like a straight boy… He must have just come out… He wasn't comfortable in his gay skin yet… Mark

never talked about Rick.... Zane always talked about them... I didn't
understand what Mark saw in him... Zane didn't like Ricky at all...

Zane said he saw Ricky going past the window...

Zane.

I stared at the picture. Where had I seen him before? It was
important to remember, and I strained as I struggled with my
memory. I stared at his smiling face: the dimples, the white teeth, the
dark hair, the strong broad shoulders, his eyes.

His eyes.

The eyes were wrong.

That was why I couldn't remember, I realized as it all fell into
place in my head. I closed my own eyes and concentrated. Change
his eyes. But how? The color? No.

Suddenly, I knew.

And as Mrs. Dahlgren told me the name of Ricky's lover, I knew.

The picture, leaning against a stack of other prints.

Those aren't his real eyelashes, I heard Dominique say. *Everyone falls*
in love with his eyelashes, but they're false. I applied and curled them
myself.

Dominique.

Ricky was her model. She knew Ricky better than she'd let on—
to me or to anyone.

She was the ex-wife of a mob lawyer.

Ricky was the white son of a judge presiding over a mob trial.

"Maybe he thought he couldn't tell us because she was black,"
Mrs. Dahlgren went on, her voice broken. "He thought we were
racists. But we weren't—you have to believe me, Mr. MacLeod. We
would have been fine with it, as long as she loved him and he loved
her." She was sobbing. "Maybe I should have told him...but then
he would have known about the marshals..."

I swallowed. "Mrs. Dahlgren, I...I have to go."

"Please..." She looked up at me. Mascara-stained tears ran
down her cheeks. "If you find him, please call me...if you find
anything..."

I walked out of the house and to the car. I noticed a dark car, similar to the one that had followed me home from Paige's, parked down the street. Two men in suits and sunglasses were sitting in it. *The marshals,* I thought as I got into my car. That's who'd followed me.

My heart sank. They'd followed me because I'd been at Paul's. He *was* involved in this somehow.

CHAPTER EIGHTEEN

Dominique had been the connection all along.

I couldn't figure out where I fit into everything. I thought about it as I drove down to the Quarter. The Feds had stepped in before Venus could question the Dahlgrens about the gun, which would have led us to Dominique. But she hadn't killed Mark; her alibi had checked out. So it had to have been Zane. She gave the gun to Zane, and he'd killed Mark for her.

But why?

And what had they done with Paul—and why?

I tried not to think about Paul. I hadn't liked listening to Mrs. Dahlgren justify her belief that her son was still alive by saying the same things I'd said about Paul. It made me think he must be—

No, I wouldn't think about that.

I stopped by my house first and strapped on my shoulder harness, checking my gun to make sure it was loaded. I put on a leather jacket to cover it up and drove to the Quarter.

My cell phone rang. "MacLeod."

"Chanse, it's Paige." Her voice was hushed.

"Speak up," I said, stopping as the light at Canal turned red. "I can barely hear you."

"Hang on a second." I sat there, holding the phone, hearing Paige saying things in the background, other voices replying to her. The light changed, and I started through the intersection.

"Okay," she said in her normal tone, but her voice still sounded funny. "I just got a tip from the coroner's office, Chanse."

My stomach dropped into my shoes. *Paul,* I thought. "Uh-huh?"

"They...they've found Ricky Dahlgren. Shrimpers dragged his body out of Barataria Bay just off Grand Isle yesterday morning." She cleared her throat. "The coroner says he'd been in the water since at least Sunday."

"Thanks." I turned the phone off.

Zane couldn't have seen Ricky Monday night. He was already dead. I'd been pretty sure it was a lie, but now I knew for sure.

I parked just off St. Ann on Dauphine, and hurried down the street to the corner. The Attitude gate had a FOR RENT sign on it. I walked around the corner and into Domino's.

Sly was stocking liquor behind the bar when I walked in. "Hey, Chanse." He grinned at me. "Dominique expecting you? She's up in her apartment."

"Yes," I lied. "I'll just go on back."

"Cool."

There were no workers anywhere. My shoes echoed against the wooden dance floor. I reached the door to the back steps, yanked it open and climbed the steps two at a time. Adrenaline is an amazing thing. I pounded on her door and could hear it booming inside.

The door swung open. Dominique stood there barefoot in jeans and a T-shirt and no makeup. "Chanse? What the hell..."

I pushed past her and walked across the room to the stack of prints. I knelt down in front of them, staring at the outer one. It was the one I remembered, and it was definitely Ricky Dahlgren.

"You can't just come barging in here like this!" Dominique grabbed my arm from behind. I shook her off and stood up.

"You've been lying to me since the very beginning, haven't you?"

Her eyes widened, and she took a step back. "I...I don't know what you're talking about. Please leave." She gestured to the door, then folded her arms across herself. She wouldn't look at me.

"This is Ricky Dahlgren." I pointed at the print. "So you lied when you said you'd only met him a couple of times." I glanced back down at the print. "His mother seems to think you knew him pretty well."

"His mother." She barked out a short laugh, sliding down into a chair. She still wouldn't look at me. "Yes, the wonderful Lois Dahlgren, coming down to the Quarter to play the gracious queen to her son's *nigger*." She spat the last word out. "'Of course we'd welcome you to the family.'" She mimicked Mrs. Dahlgren's tone and Alabama accent perfectly. "'I don't know why Ricky hasn't told us yet, but when he does, you'll always be welcomed in my home.' Rich bitch."

"She gave you a gun for protection, didn't she?" I walked over to where she sat. "That was a nice thing to do."

"I could see it in her eyes." Dominique lit a cigarette with shaking hands. "You know, I wanted to be wrong about her, about both of them. Ricky was so sure they'd be happy—he was always begging me to let him tell them. But I knew how they'd really feel. They'd pretend everything was okay—'aren't we open-minded?' But you wouldn't have to scratch too far beneath the surface to find it mattered."

"What did you do with the gun? Did you give it to Zane?"

"Zane?" She looked at me and laughed. "Why the hell would I give that gun to Zane? I gave it to Mark."

I goggled at her. "Mark? You gave the gun to Mark?"

"I didn't want it around me." She shivered. "I mean, yes, it was a nice gesture and all, but can you believe she was giving me a gun as a favor?"

"Why give the gun to Mark?"

"Because of his prison record, he couldn't get one on his own, and the Feds weren't about to give him one."

I couldn't do anything but stare. I couldn't be hearing this right. "The…the Feds?"

She stood up and walked over to a window. "There's so much you can't even begin to understand."

"Where's my boyfriend?" I shook my head. I didn't give a flying fuck what was going on with her.

She looked at me over her shoulder. "I don't know."

"Don't lie to me anymore!" I reached into my holster and pulled my gun out. I cocked the trigger and aimed it at her. "Tell me the truth."

She paled and groped her way back to her chair. "All right, man, all right. Chill, okay?" She took some deep breaths. "I swear to you, man, I don't know what happened to your boyfriend, all right?"

"Then where the hell is he?" My hands were steady, even though my heart was beating loud enough to almost drown her voice out.

"I swear, man, I don't know." Her voice was sulky. "Christ, put the gun down already—Jesus! It all started three years ago, when this guy came backstage after one of my shows."

He was a Fed, she explained, who'd informed her about her husband's connections with organized crime. "I'd had a little trouble with the law after my cocaine problem, and I was going to have to go to court for it. He told me he could make that go away, if I started feeding him some information about my husband's business associates." She ground out the cigarette. "The cops had me dead to rights. I was going to jail. What choice did I have? I didn't think…" she swallowed. "I figured Charlie was just a lawyer, right? I might hear some stuff now and then, but nothing major."

"Go on."

Dominique said she'd usually just ignore Charlie when he talked about his work, figuring he was just bragging, trying to make himself seem more important in her eyes. But once she started paying attention, she began to piece things together. Charlie wasn't just a mob lawyer. "He was in it up to the neck."

She lit another cigarette, her hands shaking so much she could barely get the flame started. "That's when I started to get scared. Charlie started acting different around me, like he suspected something. I told the Fed I couldn't do it anymore, that it wasn't worth risking my life."

She'd gone on tour for her most recent record—and had begun to breathe easier. She was away from Atlanta long enough to feel safe, and she soon decided she wasn't going back—except to ask for a divorce. "I played this straight club out in Metairie, and I saw this guy there dancing. He kept flirting with me while I sang, and after the show I sent my manager out to get him. It was Ricky."

She said Ricky was such a sweet kid, such a good-looking young man, that she went out for a drink with him after the show. They'd come down to the Quarter, and they'd held hands as they walked down Bourbon Street. "I told him about how much I wanted to get off the road, just open a club somewhere, and he led me to this dark building"—she gestured around the room—"and told me I should do it: This would be the perfect place to have one. I spent the whole weekend with him."

He was a nice guy, and she was lonely.

"I don't care about the romance," I snapped. "Get to the point."

She closed her eyes. "Look, you want to know everything?"

"I don't care about you and Ricky, okay?"

She took a breath. "When I started having trouble with the club and Mark Williams came sniffing around, I knew he was being paid by Charlie. When I left, Charlie'd made threats, you know? Ricky was pretty sure, too, so he tried to play up to Mark, befriend him."

I never saw them touch each other.

"He was so dumb—and with that trial coming up." She shook her head. "I kept telling Ricky to stay out of it—it was dangerous. But he wanted to be a Fed so bad."

He'd applied several times to be a Fed, but they didn't want him.

"He thought this was his big chance, if he could link up Charlie to the problems I was having, they'd have some leverage to use on him." She stopped talking. "Can I get a drink? I'm thirsty."

I kept the gun trained on her as she got a bottled water out of the refrigerator and sat back down. She took a drink, then looked at me with contempt. "I'm not talking anymore. Go ahead and shoot me."

"Oh, you'll keep talking." I crossed over to the table, and sat down across from her, the gun still pointed at her heart. "You know what I heard on the radio on the way over here?"

"No." Her eyes were on the gun.

"They found Ricky. In Barataria Bay. He'd been there since Saturday."

"Barataria Bay?" She looked confused.

"He's dead. They found his body."

Either she was a great, undiscovered acting talent, or her feelings for Ricky had been real. She screamed from the bottom of her diaphragm—with an earsplitting power and commitment that made the windows rattle and my eardrums stretch. The scream was primal, with an emotion that came from the depths of her soul. It was anguish, it was pain, it was deep and raw and horrific to hear. She slid off her chair and curled in a ball on the floor. The scream continued, unabated, uninterrupted as she began to pound the floor with her fists, harder and harder.

I put the gun on the table and knelt down beside her, putting my hands on her shoulders and pulling her dead weight up to her knees. I put my arms around her as she drew in breath finally, the scream's volume still echoing in my aching ears and in the farthest corner of the loft. Instead of screaming again, her entire body sagged lifeless in my arms and began to shudder and convulse with sobs. I reached over for her water and handed it to her. She drank from it, trying to pull herself together, losing control into the agony again for a moment, and I held her. When it passed, I handed her the water again.

She let out a deep breath. "You're sure?" She pulled away from me.

"Yes," I said gently.

I saw a glimmer in her eyes, deep inside their brownness, and I recognized it as steel. She was a strong woman. She'd pull herself together eventually, would get through this. I picked up the gun again.

"Charlie did this," she said, her voice quiet. "And I am going to kill him." She looked at me, one eyebrow raised, and I felt a chill. "One day he will pay."

"About the gun…"

"I gave it to Mark that very same day I hired you." She laughed, wiping her eyes. "Ricky had convinced me Mark was catching on to him, so I had to hire a private eye to take the 'heat' off. It all seems so stupid now. Why did I go along with him?" She shook her head. "Sweet little boy playing at grown-up games."

"But Ricky was already dead."

"He was going to Houston," she said, her voice devoid of tone or inflection. "He couldn't call me while he was gone. I hired you on Monday...and after you left Mark's office, he came by to see me—to confess." She looked away from me. "He knew you'd figure it out at some point. He'd called Charlie and told him he was out of it. Charlie told him he was a dead man, so Mark was going to skip town. Just disappear. He had a friend who'd help him."

Paul, I thought. That was why Paul had come to see him that night. Paul could get him on a flight as a guest, as he had done me. And there'd be no real record of him flying out.

"I gave him the gun." She smiled at me. "He needed it more than I did—I'd never use the damned thing. He left and I tried calling Ricky, but he didn't answer his cell. I was going crazy and I didn't know what to do, so I called my old friend, the U. S. marshal. I told him everything that was going down. Mark could turn, and they could use that to make Charlie turn, or at least put him behind bars. But by the time they got there, Mark was dead. Killed by the gun I gave him." She shuddered.

"And Paul?" I could hear the desperation in my voice.

"Honey, if the Feds have him, I don't know anything about it." She held up her hands. "I'm sorry. Go ahead and shoot me—I don't care. But I swear to you, I don't know anything about him."

"Who killed Mark?" I knew the answer to that: Zane. Zane, who'd been dead for a few years. "Why did Zane kill Mark?"

"Zane?" She looked at me. "You keep saying that. Why do you think Zane killed him?"

"Never mind." I put my gun back in its holster. "Look, I'm sorry about, well, you know." How do you properly apologize for holding someone at gunpoint? I'm sure Miss Manners has never been asked *that.*

I walked back out to the street. I was doing it again. I'd sworn to everyone I knew I'd never go confront a possible killer armed with just a tape recorder again. This time, I didn't have the tape recorder, but I had my gun. It was a false sense of security, I knew, as I walked down to Dauphine Street. I know the statistics of people being killed by their own guns are ridiculously high. The last killer I'd confronted had also lived on Dauphine Street.

I stopped at the corner of the 1200 block. I pulled out my phone and dialed Venus. "Hey, Venus. Chanse MacLeod."

"What do you need?" Her tone was, as always, businesslike.

"I know who killed Mark Williams."

She lowered her voice. "I told you to stay away from the Williams murder."

"I don't care about that!" I waited for a cab to go by. "All I care about is finding Paul. Besides, you can call the Feds when I get off the phone."

"Go on."

"Zane Rathburn—only that's not his real name." I went over everything I'd found out. "I am walking up to his house now."

"Stay away from there!"

I hung up and put the phone back in my pocket, then I patted my gun. I walked up to Zane's house. It was a brown brick double; with cement stairs leading from the sidewalk to the porch. Zane's half was the one to the right. I knocked on the door; I could hear a television inside and felt adrenaline rushing through my veins. My ears were ringing a bit, and my palms were sweating as footsteps approached the door. The curtains pulled back an inch or two, then swung back as the deadbolt clicked back, and the door opened about five inches. "Yes, Chanse?" Zane stood in the crack of the door. He was wearing jeans and a sweatshirt with a picture of the original Charlie's Angels on it. His eyes were about half shut and his face was blank.

"May I come in?" I kept my voice calm and level.

"Why?" He blinked at me.

"I need to ask you a few questions, and I'd rather not do it here on the street."

He nodded. *Bingo,* I thought as he opened the door and stood aside to let me pass. The television in the living room was tuned into the Weather Channel. He gestured to a sofa. I sat down, pulling out my notebook. I looked around the room. Other than the furniture, it was bare. No knickknacks, no personal belongings of any kind.

He wasn't much of a housekeeper, either. Dust balls crowded the corners, and the hardwood floor hadn't been washed in weeks.

I swallowed. *Stay calm.* "I wanted to go over your movements on Monday again."

He fluttered a hand through the air. "We've already been over this."

"What time was it you saw Ricky Dahlgren on Monday?"

He frowned. "You know, I'm not really sure it was Ricky after all. I just saw someone out of the corner of my eye, really, and I just assumed it was Ricky because who else would it be?" He gave me a very little smile. "I told the police this already, Chanse. They were here last night." He leaned forward a little bit. "If Ricky was dead already, I couldn't have seen him, now could I?"

"And you told the police that?"

"It's a common error." He sat back. "Only human, you know. We see what we think we're supposed to see. I tried to help come up with a description of the man I saw." He shrugged his right shoulder.

He was good. I almost believed him myself. I knew he hadn't seen anyone, I just couldn't prove it.

"And you left to go to dinner around six?"

"Yes, that's right. To go get ready for dinner. I had a date."

"Danny DeMarco, that's right." I fumbled through my notes. "He's straight—you know that?"

"Yes." He frowned. "Really, how much more of this is there? I'm busy, Mr. MacLeod."

"Really?" I smiled. "I thought you closed down the business."

"I'm moving back home." He stood up. "And I promised the landlady I'd be out by five today."

I stood up to. "Back to Houma?"

"Yes, to my parents. As I am sure you can understand, I can't really afford to live here in New Orleans anymore." He walked over to the door. "Now if you'll excuse me…"

"Your name isn't Zane," I said. "And you're not from Houma."

He stiffened. "Don't be ridiculous."

"Look, I don't care about that," I said quickly. "I don't. All I want to know is where is Paul?"

"Paul?" He looked confused. "I don't know where your boy-friend is."

"I'm serious." I put up both of my hands. "I don't care who you are or what your game is. I'm not a cop. Just tell me where Paul is and I'll get out of here."

Suddenly, it seemed like everything kind of shifted, even though what actually happened was that his lips tightened and his eyebrows moved a little bit. The quiet, soft-spoken, subservient gay boy was gone, and in his place was a cocky arrogant man with shrewd eyes and hard lines to his face. He laughed. "I don't know where your little boy toy is—nor do I give a shit." He kept laughing. It was a harsh sound, like cloth tearing. "I don't know what you think you know…"

"I know you killed Mark Williams." I reached inside my jacket for my gun. "You walked through the back door in his office to his apartment and shot him. You then walked back into the office and packed up your bag and went home to get ready for your date."

"Is that so?" He kept grinning at me, even after I pulled the gun out and trained it on him. "Should I be scared? You've got a gun on me."

"Where is Paul?" I cocked the trigger. "I'll shoot you."

He raised both his hands. "Go ahead."

I took a deep breath. I started a mental countdown in my head.

"Drop the gun!"

Two men wearing flack vests, guns trained on me, burst into the room from the back of the house. I dropped my gun and put my hands up. "Get down on the floor!" one of them shouted. I got down on my knees and then lay flat on the floor. One straddled me and grabbed my arms, wrestling them back into handcuffs—none too gently, I might add. Then, once my arms were secured, I was dragged to my feet and slammed back into the wall. I looked off to the right as Zane was being escorted out the front door. "What the fuck do you think you were doing?" one of the men screamed into my face. He was wearing safety goggles but had thinning blond hair. He was tall, almost as tall as me, and strongly built.

"I…I want a lawyer," I said.

"He wants a lawyer," he mimicked me. "Let's get this piece of garbage out of here."

They shoved me back through the house and out the back door. I was pushed out along a path and then to a big, dark car with tinted windows. The guy with the thinning hair opened the back door. "Get in, asshole," he said.

The guy behind me guided my head through the door and shoved me into the seat, climbing in behind me. The guy with the thinning hair went around and got into the driver's seat. "We're going for a little ride, asshole," he said, starting the car and pulling out into the street.

The numbness of the shock started to wear off a bit. I was under arrest of some sort but hadn't been read my rights. That could only mean one thing.

The Feds.

I cranked my head to look out the back window. The street was empty. Where the hell were Venus and the cops? "How did you guys get there so fast?" I asked.

"We'll ask the questions, asswipe," was the answer from the front seat.

I sat back. My head ached, and my circulation in my arms wasn't exactly the best. I was pretty sure I was bruised in a couple of places from being banged around.

They hadn't gotten there fast, I reasoned. They'd already been there. The Feds were protecting Zane or whatever his name was. I'd almost messed up their plans, whatever they were, and they weren't happy. They weren't going to listen to me, so it was best to keep my mouth shut and keep asking for a lawyer.

Loren McKeithen, to be exact. Time for him to earn some more money.

CHAPTER NINETEEN

"I want a lawyer."

I'd said it about a thousand times since the U.S. marshals dragged me into the Federal Building and put me into one of their interrogation rooms. It was grueling. I hadn't worn a watch, so I had no idea how long I was in there. They'd trade off every once in a while, playing "good cop, bad cop." They threatened me. They threw questions at me. They said they were going to lock me up for a good long time. I'd be old and infirm before I got out.

"I want a lawyer."

"We're going through your life with a fine-tooth comb," they said. "We're examining your phone records. We're searching your apartment and going through your computer."

"I want a lawyer."

"Why were you threatening Zane Rathburn with a gun?"

"I want a lawyer."

On and on it went, threats and more threats. Every so often one of them tried to reason with me. I never bothered to learn their names. Fuck 'em. Zane Rathburn was a cold-blooded killer, and they were protecting him for whatever reason of their own. *Yeah. My fucking tax dollars at work.*

I had my head down on the table. I was exhausted and thirsty and had to piss. The door opened again. I didn't bother to look up. *Fuck 'em. They can threaten the top of my head from now on.*

"I told you to stay away from the Williams case."

Venus.

I picked my head up. She set a bottle of water on the table. I grabbed it and took a long drink. I burped and set the bottle back down. "Yeah, well, I told you I didn't give a rat's ass about who killed Williams, Venus. All I want is to find Paul."

She sat down across from me, rubbing her eyes. "Yeah. I knew you wouldn't leave it alone."

"Where is he, Venus?" My voice sounded rough. "What did Zane do with him?"

"I don't know where he is." She reached over and grabbed both of my hands. "He says he doesn't know anything about it."

"That's bullshit, Venus, and you know it."

She dropped my hands and stood up, walking over to the big mirror, which I knew was a one-way window. The Feds were watching, listening. I resisted the urge to flip them the finger. "His name is actually Vinnie Castiglione."

"So fucking what?" I already knew he wasn't Zane Rathburn.

"He's a professional killer."

Yeah, right. "He's just a fucking kid."

Venus turned around. "I'm serious, Chanse. He's no kid. He's thirty-six."

"What?" I stared at her. "That's bullshit."

"He just has a baby face. The Feds have been looking for him for a long time. He has about thirty kills to his credit."

"Then why the fuck are they protecting his ass? He's the one they should be fucking questioning, not me!" I didn't have the energy to get as mad as I wanted to.

"He…he has a lot of information they're really interested in."

The truth dawned on me. "They're going to put him in Witness Protection, aren't they? He's killed thirty people."

"The Santini crime family is a lot worse, Chanse, and he can bring them all down." She sat back down. "Sometimes you have to make a deal with the devil in the name of the greater good."

"Yeah, sure, whatever." I ran my hands through my hair. "Then where is Paul? What did he do to him?"

"He doesn't know anything about Paul, Chanse. He swears to it, and I believe him."

"How can you believe someone who's killed thirty people?"

"Because there's no reason to lie at this point." She leaned back in her chair. "Chanse, he's admitted to the killings. Why would he deny one more?"

I stared at her. I fought down the rising fear, the tears coming to my eyes. Nobody knew where Paul was.

Where is he?

"So why did he kill Mark? Because of the money he stole?" There had to be something, something we were all missing.

"It's a long story that goes back to Dominique and her husband." Of course.

Venus explained. When Dominique left Charlie Wyatt, it didn't sit well with him. He was certain there was another man in her life, and he wasn't going to sit around and do nothing. When she bought the building on Bourbon Street, Wyatt figured her lover must be from New Orleans. Wyatt hired Castiglione to keep an eye on her and find out about her lover. It was Wyatt who'd bought out Mark Williams's former backer, using Castiglione as a front. Castiglione knew all about Williams's past convictions and also that he was juggling the books—overcharging an advertiser's credit card when paying for an ad in order to have ready cash and then refunding the money later by overcharging someone else. With that leverage, he forced Williams into going along with the scheme to force Dominique out of business. The five grand paid every month to Attitude PR was wired into Mark's business account from a bank in the Caymans.

I interrupted her. "So what was the connection with the Dahlgrens?"

"A sad coincidence, for Ricky Dahlgren." Venus sighed. "Of course, when all this started, they had no idea that Judge Dahlgren's son was Dominique's lover. Once Castiglione pieced it all together, Wyatt wanted him killed immediately—but Castiglione double-crossed Wyatt and went directly to Joey Santini, the head of the family. Santini ordered him to keep Ricky alive, until the time was ripe—when the trial was getting started. They figured if Ricky was killed then, Judge Dahlgren would step down and the trial would be delayed."

"So they killed Ricky last Friday and dumped him in Barataria Bay?"

She nodded. "Williams figured it out somehow. He called Paul on Monday morning. Castiglione had a bug on Mark's phone and overheard their conversation. Mark was getting ready to skip—he was going to clean out the bank accounts and run. Paul was going to help by getting him an airline pass out of the country."

So, posing for the magazine cover had been a cover story. I buried my face in my hands. Paul had just been trying to help out a friend. "But why didn't Paul tell you any of this after Mark was killed?"

She shrugged. "I don't know. Maybe he was scared. I don't know how much Williams told him—we may never know that—but he just stuck to his story. He went to see Mark and found the body."

"Zane killed him, didn't he?"

She nodded. "He went back through the back office door and shot him with the Judge's gun. Once we knew Dominique had given the gun to Mark, it all became clear. Zane didn't even know whom the gun belonged to—an unlucky chance for him. He just assumed it was Mark's. He'd seen it in Mark's desk drawer that afternoon."

"And you're sure Zane knows nothing about Paul?"

"I'm positive."

I got up and walked over to the one-way glass. "And how long are they going to keep me here?"

"You're free to go," Venus said. "You checked out. That's why they sent me in here."

"Great."

"There's one more thing you might want to know." She got up and walked over to me. "We canvassed Paul's neighbors, asking them about seeing anything strange Tuesday night. One of them remembered seeing a car he'd never seen before parked in Paul's driveway."

A burst of adrenaline went through me. "Really?"

"A navy blue older-make Oldsmobile with Mississippi plates. They didn't get the plate number, though."

Mississippi. I groaned. "Chris Fowler."

She gave me a puzzled look. "Who's Chris Fowler?"

I sank back down into my chair. "Oh, God." I started explaining it all to her...the threatening e-mails, my conversation with Jude, Paul's history of wrestling video stardom. "That's how he knew Mark Williams in the first place," I said.

"Come on." She walked over to the door and banged on it. One of the Feds who'd been verbally abusing me opened it. "I need access to a computer and the Internet—right now."

"Sure." He gave me a look. "Anything we can do to help."

How about eating your gun, asshole? I thought as he led us to an office and booted up the computer. "What server is Paul on?" Venus asked. I told her, and she pulled it up, then pushed back to make room for me. "Log in."

I typed in Paul's account name and blinked back tears as I typed "chanse" into the password line. "You've got mail!" the computer told me. I clicked on the envelope and scrolled through the e-mails till I found the one from Chris Fowler. I pulled it up. Venus read it quickly, then clicked on the printer icon. A printer on top of the file cabinet next to the desk began printing. She turned to the DMV terminal on the credenza behind the desk. She logged in, then typed in "Mississippi + 'Chris Fowler'" and clicked SEARCH.

The registration came up within seconds: Christopher Fowler, of Forest Road in Bay St. Louis.

A 1988 Oldsmobile Delta Royale 88, blue.

"Now, that's probable fucking cause." Venus snapped her fingers. She pulled out her cell phone and dialed. "I need you to patch me through to the district attorney's office in Bay St. Louis now." She walked over to the window, tapping her foot. "Yes, hello, this is Detective Venus Casanova with the Eighth District of New Orleans..." I tuned her out as she explained what she needed, what was going on. "Bingo!" She clicked the phone closed and then faxed the e-mail printout to a number. "You up for a road trip?" she asked.

"The sheriff is going to meet us at the house with the warrant. You can't go in."

"Try and stop me from going." I glared at her. She just nodded and motioned for me to follow her.

Five minutes later we were in Venus's SUV, her bubble light on top, the siren blasting as she headed for I-10. I stared out the window as we flew down the highway, weaving in and out of cars at a speed I didn't care to know.

He'd been there. I'd been so fucking close. I'd sat on Chris's fucking sofa while he had lied through his goddamned teeth to me—Paul had been there the whole time. He wasn't hiding out there. Paul knew I'd be worried and Paige would be worried. If he'd heard my voice and had been able to speak, he'd have let me know he was there.

He hadn't been able to.

The fucking ghost man was keeping him a prisoner.

Or he's buried in the back yard somewhere, an insidious voice said in my head. *Or maybe there are pieces of him wrapped up in butcher paper in the freezer.*

No, he's not. I'd know. I would know if he were dead.

I heard Mrs. Dahlgren's voice in my head: *A mother would know if her child was dead, wouldn't she?*

She hadn't known. Ricky had been at the bottom of Barataria Bay for days when she'd said that to me. She'd been in denial, that's all. But I knew Paul was alive. I knew it.

Hang on honey, I'm on my way, I telepathically told Paul. Paige believed in that kind of stuff—in sending out positive energy and drawing strength from other people's positive energy. I wasn't sure if I was doing it right, but I closed my eyes and thought about Paul and about how much I loved him. I knew that he would sense it and keep himself alive. He was alive.

He had to be. There was too much I had to say to him; we had too many things to do together yet. We were going to grow old together. We'd joked about it: the two of us in a gay retirement home in rocking chairs with comforters over our legs. "With cute, young male nurses," Paul would say with a big grin on his face.

"You doing okay?" Venus asked as we flew over the lake bridge.

I nodded.

"It could just be a coincidence, Fowler having the same kind of car, you know." Her mouth worked. "You got any smokes on you?"

I reached into my pocket and shook one out for her. She rolled down her window, then lit it. "I think I've run out of coincidences lately, Venus. I've had more than my fair share."

She patted my leg. "It's going to be okay."

I just looked out the window as the neon lights of Slidell flew past. We had to be going over a hundred miles per hour. The siren kept screaming while we passed cars as if they were standing still. We crossed the state line and zipped right through Waveland as if it weren't even there. When we reached the city limits of Bay St. Louis, Venus radioed for the sheriff, switching off the siren. "Have you got the warrant?"

A thick Mississippi voice replied, "The judge just signed it, ma'am. We'll be at the house in a few minutes."

"We'll wait for you."

I guided Venus through the city, and then we were driving down Forest Road. "That's the house up ahead," I said. Venus stopped and parked the SUV on the side of the road. She pulled her gun out of its holster and took the safety off. "Stay behind me," she said. She gave me a lopsided grin. "I'd tell you to stay here, but you wouldn't do that, would you?"

"No."

We got out of the SUV, closing the doors carefully so they didn't make a sound, and walked through the darkness to the foot of the driveway. The house was dark and silent, but that didn't mean anything. He didn't like the light.

A police car came up Forest Road from the other direction and stopped in front of us. Both doors opened, and two uniforms got out. One was in his late fifties, but he wasn't the stereotype of the small Southern town sheriff. He was in good shape, his body all lean hard muscle. The other was younger, about my age. Venus flashed her I.D. at them. "You guys lead the way," she said.

"Who's this?" the younger one said, indicating me and shining a flashlight into my face.

"My partner," Venus lied without missing a beat.

We followed them up the driveway onto the porch.

Something was wrong. I could sense it once I stepped onto the porch.

The sheriff started pounding on the door. "Mr. Fowler! Mr. Fowler! It's the sheriff! Open up!" he shouted.

Nothing.

He looked over at Venus. "I've got a warrant."

"Break it down," she ordered.

He nodded at the younger one, who stepped back and raised his foot. The door exploded open from the force of his kick, the doorframe breaking and splintered wood flying in all directions.

I recoiled. I smelled death.

The sheriff shone his flashlight inside over piles of garbage. Cats ran back and forth, making plaintive noises. A couple made their way over to us, rubbing on our legs. The younger cop shone his light on the walls, finally finding a light switch and flicking it. The room flooded with light. It was even worse with the lights on.

I turned my head to where the poster of Paul had been the other day.

It had been slashed to pieces in its frame, except for the face. "Venus." I pointed to it.

"Oh, Christ," she said. She walked over to it.

The local cops walked into the kitchen and turned on the light in there. I could see through the door. It was just as disgusting as the living room. Fowler lived like a pig. The odor of cat urine was overpowering. Cats scattered. "Looks like we're gonna have to call Animal Control," the young cop said.

The sheriff turned on the hall light and started opening doors. "Oh, Christ!" he half shouted. "Detective Casanova! Can you get in here quick! Shelby, call the paramedics!"

My heart leapt into my throat as I followed Venus down the

hallway. We carefully stepped over trash, dirty clothes, and piles of cat shit. Venus stopped cold in the doorway. "Oh, dear God in heaven." She turned. "No, Chanse, don't go in there."

I pushed her aside and stepped through the door.

"Paul," I managed to croak out as I moved in what seemed like slow motion to the bed.

He was naked and shackled to the bed, spread-eagled over the mattress. The sheets were filthy with human excrement. His skin looked white, too white. The sheriff was trying to find a pulse. Paul's eyes were closed. Dried blood covered the left side of his face. "He's alive," the sheriff said, "but barely."

I reached for his hand. It was cold. "Paul…" I whispered and started shaking.

I rode with him to the hospital in the ambulance. The paramedics pumped adrenaline into him. The head injury was bad, and I could see the size of the blow as they cleaned the wound. He remained unconscious the entire way.

"Wake up, honey, I'm here," I whispered, sitting in my little corner of the ambulance as it screamed through the Mississippi night. "You're going to be okay, you know."

They took him into the emergency room, and I answered questions for a kind-faced nurse. When we were finished, Venus led me into the waiting room. "He's going to be okay, Chanse." She held my hand so tight it hurt. "You'll see."

And we waited.

And waited.

Sometime, I don't know when, Paige arrived, her face white and her lips trembling. Her makeup was smeared with tears. She threw her arms around me before I could even get up and sobbed for I don't know how long. "Have they said anything?" she asked, her voice shaking.

I just shook my head.

The Maxwells came in right behind her. Their faces were just as white and strained, but Fee gave me a big hug. "Now, Chanse, my love, don't you worry. Everything's going to be just fine. My Paul's a

fighter—you wait and see." But her smile and her tone were lies. I
could see the fear in her eyes and in Ian's. It was also there in the way
they gripped their rosaries as they paced around the waiting room.

A doctor came into the waiting room and cleared his throat.
"Mr. and Mrs. Maxwell?"

We all rose. "May I speak with you privately?" he asked.

"We're all family here," Fee said fiercely, putting an arm around
me while Ian put an arm around Paige and Venus.

"I'm sorry, but the head injury is too severe. We can't do anything
for him here," the doctor said. "I've arranged for a helicopter to take
him to Touro in New Orleans. They'll be able to do a lot more for
him there."

My knees buckled, but somehow Fee managed to keep me
standing.

"They'll take him right into surgery," he went on.

"So, we'll be needing to get back to New Orleans, then?" This
from Ian.

The doctor nodded. "He'll be leaving soon."

"Thank you, doctor." Fee gave him a hug, which startled him,
and then he walked back out.

"Well, who'll be riding with whom, then?" Fee asked.

CHAPTER TWENTY

I rode back with Paige, but I don't really remember much of it. She was blaring Norah Jones on her car stereo and chain-smoking, lighting a new one from the butt of another. All I could remember were the blurry shapes of things as the car went past. Paige was driving fast. This usually worried me, but I didn't really care this time. All I could think about was how messy Fowler's house had been, how much that must have bothered Paul. Paul liked everything just so. I mean, he organized his clothes by type and color. His socks all had to be lined up the same way in the sock drawer. His underwear was folded *this* way and was also sorted by color and maker. The filth, the clutter, must have driven him insane. But then again, it was also probably likely he'd been unconscious the whole time he'd been there, which was what—three, four days? That couldn't be good. That head injury must have really done a number on him, and that would explain why there was so much blood. Fowler must have conked Paul in the kitchen in New Orleans, carried him down the stairs and to his car, missing the walk with his first step down and stepping into the flower bed. Then he probably just put him in the trunk, went back upstairs, beat off on the bed, stole the print, and defaced the other.

And I had sat in that disgusting living room, in the gloom, with the cats and the smells and a fucking psychotic murdering fuck just a few feet away—and Paul unconscious just down the hall, shackled naked to a bed and covered in his own filth. I started shaking, my stomach lurching. I rolled down the window and gulped in fresh air. We were just reaching the lake bridge.

GREG HERREN

Paige turned down the stereo. "You doing okay, babe?"

"No, not really." The cool lake air felt great on my hot face, and the sweat forming at my hair line dried. My stomach settled down a bit.

"You wanna talk about it?"

"No." I couldn't. I didn't want to hear the words I would say out loud. I didn't want anyone to hear them, at least not yet. I might be ready later, but not quite yet. It was odd. I was feeling so many different emotions all at the same time—I would switch from one to another before any single feeling could take over completely. I wanted to laugh with relief. I wanted to cry. I wanted to scream. I wanted to throw up. I wanted to get my mind to slow down.

And I wanted to feel something. Anything. Anything other than this horrible distortion of reality, this nightmarish thing my life had become in just a few hours—wake up from it and let it fade with the light of the next morning.

Nothing I could have done would have altered this.

Bullshit as it was, it was something. I'd had no control over the sequence of events. I hadn't known Paul had made videos and therefore was afraid to tell me he had a stalker. Had I known, maybe...

But then again, Paul felt like he couldn't tell me about any of it. Why would he have felt I was capable of hearing it in a rational, calm manner and not been jealous? I'd proved his fears right, hadn't I? But then I could convince myself that my violent reaction was partly due to finding out after he'd been arrested for killing someone. I'd been in a vulnerable, emotionally raw state, and had not reacted the way I would have under ordinary circumstances.

"Well, I need to talk," Paige said, throwing a cigarette out the window.

I reeled myself in from the discussion in my head and turned my head to look at her. She looked terrible. She'd been driving with her window cracked for her cigarette smoke escape, and her hair had been blown to shit. She'd been crying, and now her mascara hung in big clumps at the end of her lashes. I'd never really noticed she wore a bit of foundation before, but now I saw where the tears had run through it. Her face was paler than I'd ever seen her, and there were dark circles of worry under her eyes.

"So, I'm sorry, if you don't need to talk—that's fine, and if you don't want to listen to me, just tune me out." She went on without even looking over at me. Her eyes were focused on the road in front of her and weaving around cars. "I mean, he's going to be fine, right? I mean, surgeons are miracle workers these days, but he'll make it— he isn't going to die, right? I mean…"

I turned my head back to the window and watched as we reached the south shore. I could hear her voice going on, but I couldn't understand what she was saying without looking at her. I didn't want to look at her. It was fine, really. She loved Paul, too, and the way she had to deal with all of this was to talk to convince herself the worst wouldn't happen. Maybe she was talking herself into it. I wished I could.

I wish it was Monday morning. Sunday night, we had rented a couple of tearjerker women's movies. Paul and I were both suckers for a good old heroine-suffers-bravely-to-die-at-the-end movie, and we had gone to bed after Susan Sarandon finally accepted Julia Roberts as her replacement in *Stepmom.* We had argued a while about whether or not the movie fit the genre. Paul's theory was that it didn't since Susan's character didn't die until after the credits rolled; mine was that the film did since it was still about fatal illness. We had finally compromised by moving it into the fatal-disease-of-the-week movie category. When we'd gone to bed, Paul was in the mood but I wasn't. I was tired. I had been doing my quarterly report for Castle Oil, one of my bigger security clients, and had been staring at my computer screen for three days. So instead, Paul had gone back into the living room to watch a sex video and pleasure himself. I 'd been asleep before he made it to bed that night. The next morning, though, I'd woken up with him right up to my back, with one of his legs and both arms thrown over my body. I had felt his breath on my neck. I'd woken up before the alarm, but rather than get up I had just lain there, thinking how nice it felt.

It might have been the last time.

Everything came over me at once. *Paul could die, Paul could die—he might be dying now. I might not ever get to talk to him again, I might not get to tell him anything—my God, the last night we spent together I didn't want to have sex. Oh, my God, please let me have that chance back—please give me another moment to hold him, to kiss him, to tell him how much I love him...*

My lungs felt as if they were going to explode, so I stuck my head back out the window and opened my mouth. Centrifugal force pushed air down into my windpipe until I finally coughed it back out and began to breath, deeply and slowly, making that horrible gulping sound every time I inhaled.

"Are you okay?" Paige's hands were shaking on the steering wheel.

"Now—now I am." I took a couple of deep breaths and put my hands on the dashboard to keep them from shaking. "I'm melting down, Paige. I'm trying to hold it together, but I don't know if I can."

"When your mind starts going fast, it's time to slow down and take deep breaths to fight off." She tossed her pack at me. "Can you light this for me? I can't drive, hold it together, and light a cigarette at the same time anymore." She laughed. "I guess I'm getting older. I used to be able to do this quite easily."

There was pain in her voice, pain from a distant place she'd locked away in her head.

She wiped a tear away with a trembling hand and then took the cigarette from me. After a long inhale, she blew the smoke out the window through the side of her mouth. "Yeah. I always thought I'd gotten used to it. But I haven't."

"Paige..."

She slowed as we descended the off-ramp at St. Charles. "You better?"

"Yeah. For now." I felt calm. But I could sense the hysteria, trying to get enough momentum to force its way out again. Paul was going to be fine. He was young and strong, and he was healthy, God knows. All that eating right and exercise had to have been for something, right?

We parked in the hospital garage and walked over to the main hospital. We held hands. Paige's palm was hot and dry, and I kept squeezing it. I could tell she was still trembling a little. The nurse at the front desk sent us up to a waiting room on one of the upper floors. I took in the antiseptic smell, the harsh lighting, the people talking in whispers. Fee and Ian were already there, drinking coffee that looked like it could peel paint out of Styrofoam cups.

"They haven't told us anything, but he's in surgery now," Fee said after hugging us both. We all sat down on the uncomfortable furniture. Her face was resolute. "But I know he'll be fine. He's strong, that one is."

Her accent was comforting somehow.

"We've called the other kids," Ian said. "They'll be here in the morning. They wanted us to give you their prayers."

"How...how nice." I didn't know what else to say. I probably should have just said nothing.

Fee gave me a faint smile. "You're part of the family, Chanse."

This time I didn't say anything. I couldn't. I just somehow got to my feet and walked out of the room and down into the bathroom. I stood in front of the sink, and sobbed. I went down into the dark place of pain and sorrow I'd always avoided and gave vent to everything. *What if Paul dies? What if I never get the chance to tell him how much I love him? What will I do? How will I face life without him? Why is this happening to him? Why not to me?*

And then, it was gone as quickly as it had come. Deep breaths, slow and easy. I threw cold water in my face and rubbed it dry with a paper towel that felt like sandpaper. I took one final deep breath, and walked back into the waiting room.

I don't know how long we sat there. Time was of no relevance. Paige kept getting up and buying sodas and chips out of the vending machine. She'd taken her shoes off and curled up in a chair, paging through three-year-old issues of *Good Housekeeping*. Fee had a book of crossword puzzles in her purse, and she and Ian sat together and figured out the answers. I watched the television, without comprehending any of the programs or hearing the sound or laughing at the jokes. Nothing was felt or thought about except the passing of time. I was afraid to ask anyone what time it was, because I was afraid I would start asking every five minutes and get on everyone's nerves.

I'd just gotten back from getting rid of about a gallon of Dr. Pepper when the doctor came in and asked for Fee and Ian. I walked over and put my arm around Paige.

"He survived the surgery," the doctor was saying. "But the head injury was pretty severe. It drove bone fragments from his skull into his brain, and we had to remove those fragments."

"But you were able to?" Ian asked. He was clutching Fee's hand.

"Yes, we were able to get all of them out." The doctor took a deep breath. "But the bad news is there's no brain activity."

I sat down on the arm of a chair, hard.

"There wasn't any when he was brought in," the doctor went on. "But those fragments had to come out. He would have died had we left them in."

"But his brain is dead, isn't that what you're telling us?" Fee's chin went up.

"I'm afraid so, yes."

"Is he breathing on his own?" Paige's voice broke.

The doctor shook his head. "I'm afraid not. But that could change, of course, once he recovers his strength from the surgery…"

"But people who are brain-dead…" Paige gulped, choking off a sob.

"What are the odds of his waking up?" Fee asked.

The doctor just shook his head. "We can just wait and pray."

"When can we see him?" This from Ian.

"In the morning, when he's rested some." The doctor looked sad. "I'm sorry, folks. All I can tell you to do is pray."

"We'll do that," Fee said.

The door shut behind him. Fee sat down. "You kids might as well go home and get some sleep. There's nothing you can do for him now."

"Are you sure you don't mind?" Paige stood. "I can come back in the morning and bring breakfast."

"That'd be nice." Fee smiled at her. "Now, Chanse, you run along with her. You get some rest. Ian and I will be fine. It won't be the first time we've stayed in a hospital overnight with one of our kids."

"I...I wouldn't feel right."

"Go on, son." Ian put a hand on my shoulder. "We'll call you if there's news."

And we left. Paige took me back to where my rental car was parked in the Quarter. I had two tickets. I threw them in the car and drove home. Once inside, I thought about rolling a joint but decided against it. Pot might just heighten my anxiety, rather than help me relax. Instead, I just went to bed.

And somehow, I slept.

I woke in the morning and drove over to Touro around eleven. I'd forgotten to set the alarm, and I'd slept deep and long. Exhaustion from the overdose of adrenaline, maybe—I don't know for sure. When I got there, the waiting room was full of Maxwells. Paul's three brothers had all arrived. It was spooky how much they all looked like Paul. Paul was more handsome and well-built, but the resemblance was there in the frame, the body language, and the way they all walked. His sister, Siobhan, was also there, and she looked like her mother must have as a young woman. I got hugged and kissed by all of them. Paige was there with several boxes of donuts. "Why don't you go in and see him?" Fee said, sensing I was a bit overwhelmed. She took my by the hand and led me back to the intensive care unit, where she introduced me to the nurse as her other son, Chanse, so they could give me a badge to get me in. She led me to where Paul lay inside a curtain and then kissed me on the cheek and slipped away.

He looked better than he had chained to that bed, but he still...I swallowed. His skin was bluish white, and his stubble was growing in. The machines he was hooked up to around the bed wheezed and hummed and beeped. His eyes were closed and weren't moving beneath the lids.

I sat down on the chair next to the bed and reached up to take his dry, cold hand.

"Paul, it's me Chanse. Can you hear me?"

Nothing.

I started talking. But I didn't say anything of the things I thought I would. I started talking about things we'd done, like the time we'd gone to the Aquarium and the IMAX theater, and how bad the IMAX movie had been. I remembered how much we'd liked the fish and mused on how Zen-like a fish's life must be. Afterward, we'd bought bottles of water and walked along the Moonwalk and the top of the levee. Finally, we had just stopped and leaned on a railing to watch the barges going by and the currents in the muddy water swirling and rushing. We hadn't talked because we hadn't needed to. Just being together, knowing that the other was right there, had been more than enough. Sometimes, what I liked the most had been the silent times, when we were both in bed at night, reading books with our night-lights on, or just lying in bed on a Sunday morning half asleep with our bodies wrapped around each other. I talked about how much I liked making him pancakes in the morning, how much pleasure it had given me to make him so happy and how he'd made me happy just by being there. Sure, he got on my nerves from time to time, just like I got on his, but that was okay. The other times had made up for it.

No response from him at all.

I walked back out to the waiting room. Every few hours I'd go back in and talk to him some more, but nothing. There was no response to anything.

The Maxwells made the waiting room not quite so intense and gruesome. I liked them all. They told stories about Paul, stories that made them laugh until they cried, stories that showed how much they loved him. And I loved them for loving him and for sharing the stories with me.

And every night I'd go back home, and Fee and Ian would stay the night. They'd go back to their hotel room and sleep during the day when the rest of us were there. They'd always take the overnight shift; they wouldn't hear of anything else.

The fourth night, as I was leaving, I thought, *So this is what "family" feels like.*

Paige came as often as work would let her. She was the one who told us Chris Fowler had been found in his garage after we left. He'd hung himself. I didn't feel anything but pity for him when she told us. The poor, lonely, warped man had fallen in love with Paul. There's such a fine line between love and obsession. Who knows how I would have reacted if Paul had ever stopped loving me— or had never wanted me in the first place?

I was less aware of the hysterics with each passing hour; with each time I went in to sit with Paul, hold his hand, and talk to him about silly things that didn't matter, like movies and TV shows and the gym, the kinds of things we always used to talk about together. I wanted to say the other things but still couldn't. And when I thought about the situation, I just thought, *Paul's alive—he's going to wake up, and everything is going to go back the way it was.*

Until the fifth day.

When I got to the hospital, the Maxwells were all there. Their faces were grim, and as I looked from one to the other, I feared the worst. "He's dead," I said.

"Sit down, honey, please," Fee replied. "He isn't dead." And then she started to talk. They'd been talking to the doctors. It didn't look good for him. The machines were keeping him alive. He'd often talked about it, how he didn't want to be kept alive that way. *Turn the machines off, let me die, and harvest my organs,* he'd always said. So they'd decided.

"He never said that to me," I heard myself say in a thick voice.

"It's what he would have wanted, you know that," murmured one of the brothers, I don't know which.

And I knew they were right.

"When?"

Fee finally cracked. "I wanted to wait until you saw him again."

I nodded and walked back to where Paul lay, and I stepped inside the curtains.

"Hey, honey." I reached down and touched his cheek.

"They...they tell me..." My voice broke. My eyes begin to fill. I cleared my throat. "They tell me they're, um, going to turn your machines off." My nose began to run. "I know—I know they're right. I know you would have wanted that. It's just...they just, you know, told me so I wasn't prepared for it, you know?" I wiped tears off my cheeks. "You deserved better than what I gave you, honey. You deserved someone you could tell things to, someone who loved you no matter what. I do, you know. I'm only sorry it's taken me this long to understand it, you know? You made me so happy." I reached down and kissed his cheek and touched my forehead to his while I cried for a few minutes.

Nothing. No response.

I leaned down and kissed his cheek. "I love you, Paul."

I walked out of the ICU. I walked down the hall and out to the parking garage. I got into my rental car and drove out. The sun was bright. My eyes watered as I headed home.

But I drove past the turn to go home and kept heading downtown to the Quarter. I parked and walked down to Bourbon Street and St. Ann where I stopped at the Attitude gate. The FOR RENT sign was gone. I stood there for a minute and looked inside. I saw the front door open and my beautiful, sweet Paul walk out again. My eyes teared, then he faded away again. I walked on down and around the corner.

Sly was behind the bar, just as he always was. "Hey, Chanse." He shook my hand. "Hey, man, was really sorry to hear about your boyfriend."

"Thanks." New Orleans is really a small town.

Dominique came walking in from around the corner. She looked tired, haggard, as if she hadn't been sleeping well. She slid down onto a barstool next to mine. "I'm sorry, Chanse."

I nodded. "I'm sorry about Ricky."

"Yeah." She motioned to Sly. "Get me a glass of Wild Turkey." She looked at me. "Want one?"

I looked at my watch. Quarter till noon. Hell, it was five o'clock somewhere. I nodded.

Sly slid the glass down to me. We raised our glasses and clinked them together.

To love," she said, her voice aching.

"To love." My own voice broke, but I forced a terrible smile on my face.

And I knew, at some point, the whiskey would bring the numbness back.

ACKNOWLEDGMENTS

As always, I have an enormous number of people to thank for their help, encouragement, and support, not only during the writing of this book but also just for being in my life in general.

My editor at Alyson, Nick Street, is not only a saint but a martyr. Bless his heart, I am sure he had no idea what he was letting himself in for when he signed on to work with me on this book. He's talked me in off the ledge more times than I care to count, and I not only thank him but apologize for being such a royal pain in the neck. Bless you, Saint Nick. I promise I won't be such a problem if there is a next time.

Julie Smith's heart is as big as her talent. I doubt very seriously whether I will ever be able to write as brilliantly as she does, but I aspire to be as good a person as she is someday. Thanks, Lady J. Your work and your life are a constant inspiration to me.

Peter Sabi very generously explained to me how the Vieux Carré Commission works and what it really does. Without the commission, there might not even be a French Quarter. Thanks, Peter, and also to all of your coworkers for helping to keep New Orleans the unique and special place it is.

The following people make my life better just for being who they are and for their kindnesses day in and day out: Mark Richards, Johnny Messenger, Felecia Wong, Roberto Rincon, Larry Stillings, Linda Ireland, Jack Carrel, Sharon Brown, Jean Redmann, Kelly Smith, Jay Quinn, Bill Cohen, Poppy Z. Brite, Felice Picano, Trebor Healey, David McConnell, Carol Rosenfeld, William Mann, Diane Trice, Randal Beach, Sheila Wilkinson, Debra Voelker, Kiki

Reineke, Margaret Coble, Victoria A. Brownworth, David Rosen, Erin Welker, Patricia Brady, Dorothy Allison, Robin and Lou Ann Morehouse, Eddie Coleman, Harriet Campbell Young, Richard Read, Julie Fitch, Barbara Brown, Ben Weston, Noel Twilbeck, Patrick Merla, Sarah Schulman, Laura Lippman, Dean James, Philip Rafshoon, Jim Gladstone, Crystal Little, Katherine V. Forrest, the lovely and talented Jess Wells, Michelle Tea, Ian Philips, Greg Wharton, Ron Suresha, and so many, many more...

And of course, my own Paul Willis, who's still the best thing that ever happened to me.